CRYSTAL EYES

N. B. AUSTIN

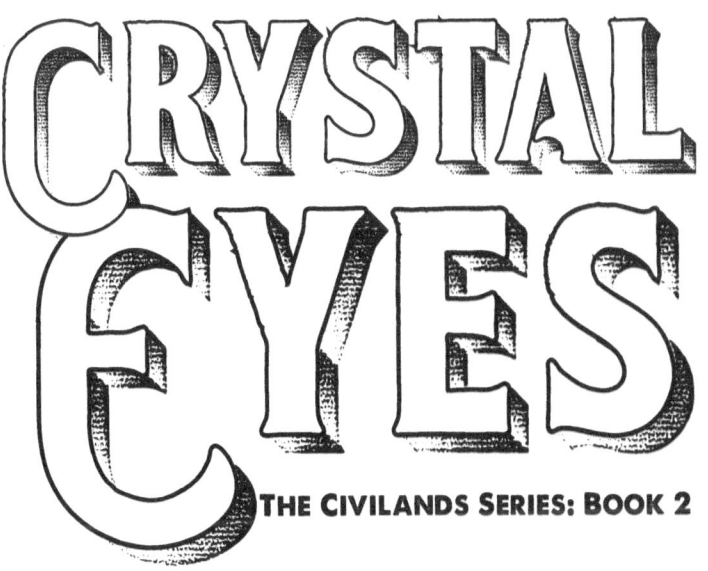

CRYSTAL EYES

THE CIVILANDS SERIES: BOOK 2

MOORE BELL

~

To one who's lesser in years but greater in heart:
Thanks for teaching me so much and shining a light in the
lives of everyone you've met.
My pride in you for those things transcends any words I
could write,
But it's a fuel for the fire that's been started here.
I'm excited to watch it burn together, and I'm blessed to
call you my brother.

This one's for Spoon

~

CHAPTER 1

FEEDING TIME

The Hold was a bustling place, one Latera might have enjoyed under different circumstances. Unfortunately, in the months since the Keagans first captured her people, she had experienced everything but joy.

When she had stepped into her new, unofficial role of leadership on the journey south, she could not have prepared herself for this. Throughout the Hold, the V'ahani of the Riverlands were treated as inferior—by both the Easterners and their rival clan, the Tokali, alike. They were packed into small shelters with cots that were on top of each other. The lack of privacy was very difficult to endure, and the stench of her companions, who were limited in their ability to bathe effectively in these packed circumstances, was quick to spread. Yet that was not the worst of it by any means.

While the natives of the southern Murrieta berated and ridiculed them, the Keagans did the same, and, when they wanted to, also got physical. Latera had taken it upon herself to console several of the V'ahani women who had experienced forceful advances. Each time, she felt more angered and heartbroken, a feeling amplified by the fact that she had no idea what she could do to prevent the attacks. She wondered constantly if she'd be next, though she truly would have accepted it if it had meant she'd never have to see any of her V'ahani live another day with such shame and lack of dignity.

On a particularly dark, rainy afternoon, rather reflective of her mood, she thought with all the bitterness inside her, she was leaving one of the most difficult discussions of them all. One of her closest friends here at the Hold and a fellow nurse, Winona, had sent her an urgent message earlier: her husband, Mika, had been beaten. Latera had rushed over the moment she received word.

Though Winona and her husband Mika were several years older than Latera—both were in their late thirties—Latera had known Winona since she was a child. After Latera's mother's death, and far before Arkouda's murder, Winona had been kind enough to be there for her during her grief, and the two grew close in their shared occupational experiences. Somewhere along the way though, they'd drifted apart. Latera always thought it was because she was unmarried. So much of their people's social structure was divided into the married and unmarried, and it simply became harder and harder to find common ground. But once they found themselves captive in the Hold they reunited both in friendship and purpose. With Latera leading her people, she depended on Winona's friendship to steady her.

As for Mika, he was not the grizzled warrior many of the V'ahani men tried to be. Any time Latera visited the couple, he would gush about new discoveries in his research of the philosophies and religious history that guided their people.

As Latera stepped out into the rain, she replayed the conversation.

"The men who attacked him tried to make a move on you first?" Latera had asked Winona.

Winona was shivering and her teeth chattering. "That is right," she said. She, and the rest of them, were cold from the wet caused by the leaks in the roof of the shelter. It was difficult to find a dry place, and she'd given the only one she could find to Mika. "My Mika was just defending me, and at first they backed off. I thought it was because of the forcefulness of his defending me. But that is when I saw *they* had come—Clovis and Walter Keagan. Clovis did not take kindly to the strength Mika showed, so he . . ."

"It is okay, Winnie. You are strong."

"He toyed with him. It was like a cat playing with a mouse and there was nothing I could do but beg for it to stop as the others held me back," Winona said, pausing for a breath. "Walter ended up having to pull Clovis back and thank the Mother he had done so or who knows? And you saw the 'X' shaped scar on his cheek. These terrors we endure here will remain with us for life."

"I am so sorry, Winnie. I should not even call those animals 'men.' They are not men. Just as the councilmen were met with justice for their crimes, the Keagans will suffer even worse. Each one of them—I promise you."

"Mika is so brave. Do you know what they would have done to me, Latera, if he had not been there? This happened to him because of me. I knew we should have followed your order to only travel in larger groups, but I thought it would be okay with us two."

Latera was losing patience with her own inability to find some solution for this pain. She had brushed the damp, brown hair out of her friend's face, which was turned toward the ground, and touched her forehead to Winona's, who was beginning to well up with tears.

"Do not dare blame yourself for any of this, do you hear me, Winnie?" Latera had said. "Our lives are defined by how we endure. We will get out of this. I will get us out of this."

As Winona began to breathe deeply, she had stepped away and looked straight into Latera's eyes. "I will never understand how or when you became this—this force, Latera. You have become hardened for our sake, and we can all see it. I just pray you will not allow this burden you bear to break you. There is already so much you have given, but you should not have to be the one to give everything."

"That might be where you are wrong, though I do appreciate the sentiment. For as much as I spend my time scheming, I do not even know what I can do right now. It is all I think about. Even if there was an option with only the slightest chance of success, I would take it, but nothing has come to mind yet."

"Well, do not consider the responsibility yours alone, because it is not," Winona had said as she grabbed Latera's hands. "Since the executions of the councilmen, Clovis and Walter have not made a formal public appearance. They simply hung, beat, and *executed* our Councilmen in a public spectacle of violence and have only appeared in the shadows ever since—today, it was Mika." Winona paused, her voice cracking. "But tomorrow it will be another. There is nothing we can do right now until our people in the Mountainlands come and kill those two bastards. Without those two, these men will be nothing."

"Of that I am certain," Latera had said, blowing into her hands for warmth once Winona released them. "Tell Mika I said to keep his head up and be patient. The pain he is going through now will only make him stronger."

The sliding of Latera's feet on mud snapped her from her reverie. The rain continued to come down as she jogged back to the shelter, and the streets of the Hold were thick and muddied. The whole place was dark and felt so empty, with only the faintest candlelight peeking between the cracks in the doorframes of the homes around her. It was as if everyone was hiding from what was becoming of this massive territory. In their darkest hour, Latera hoped she could somehow preserve whatever faint light still existed in the hearts of her people.

Just as she approached her destination, three Keagan men jumped out to surround her. They grabbed her, and one covered her mouth from behind before she could scream. As she desperately resisted and analyzed her surroundings, it seemed the lights in the homes around her had all gone out. The men dragged her into an alley off the road. She dug her heels in the mud and kicked out to fight as much as she could, but it was to no avail. After the past few weeks, she had known it would only be a matter of time before her distraction with everyone's safety but her own would be costly.

"Stop struggling, and this shit'll be over quicker," the attacker with his hand over her mouth grunted into her ear. His breath was eerily warm on her neck and was visible in the chilly rain. She shook her whole body, blind with a furious disgust. Trying desperately to voice her resentment, she could feel his hand only come down on her mouth tighter.

"Let's get this show on the road," another man said hastily. "We want our turn, too, and this bitch is only staying quiet for so long."

"I think I'll take my time." The first began to forcefully grab for Latera's clothes.

Knowing she needed to act fast, Latera shook her head violently until she was able to bite down into the man's hand. When she did, he yelled out, and a struggle between them ensued. In the scuffle, Latera noticed the man's pistol in his open holster.

"You need help controlling a young girl?" one of the others joked, which made the third laugh.

"Don't you dare take another step," the Keagan man wrestling Latera yelped before they could approach.

With the man's attention on subduing her, Latera noticed a window of opportunity. She lifted his pistol off him when it was out of sight of the others. When she succeeded, without him even having noticed it, she was thrilled, but as a figure wearing a hood appeared at the mouth of the alley, she abruptly stowed it away inside her dress. The hood covered the figure's face entirely, but Latera could guess it a man by the height and breadth of his silhouette. A revolver with one of the longest barrels Latera had ever seen rested loosely in his hand, but that was the only thing she could make out from behind the droplets of rain before her attacker held her tight again. She breathed a sigh of relief that she'd managed to hide the revolver near her armpit, a place he couldn't feel it.

"It's raining cats and dogs out here!" the man hollered merrily. "Did you know the origin of that phrase isn't known for certain? What a crazy thing, huh?"

"Look sir, I—."

"Crazy indeed," the mysterious man interrupted. "One theory is that since people have seen freak occurrences of it raining frogs or fish, raining cats and dogs would mean it was a particularly intense downpour. But if that were the case, don't you think the phrase should have included heavier, less tame animals? Like perhaps, lions or grizzlies?"

So, this person is familiar with the struggle between the Keagans, known for their lion insignia, and the V'ahani, known for their relationship with the grizzlies of the Northern Murrieta, Latera thought. The man who was holding her slowly began relinquishing her from his grip. She could feel his hands beginning to shake as she shoved him off her, and she wondered about the effect this person had on her attackers.

"We're gonna be on our way now," the attacker called after giving Latera a look.

"Yeah . . ." the hooded man acknowledged. "You will be, because if you don't leave, I'm gonna be the one making the dogs rain down upon you. Hounds to be exact. Maybe some wild cats, too. Then the phrase might have some real meaning for us after all, huh!?"

With that, the men were off in an instant, but Latera's anger only exploded at their retreating backs. "I will not forget your faces!" Latera screamed at them. "I will forget nothing. Each of those who has wronged the V'ahani will pay—whether by my hand or not. They have and will continue to face my wrath. You three are on my list now. So, run, hide, do what you must. But I will find you, because I will not ever forget."

Once Latera noticed they were out of sight, she turned back to the mouth of the alley only to find it empty as well. All she could do was take a deep breath and fix her clothes as she darted back to the shelter. The whole way, she wondered what she would now do with this pistol she had stolen and worried about the repercussions she'd face if it was discovered she'd taken it. Then, as she approached the shelter, Latera was terrified to see Elan waiting by the entrance under the cover of an overhang.

Elan and she had not spoken since the capture of the V'ahani of the Riverlands. Latera hated him and the Tokali almost as much as she hated the Keagans themselves—perhaps even more. Especially now, with the condition they were in, her animosity was only growing by the day. Though she understood he did what he needed to do for his people, it did not change what he had done to hers.

"Elan...it really is not a good time. What are you doing here anyway?"

"I do not know." She noted his clothes were drenched, and the bun in his hair was becoming unraveled. "I have been waiting for you but...but now that you are here, I do not know what to say."

"Then say nothing and leave. I do not have time for your childishness anymore. I want nothing to do with you, just as you wanted nothing to do with me. Do you even know—"

"I do know, okay? I know what I have done, and I am sorry. And it is not that I wanted nothing to do with you. I wanted everything to do with you! I still do."

"Oh, are you f-fucking kidding me?" she exclaimed, using a word she'd heard the Keagans use regularly. She wasn't entirely sure what it meant—only that it was some kind of curse. Somehow it felt right to her to say it then, and he seemed as surprised by it as she was. "The only thing you can do for me is find me a way to end the misery my people and I face every single day in this place. Until you do so, there will remain nothing to say."

Elan looked away as he thought for a moment. "Do you want to come out of the rain and under this cover? It is pouring out there."

"I will not come near that entryway until you remove yourself from it."

Elan rolled his eyes at her in frustration—a telling reply, she thought. "Look, if your people just assimilate, we can truly have the unity we all want. I understand things are hard now, but they will improve with time, just as they have for us. As a matter of fact, Clovis is going to be addressing the Hold for the first time since your people have come here. His men can be a hassle, but he may bring them into line for the sake of maintaining the order William Keagan desires. He seems to be set on keeping William out of his hair when possible."

"He is going to address the Hold? When?"

"Yes, this week—the gathering will be held in three days in the Square," Elan answered. "I was not supposed to tell you, so please, do not tell anyone. But...do you see now that I want to help?"

Latera said nothing at first, her mind racing a mile a minute. "Uh, yes, of course. That helps a lot Elan. I appreciate being informed. So, thank you."

"You are welcome," Elan said, smiling wider than he should have been. Latera was only grateful for the news. But his desire to please her might prove useful. Let him think she could forgive him, if it loosened his lips. "I really think things will work out now that we are all together. It is my hope that pretty soon the whole Murrieta will be united."

Her vision flashed red at his stupidity. Unity? This was slavery.

"Thank you again, Elan. But I must retire now."

"Of course," he said, moving away from the door. "I will see you soon, I hope."

Latera nodded at him but said nothing as she entered the shelter.

Finally, she had it. She had what she needed to save her people. Winona was right: they needed to cut off the head of the snake if they were to gain their freedom. Now, Latera had a weapon, a time, and a place.

In three days, she was going to kill Clovis Keagan.

*

Each and every night, Daniel Keagan ensured there was nothing to hinder the morning's light from seeping through his bedroom window and shining directly onto his face come dawn. It was his ritual, which he felt was the reason for any success he might experience. From a young age, he had promised himself he would work harder than anyone around him. This included the need to have as much time available in the day as there could be.

This morning, however, he wanted the sun's rays to illuminate something in particular. Lying next to him, stark naked, was the goddess of a bar-maid, Johanna Fontaine. Since awakening, he had experienced the joy of admiring her radiant blond hair, lavish breasts, and extensive legs in the glowing light. After how far his brothers and he had come, it felt like he had earned such brilliance. Though he was not a materialistic or showy man, there were times when he simply needed to admire the things he was fortunate enough to have.

Daniel lay straight on his back with her on her side, leaning against him with an arm and leg stretched over him. Her skin emitted a warmth against his. As the sun began to spread through the room, Daniel noticed a squint of displeasure twinge across

Johanna's face. Her expression soured even more once her eyes had crept open.

"What the hell? What time is it? Why isn't the damn curtain down?" she moaned as she turned off Daniel and faced the other direction, burying her face in the blanket beneath her.

"What better instruction could our world give us to rise than the dawn?" Still in awe of the morning beauty and not complaining about the sight of Johanna from behind, Daniel stretched his limbs.

"What better instruction could my body be giving me to keep sleeping other than feeling tired?" With her face buried in the sheets, she groaned aloud.

Daniel stood up and began to dress, too ready to get down to business to mind her laziness. "Our bodies can be deceitful about the things we need," he said.

"Are you this serious all the time?"

"You didn't seem to have any problem with how serious I was being last night," Daniel joked as he came by her side of the bed and spanked her.

Johanna jumped in surprise and perked up with a smile. "No, I suppose I didn't. But maybe our relationship isn't meant to exist beyond the walls of the bedroom then."

"Who says it would have anyway?" Daniel chuckled.

"Daniel Keagan! The nerve of you sometimes, I swear!"

"I kid, I kid. I do need to be off now though. Always work to be done, and there are some people I need to see. I'll swing by the saloon tonight, though, so how about you have us some whiskies ready?"

"Whisky?" Johanna said with her face scrunched. "Sick. I'll

leave it to you to be drinking that shit, but sounds like a plan for later, hun."

Daniel didn't actually have anything urgent planned for the morning, but he was ready to get out of his room. Sex with Johanna was great, and she was beautiful, but there were times when he found himself bothered by her. He had a hard time putting his finger on any one thing that caused it. There wasn't any way in particular she was wronging him, but something about their relationship wasn't right. In a way, he felt like a train moving at full speed, but rather than her being the steam that pushed him forward even faster, he feared she would only slow him down. As cold as it seemed to him, he couldn't shake the feeling.

As he worked his way toward the lobby of the hotel, he noted how empty it was. In a place where there was usually a Keagan man or two to be seen, there was none. Only the old owner, Donald Schneider, sat mindlessly behind his desk at the front. He was a wrinkly fellow, whose whole face seemed to be drooping off his skull. While sitting behind the desk, his eyes always appeared closed, but when he perked up, there was a sweetness about him. His strange accent and little, cylindrical hat he always wore were funny as well. One of the most well-known and liked people in Harran, Donald was one of the first people Daniel had met here, and Daniel was fond of him.

"Hey there, Don, how are you this morning?" Daniel greeted him.

Donald sat slumped back in his chair and let out a loud snore. Daniel figured it would be best to let him sleep and began to turn toward the door.

"Daniel, is that you tryna go sneakin' off without so much as a how-do-ya-do?" Donald asked, scaring Daniel half to death.

"Oh, I'm no sneak, sir. I was just trying to let you get some sleep. But good morning to you, Don," Daniel greeted him again.

A dismissive, shaky old hand was waved Daniel's way. "Well, heck, don't get yer knickers in a bunch, boyo. I'm just givin' ya a hard time is all. It's right and proper to refer to yer elders with a 'mister,' by the way."

"Oh I kno—"

"Though I do hate bein' called Mr. Schneider," Donald interrupted. "Makes me feel old, ya see, and I don't need to feel any more-a that than I already do. Please stick with Don."

"Alright, Don, will do," Daniel said as respectfully as he could. He was used to this routine with Donald, who repeated himself frequently. Daniel enjoyed their conversations though, no matter how repetitive they were. In a way, he thought of them as a kind of challenge. He often would try to figure out how to approach them so Donald wouldn't need to repeat anything he said at all. Needless to say, Daniel hadn't gotten all that good at it to this point, but he was having a fun time trying. With so many interesting characters throughout the endearing town, Daniel felt fortunate at times to have landed in Harran.

"Did ya know I'll be turnin' seventy-five in only seven months? Hell-of-a-thing ain't it? Three quarters of-a century I'll have been alive, and the world only seems to have gotten more and more rife with turmoil as the years've gone by," Donald reveled in awe. "Sometimes I think, 'ya know, maybe I didn't do enough to help stop it all. Maybe it's partly my fault it hasn't seemed to have gotten any better in all that time.'"

"I did know about your age, sir," Daniel chuckled. "You mentioned it last month, only difference being you said there were eight months left at the time. Sure is a hell-of-a-thing too. You're a special kind of man, you know. But we all have our roles to play, and yours is to bring people one of the most foundational necessities of life: shelter. You can't be expected to save this world on your own. No one man could."

"Hm," Donald responded with a pause. "I s'pose yer right about that one there. Kinda how I like to think of it too sometimes. Almost like ya plucked that one right out of my head, ya little thief."

Daniel laughed with Donald, basking in the little victory of cutting a typically very long, existential conversation down to a brief exchange.

"Great minds think alike. I can't lie to you, though, there are times I've been starting to think the same thing too. Like…I look around at the people in this town—people like you, Donald—and think about how much respect I have for y'all. Y'all just seem to live a simpler way—a more neighborly way in general. I look at that, and I start to worry the same way you do. And even though I ain't got the years you got, the question I'm thinking about isn't as much if I've done enough to fight the storm, but if I myself am contributing to it."

"Yer young, so of course yer contributin' to it," Donald quipped, Daniel forcing an uneasy chuckle. "Ach, thinkin' though…seems ta be just about the worst thing we could do at times. Keep everythin' in moderations though, I s'pose, and maybe there'll be hope for ya yet."

"I know it too well. But I bet you know same as me how hard it is to shut the mind off when you're a thinking man! So, hey, you know why it's so quiet? Where's everybody at?"

"Oh, I wouldn't know seein' as I'm usually the last to hear things 'round here. A bit odd, that, considerin' I own a place where the comin's and goin's generally tend to happen. Sounded like some kind-a nervousness outside amongst yer men though," Donald answered with a yawn. "Yer name seemed to have come up quite a bit, too, so seemed it was somethin' they each didn't wanna be the one to tell ya."

Daniel scratched at his cheek with a sigh. "I see. Another fire to put out as usual, I guess. I do hope I can feel like I made this world a better place when I get to your age, Don. With all the shit I've had to go through—hell, all I'm still bound to go through. But, anyway, nice talk. I'll be seeing you."

"It sure can all be fixed, and at some point, it will be." Donald's tone was stern now. "Until then, though, Daniel."

Daniel paused to consider this strange final note before gesturing goodbye and marching toward the door. He wondered if this was some sort of new wrinkle of hope that had somehow recently been inserted into Donald's repetitive mind. There was no point in dwelling on it, though, as by now everything Donald said felt like some kind of déjà vu.

When Daniel reached the door, there was one of his men, quivering outside. Based on what Donald had said, Daniel presumed this man had drawn the shortest straw. "Daniel," the fellow called out. "There's something you need to see, sir."

Anticipating this kind of remark, Daniel gave only a brief nod and followed the man to one of two horses waiting nearby. Once his man stormed off, he was quick to urge his horse on to follow. Their path led them toward a trail to the northeast, away from the town. As they reached the outskirts, a spattering of blood could be seen along the road. It only seemed to get thicker the further they went, and soon enough, they came upon the burned down Morrell home.

At this point, Daniel had inspected and was familiar with the scene of the house, but he now saw a group of his gang members standing out in front of it where the trail of blood led to. When he rode up, they whipped around and stood at attention, moving fearfully out of his way. Once Daniel made it to them, he jumped off his horse and crept over to the subject of their attention.

Before him sat a wooden sign, dug into the ground in front of a boulder. On top of the boulder was a dead man, pale as a ghost and draped in a wolf carcass, which looked almost alive, as it was staring right at him. Daniel began to feel sick at the sight and the stench as he also noticed a lion's paw pin stuck in the place of one of the wolf's eyes.

"Needless to ask, but this man is definitely one of ours, yeah?" Daniel turned to the group. They nodded in silent confirmation.

Daniel looked back down at the sign. Written in blood, it read ". . . and thus, my friends, your hunters shall become our prey." Daniel crept over to it. Though this message was facing their direction, away from the body, he noticed it was actually written on the backside of the sign. When he looked at the other side, he could see the front was painted a bright but fading yellow. Written on it in black in friendly handwriting were the words: "Welcome to Harran!"

CHAPTER 2

CANVAS

"Hanzah, I like to think I know these ranges rather well. I know them better than a hound knows the scent of another's piss. Unfortunately, it would seem we have searched every crevasse of these Mountainlands to no avail," Orrin explained as he led Hanzah along a narrow trail.

Hanzah chuckled under his breath despite the deflating news. It had been months since he had lost Dominic and the Morrells in the avalanche. Between his fears for the safety of his sister, Latera, and his worry over his missing traveling companions, only his uncle's odd disposition could lighten his mood. "The things you say sometimes, uncle."

"What was that?" Orrin asked as he swiftly halted and whipped his body around. As he did, he slipped, losing his footing on some loose rocks along the uneven path. Hanzah observed the spectacle Orrin created as his hands shot up into the air to maintain his balance. Though Hanzah was always startled by his uncle's erratic behavior, he had grown less and less surprised by it in the months since they had been reunited.

"Are you alright?" Hanzah giggled more loudly this time as

Orrin beamed back, his lips curling beneath his thick, lengthy moustache and beard.

"Alright? I am more than all right! Did you see that save?"

"Oh, I saw it, and it was impressive but in a different way than I expect you are thinking it was," Hanzah said, and they laughed together.

"Impressive is good." Orrin took a moment to remove his big, fluffy winter cap to scratch his thick head of long, graying hair. Though it was already transitioning into spring, and the snow was beginning to melt away, Orrin was known to wear his hat until the hottest days of summer forced it off his head. "I will take impressive any day of the week—especially when it pertains to being odd. Because being odd means we are being different from everyone else. Did you know that, my boy?"

"Yes, un—" Hanzah started.

"I hope you do, and I hope you do not ever forget it either, because it is the most important lesson you can learn. Truly."

"Un—" Hanzah tried again.

"Your father might not have thought the same way I do on the matter, but he definitely had his own unique qualities as well, as stoic as he was."

"Impressed" was truly the only word Hanzah could think of to describe his feelings toward his uncle, who spoke at times with so few pauses he'd exasperate himself, needing to stop just to catch his breath. How a person so airy and joking in manner could command such respect was something he had a hard time grasping, given his late father's more determined nature. They were both easy-going, though, and with Arkouda having only been two years Orrin's junior, Hanzah supposed they must have learned a lot from each other. Perhaps that was how Orrin could so swiftly flick the switch of leadership on and off—at least, Hanzah liked to think his father had had a positive influence on his uncle.

"I will try to remember odd is good while also trying to maintain my footing to the best of my ability," Hanzah joked. "As for our search, we can turn back to camp now. I do appreciate all you have done to try and help me locate my friends over the past few months. The fact that even with your tracking skills, we were still unsuccessful is very troubling, though. It is as if they vanished in the time since you found me. Perhaps Grand Chieftain Varek at the Fortress might have located them."

"It is sad," Orrin admitted as he put a hand to Hanzah's shoulder, guiding him as they began to walk back up the trail from whence they came. "I very much would have liked to thank the kind folks who helped bring my nephew safely to me. They would be welcomed with a feast and shelter and friendliness and kindness and gratitude the likes of which they never could have experienced before. Perhaps I have said all of that previously though. Did I say all of that previously?"

"You did, uncle, and I do appreciate the sentiment nonetheless," Hanzah said. "Do you not think Varek could have found them by now?"

"Please accept my apologies if I ever repeat myself, Hanzah. Age tends to make a person do that from time to time."

"Actually, this is not even the first time you have apologized for repeating yourself," Hanzah chuckled. He gave up trying to get his question answered. That was just the way with Orrin. He answered things how and when he liked. Since Hanzah's attempt to locate his friends had again resulted in failure, he figured he'd call to the wind again and see if anyone at the Fortress had found them by now. He'd asked Orrin to do so for him once each of the last months, just in case. But this time he felt the need to overcome his initial shyness to contact the Grand Chieftain and act himself. As confused as he was about his position in the world without his father, Hanzah realized the Morrells had become his new normal, and he hoped he could at least ensure their survival.

"If you could give me a moment, uncle, I am going to go relieve myself."

"I might do the same," Orrin said as Hanzah began to turn away to walk off the trail toward the trees. "It is a possibility."

"What?" Hanzah stopped in his tracks.

"You did mention Varek could have found them, do you not remember?" Hanzah rolled his eyes with a small grin. He never could tell whether his uncle was being serious or not, but nothing about his tone suggested he wasn't. "It would seem like there are not too many other possible outcomes in which they could still be alive—though Varek finding them would still be rather… unfortunate."

That was the first time his uncle had mentioned the idea of an "unfortunate" find.

"Unfortunate? Why?"

"Could be because Varek has to fend them off when they attempt to intrude through the land bridge, but Varek does not like Easterners. That is for certain. He is not as familiar with the Morrells as your father and I, either, since he is so far north. It was our word alone which allowed for that alliance to exist."

"Do you think he would hurt any of them?" Fear was brewing within him, but it was much like a double-edged sword. First, he worried that Varek, with his hatred, may not tell him if he'd found Hanzah's friends, and then he also began to worry what the Grand Chieftain might think of the V'ahani of the Riverlands—and, by extension, him—considering their alliances with Easterners like the Morrells. He knew he'd likely have to meet the Grand Chieftain and wanted badly to impress him—Hanzah's place among his people, his future, depended on it. "And does Varek resent us for our relationships with them?"

"It is a possibility." Orrin caught his breath and pondered as Hanzah began to sulk. It seemed Orrin took note of Hanzah's reaction. "No, no, no. It is a very small possibility considering they are both young, I think. He is just very untrusting of them— Easterners I mean. And he does not resent us, no. Varek is a stone the mightiest ocean could not move. But over an extended period of time, with a little extra effort, the strongest stones may weather. Oh, I know! While you do your business, I will go ahead and call up to the wind to send the message to see if anyone at the Fortress has seen the young Morrells. How about that for an idea?"

Hanzah sighed. He had wanted to call the wind himself, but the most important thing now was getting the information. "You know what, uncle Orrin? That sounds brilliant...Thank you."

Orrin lit up with the approval and hopped to a knee as Hanzah made his way to the trees. He didn't even need to go that bad but decided he would still take his time.

As Hanzah weaved his way through the first of the towering trees, he inhaled the crisp scent of pine. The forest emitted it all around him. With the onset of spring, he recognized the strengthening hue of the greenery throughout these Mountainlands. But there was something about his current rest stop in particular he found strikingly beautiful. It could have been the silence, he thought, or perhaps the roughness of the bark that lined the aging trees. Whatever it was, a peacefulness spread through him that was long over-do but extra pleasant now that he was with his people again and his broken arm was almost fully healed.

Hanzah remembered what he had entered the forest to do in the first place and was preparing to undo his pants when he noticed something odd about a broad tree in the distance. He began to retie himself as he crept in its direction. As he got closer, Hanzah could make out an intricately carved etching of a faceless woman. The figure and the designs surrounding her were not simple illustrations, however. The craftsmanship was masterful. The tan inner layers of the tree could be seen, wrapped all around the wider trunk. Hanzah was in awe of how detailed it all was. He ran his fingers through the cuts, which were cleanly made—the wood completely smooth. His eyes scanned every bit of the magnificence as he worked his way to the opposite side and wondered how this could have possibly come to be. Then, out of the corner of his view, he saw another carved tree, parallel to the first. However, this one was only altered on one side, on the half of the trunk facing away from the trail he had come from.

Hanzah darted over to it, inspecting both sides back and forth to ensure what he was seeing was real. He was amazed at how these etchings were completely hidden from the trail. With his curiosity buzzing, he turned to jog deeper into the forest. As he went, he saw the faces of unaltered trees. After he had gone about fifty paces or so, he spun around. Before him, as he'd hoped, were thousands of images carved into the trunks—all of which spoke volumes. They were all as magically engraved as the woman at the head of them all. Hanzah could not begin to soak them all in fast enough. There were landscapes; there were writings; there were animals; there were people. All were immaculately detailed. As much time as it must have taken to design, he felt it would take equally as long to fully appreciate.

On one of the widest trunks, he next spotted the image of a massive grizzly. All Hanzah could think about as he beheld it was his father. How he missed him now every bit as much as the moment he was taken. It made him wonder if there could ever truly be a new normal without Arkouda. As much as he loved his uncle, Orrin, and was beginning to feel at home in the Mountainlands, he struggled with the fact that nothing would ever be the same—especially with Latera still in danger.

"Marvelous, is it not?" Orrin said from behind, almost making Hanzah jump out of his shoes.

"For the sake of the Mother, you scared me half to death," Hanzah exclaimed.

"The Mother indeed," Orrin confirmed. "This place you've stumbled upon is known as the Maiden's Canvas. It is said that the carvings at Her back represent things that have come to pass in Her domain. Things that are behind Her for better or worse. While the Territory is Her magnum-opus, Her Canvas is a micro-masterpiece only She could have created."

"She did this? How can you be sure?"

"She has done all of this, Hanzah. Not just the Canvas, but everything you see around you. Between our having originated in the Territory, our connection to it, and the Canvas, there is no more evidence we could need. Anything beyond that is called faith, my boy."

Hanzah pondered this for a moment or two, until his attention was brought back to the image of the bear.

"You feel him here, do you not?"

"I do," Hanzah confirmed, knowing right away his uncle was referring to his father. Internally, and in good humor, he acknowledged it was one of the few times his uncle and he were on *exactly* the same page.

"Men do terrible things, even to the ones they claim to care for. It is one of the only certainties in life." Orrin's gaze appeared to go on for miles, with his tone more stern now than Hanzah had ever heard his uncle speak. "When the scoundrels of the world rise from the holes they burrow themselves inside, though, they will only be burned by the rays of the sun they so long hid from. There is no escaping the crumbling that comes to all greedy hearts sooner or later. All we can do is learn from them, resist the urges they cave into, and try to make the world a better place despite them. That is what your father's legacy will always be. And because of it, he will live on. I have faith the Mother will be sure of that."

Hanzah smiled at his uncle, who was now lightly panting once again. "I have faith in it too."

"Well, good," Orrin coughed. "Now, may we be getting back to camp? My stomach has been making noises that are rather unnatural in its protest."

Hanzah nodded and began to instinctively march back, but he became distracted by the elaborate designs once again. Soon he became focused on one in particular. This carving was on the opposite face of the tree at the beginning of the Canvas. On this face, there was an image of a big eye that seemed rougher than the rest. He could not tell whether it was cut poorly or it was purposefully deformed.

"What is this, though, and why is it not as well done as the others?"

"The Mother makes no mistakes, my boy," Orrin answered, shaking his head. "That is the blinded eye. It is meant to represent that our connection to this land is null while we explore the Maiden's Canvas. None of the Mother's creatures may come into it, or see into it. But come now, Hanzah. I will bring you back here another—" Orrin paused as a rustling could be heard from somewhere in the forest. He motioned for Hanzah to be on guard.

Hanzah noticed Orrin had silently yanked out his blade and had begun to creep forward toward the sound. He found it odd his uncle was not only using his eyes to rapidly scan their surroundings, but he was also sniffing the air. Hanzah was on edge now that he knew the nature of the Canvas. Besides their own skills, they would have no advantage here. No animal could enter, so no grizzly could be called or bird's eyes employed. Without warning, Orrin darted off, without any additional sound having caused alarm as far as Hanzah could tell. Hanzah tried to keep up, and a moment later he could see his uncle tackle a person who seemed to have been hiding behind a tree to the ground.

"Please, stop, don't hurt him!" a female voice Hanzah recognized rang out. As it did, Hanzah spotted Jeannie Morrell, pointing a gun at his uncle. "Please, get off him, or I'll have to—"

"Jeannie!" Hanzah screeched, overcome with joy to see his friend but also equally frightened about the pistol in her hand. She turned until she saw Hanzah, and then she dropped the gun, darting over to embrace him. Hanzah was nearly knocked off his feet by the force.

"Is the coast clear, my boy? Do you recognize this sneaky fellow?"

Hanzah walked over with Jeannie by his side until he spotted his uncle, who was perched over none other than Harrison Morrell. "I do, and I could not thank you enough, Uncle Orrin," Hanzah exhaled. "Please do release him, though. The coast is most definitely clear. After all this time we have found the Morrells. After all this time we have found my friends."

As Orrin eased off Harrison, Hanzah looked around. He waited a moment for someone else to pop out from behind a tree or some other hiding place, but no one did. As such, he turned to the Morrells and asked, "But where is Dominic?"

*

Dominic Turner sat on his knees, slouched over with his hands tied to a pole behind him. The cell, which he had grown accustomed to, was filthy, and only the faintest rays of light managed to crack through the base of the door. The stench of rot filled the place, and the rats that occasionally scurried around seemed to bask in that fact. His body ached all over from the frequent physical interrogations he suffered—ones inevitably resulting in nothing but his begging for mercy. There were times when he simply wanted to tell his captors whatever it was they were wanting to hear, but he couldn't get himself to do so. Why should he have to lie after all he'd done? He doubted it would even save him any more pain to do so, despite their telling him otherwise.

The door before him swung open yet again. Blinded by the sun as it burst into the cell, Dominic remained still, too exhausted and degraded to even flinch. He squinted his eyes at the person whose silhouette stood before him and used whatever strength he had left to find his voice.

"Please, I have nothing more to tell you people," Dominic begged frantically. "I've given you only truths for weeks, and still you badger me to confess to things I didn't do. I'm *not* here to harm the V'ahani. It *is* the truth that I helped guide Hanzah back home. I *did* lose him along the way, and I *was* traveling alone to try and find him!"

The figure merely stood there, silent. Dominic felt himself beginning to shake. When the door closed and darkness fell again, he could no longer locate the person. He turned his head back and forth, until he heard footsteps coming from his left, then his right. It sounded as if they were circling around him.

"Who's there? Please, answer me. I beg you to answer me. I'm not a bad man. I'm not like the other Easterners."

"Not...like...the other...Easterners," a deep voice whispered, now from directly behind him but still working its way round and round.

"No—no, not at all like them. I want to help your people. I do."

"So, if you are not like the other Easterners...are you like me?"

27

the voice asked, now to Dominic's right. Dominic's eyes were beginning to adjust back to the darkness, and he could see the person's legs in his peripheral.

"Well…I—I don't know who you are. But I'm sure we share a lot in common, as I did with Hanzah!"

The person finished his circle and came to a knee straight in front of Dominic. Dominic could not utter a word as he came face-to-face with a man he had never seen before, who looked at him with his head tilted as if to analyze him. The garb that covered this man made it evident he was decorated. His grizzled face featured a deep scar splitting diagonally across it with long, dark side burns on either side. Dominic found it hard to look at the wound where it went right through the left eye, which was still in its socket but was a foggy white and blinked excessively.

"My name is Varek, and I am the Grand Chieftain of the V'ahani." The leader's whisper was hinting agitation.

Dominic was having an even harder time finding the right words now that he knew it was the leader of the V'ahani standing before him. "Grand Chieftain, it's an honor," he gasped. "I do understand what you're saying—I think. I…I've been trying to tell your people for weeks I'm on your side, but my words seem to have fallen on deaf ears."

"Not here to harm us, you say?"

"No, of course not!"

"And you helped guide Hanzah back home?"

"Yes, sir. The young man is an impressive fellow and a friend. In fact, I saved his life more than once along the way!"

"But you did lose him?"

"I, uh, yes, unfortunately—"

Varek seemed to revel in Dominic's loss for words as a half grin crossed his face.

"And you were traveling alone?"

Dominic was becoming confused and worried about where this was going. He'd protected the Morrell children by not sharing their whereabouts with the V'ahani. He'd pretended it had been him and Hanzah alone. The way the V'ahani have captured and beat him— he didn't want Jeannie and Harrison submitted to the same fate. But now, worry began to creep in. Had they been discovered?

"Do you know what all people who lie share, Dominic Turner? Their motivation is greed—slimy, filthy, stinking greed. Whether they admit it or not. Whether they accept it or not. Sometimes it may be well-intentioned even, but nonetheless, there is still no way to disguise it as anything other than what it is. You and your Easterners are filled with a tremendous ocean of greed. For the life of me, I have never figured out why this is. Might you be able to tell me?"

"I wouldn't know about the greed you've seen in them. But I know I'm not lying to you, Chieftain Varek."

"And still, we continue down this road," Varek spat. His tone swelled with a thick menace. "Perhaps I will never find the answer."

Dominic remained silent, uncertain of what to say.

"Regardless, you scum-eating pig, we received word, months ago, from Orrin that he has retrieved Hanzah."

Dominic's stomach twisted in anger. They'd heard months ago and yet continued to beat him?

"And each month since, Orrin has asked us if we have come across any Easterners—'friends.'"

"I told you—"

"Save your lies," Varek scolded him. "Orrin has always asked for *three* of Hanzah's friends. And yet, you always claimed you were *one*. And so, either you lie, or you are not the friend he speaks of."

"No, I—"

"*Silence.* We have given you months to clarify which it may be, and yet, here we are. So, which is it, Easterner?"

Dominic became horrified. "I'm sorry," he gasped. "I had to protect the Morrells. We were separated from Hanzah by an avalanche and—"

"Ah, the Morrells, you say? Well at least the boy has not been utterly lost. But were you with them, or were you one of the many who have hunted them?"

It seems Dominic's worry for the Morrells was unfounded here in the Mountainlands. He took a breath. "I felt I needed to protect the children. The Morrells were sleeping when I stumbled upon your people. After what happened with Arkouda's councilmen and the way your people attacked me when they found me…I just didn't know if I could trust them and didn't want any ill to come to my companions. They had been through so much already."

Varek tilted his head, his eyes once again blinking rapidly. "What you say could be true. But again, it can be equally true you are with the very gangs that are after them."

"The Keagans? No!" Dominic shook his head as Varek began to stand up.

"Whether you are or not, though, you *are* an Easterner." Varek stood up to march toward the door. "The Morrells are a lucky few to have even been given the opportunity to earn our respect. But you…why should we believe anything after your months of lying?"

"It was a misunderstanding, please," Dominic begged as Varek opened the door, once again blinding Dominic with the burst of light.

All Dominic could see was Varek's shadow as he paused and turned. "You are just like the rest of them, Dominic. And you will perish like the rest of them." He gave his final damnation before slamming the door behind him.

Hunched over and weeping on the floor, Dominic repeatedly whimpered to himself, "I'm not like the rest of them. I'm not like the rest of them!"

But stuck in such a desperate situation for so long, he began to wonder how true the statement actually was. The fear crept inside him that perhaps, with his past, even with all he'd done to redeem himself, he deserved this after all.

*

It was good to be fed; it was good to be warm; and most important, it was good to be among friends. Jeannie Morrell was the happiest when she had all three—like she did now.

She sat with Hanzah and Harrison inside what Hanzah had told her were the chambers of his Uncle Orrin's council. They talked and laughed as they reminisced, only now calm enough to do so. It'd been a few days since Hanzah and his uncle had found them, and it'd taken as long for a sense of normalcy to return. Yet Jeannie still worried about her brother.

Harrison was becoming increasingly stressed about how they'd restore their family's place in the Riverlands. Every day before they went to sleep, he spoke about it. Their father's legacy was the most important thing to Harrison, and it weighed heavily on his mind. Jeannie could understand that, and she wanted to restore their family's place, too, but she felt Harrison might be putting too much pressure on himself. In his obsession, she worried he might not think reasonably enough to handle the situation the right way. His irrationality, she thought, might have also been amplified by his frustration with Dominic's sudden disappearance.

Now, as the councilmen of the Mountainlands began to file in to listen to their story, Jeannie hoped Harrison would say the right things.

Once they were all seated, Orrin started by introducing each of his councilmen to the Morrells. After Jeannie and Harrison greeted all in attendance, Orrin paused for a moment. He looked down at the floor, smiling and twisting the corners of his thick moustache. The oddity of him was entertaining and almost made Jeannie chuckle out loud.

"Okay, okay, well, okay then! Let us get right down to the business at hand that has led us to be gathered here today. Jeannie and Harrison Morrell, I submit the floor to you."

Jeannie wanted to start by thanking Chieftain Orrin, but Harrison spoke the moment Orrin finished his sentence.

"I first want to say I'm very glad my sister and I were found by you of all people, Chieftain Orrin," Harrison said. "I just want you to know that despite all that's happened in the Riverlands, the alliance between the V'ahani and Morrells won't ever die. My sister and I remain committed to our father's vision of unity in trade between the Easterners of the north and your people."

A confused curl of Orrin's lip showed from behind his beard. "Hmm. It would seem your father is gone and you no longer have any control over the Easterners in the Riverlands. Since that is the case, I would find it difficult to understand how you would provide the alliance of which you speak. Without Adonis and without a V'ahani presence in the Riverlands, there is no one to control these newer, dangerous Easterners, let alone speak of trade. So I wonder why this is the topic of conversation we would begin with."

Jeannie's heart sank for her brother.

"What my uncle means," Hanzah interjected, "is we thought we were going to discuss how you both ended up stranded in the Maiden's Canvas."

"Maiden's Canvas?" Jeannie was eager to leap in when she saw her brother frown.

"That is the area we found you in, the one with all the engraved trees," Hanzah said.

"When we were separated from Hanzah after the avalanche, Harrison, Dominic, and I managed to remain together," Jeannie explained.

"Dominic?" Orrin sang. "Ah, yes, the third." He turned to look at Hanzah. "Correct, Hanzah? Your third friend, Dominic...Turner, was it? Yes?" Orrin turned back to Jeannie once Hanzah nodded in confirmation. "And where might this fellow be at this time? I do not see him among you unless my eyes deceive me."

"Something we'd all love to know," Harrison said in frustration. Jeannie saw his anger rising but could do little to stop it.

"After the avalanche, we got completely lost," Harrison said. "We wandered for days in hunger and desperation until fortunately, the sky began to clear. That's when we reached the—the Maiden's Canvas. It was amazing to see, and it seemed safe, so we spent the night there. When Jeannie and I woke one morning, though, Dominic was nowhere to be found." Jeannie didn't have the chance to finish breathing a sigh of relief before he added, "He left us there. After all we'd been through."

"Don't say that." Jeannie just now found her window of opportunity. "We don't know that he left us."

"You keep saying that, but the simple fact is he was there, and then he was gone, Jeannie." Harrison did not look at her but instead addressed the others. "I know it's hard to understand when you're so young."

"I'm *not* a child! Without Dominic, none of us would be here right now! He saved us countless times during our journey to the Mountainlands and is much more than an acquaintance or friend—he's a part of our family!"

"You two are about as funny as a fox fighting with a foal for a fern," Orrin said, running his fingers through his beard.

"Is that even…funny?" Jeannie's shoulders sank as she looked up to ponder it.

"So, if we understand the story right, there is some mystery behind the whereabouts of your third companion," Orrin said, seeming to either not hear or make any note of Jeannie's comment. "Sadly, it sounds like the two most likely outcomes are either he abandoned you—sorry Jeannie…or he is not alive at all. But, either way, we need to make our way to the Great Fortress, I believe. I am not entirely sure of any other course of action."

"Yes, of course, Chieftain Orrin, but when we arrive, and there is talk of action regarding the threat to the South, I ask you to consider that we can help you take back the Riverlands," Harrison said. "We have plenty of allies in Harran—allies who would fight for us because of who we are and the life our father provided for them. If we get those forces to join with yours, we can take the Keagans down, which is a necessity for peace to be restored in the Murrieta. They are a curse on this place. Please…we've come all this way for this purpose. We've made it through fires and attacks and wolves and avalanches. At this point, we're desperate and need our allies more than ever. Will you not stand with us against them?"

"I made no mention we would not, Harrison Morrell. But based on the decision of my brother Arkouda in particular, I think, this choice becomes even more momentous for the V'ahani. It will determine our present; it will determine our future. We will be measured upon it for all time. So this is not a decision we can make as a faction of our greater group. We must travel to the Great Fortress and make it together with all our people."

"Thank you, Chieftain Orrin." Despite the gratitude of his words, Harrison did little to disguise his unhappiness. Jeannie wanted to punch him.

Orrin nodded and spoke again. "What do my councilmen say? Please note that I value your opinions, and while I want no one to forget the disgusting murder of my brother by his own councilmen, which weighs heavily on my mind—Hanzah, I pray to the Mother you in particular know that fact—I also hope my advisors will be honest with me in this matter and share their true thoughts for our next step. I promise you all I am on your side, as I always have been."

Jeannie was unsure she'd seen a person so blunt but well-intentioned as Orrin. Any other person speaking in the way Orrin did may have seemed rude, but Orrin seemed genuine, and often jolly and silly, as well. Again, though, she wondered how Harrison would handle Orrin's odder moments. Their father must have needed patience to deal with both Arkouda and Orrin. Could Harrison handle that burden?

"I agree, Orrin," one of the councilmen said. "There does not seem to be any other plausible option at this point. Safety and logic dictate only that we learn from our past mistakes, and I would challenge my fellow councilmen to disagree. We would be no better than Lennox, Castor, and Parish if we were to suggest anything other than a gathering of all of our V'ahani partners."

"Does any of my council disagree?" Orrin asked.

"Not at all."

"Nay."

The third and fourth councilmen were prompt.

"Well then, may the Mother praise us on the agreements and positive outcomes of our todays and tomorrows and yesterdays. So it shall be that we will venture to the Great Fortress, where we will decide upon the future of the V'ahani. Harrison and Jeannie, I would thank you for any information you can provide on these Keagans before then. I think we must go into this trip with great insight into the mindset of our enemies so we can educate our Grand Masters on how best to stop them."

Harrison nodded tightly. "The Morrells are at the service of the V'ahani from here on out. In that you have our word. We'd be more than happy to share all we know. I would just plead for you to consider what I said earlier, as well."

All Jeannie could do at this point was nod. This meeting made her feel her voice was neither important nor taken seriously. It seemed like it was accepted for Harrison to talk over her. What could she do about it now though? She was a young girl among men of power. Would she speak up and continue to be ignored, or sit back and stay silent?

All she knew for sure was she needed to do something, or Harrison's impatient, insatiable hunger for restoring their family's legacy might eat them both alive.

CHAPTER 3

PRAYER'S PASSAGE

With his legs kicked up on a footrest and a tall mug of thick, dark beer by his side, Gregory Calloway found a minute to relax in the study of the Keagan Mansion. The weeks following William's departure for New Berkeley had been stressful for Gregory. Not only was he now the "man of the house" in the mansion, but he was also essentially the "man of the whole operation" in the Murrieta. Leading others was not a role he had ever taken on before, and as much as he was willing to bite the bullet for William, he couldn't say he particularly liked the responsibility. He also knew a moment like this one was a rare, peaceful escape for him in the time until the eldest Keagan returned.

After taking a long swig of beer and scratching his fuzzy, balding head, Gregory eased back into his cozy armchair. He closed his eyes, immersing himself in the calming darkness of his mind.

A small fist slammed sharply into the side of his upper arm.

"Ow! What the f—heck?"

Gregory caught himself and his language when he spotted it was the young Donna Keagan who had punched him in the arm. William wouldn't tolerate Gregory teaching his cousin any fowl words while he was away.

"Donna—my goodness—you can't go around punching people who are trying to sleep and have done nothing wrong to you." This time he spoke in an intentionally less-fiery manner.

The look on Donna's face showed no remorse. She appeared furious.

"What is it you want, dear?"

The compassion and calm Gregory was trying to show Donna appeared to be having little effect. Her face turned bright red, and she stomped her foot on the ground. She looked like a plump, angry tomato.

Over the past few months, Gregory had begun to notice Donna appeared to be getting a bit chunkier—and this was yet another cause of stress. He didn't want to allow the girl to balloon while her brother and cousins were away, but also had no idea how to tell a young girl she needed to stop eating and lose weight.

As Gregory's thoughts wandered off, Donna stomped again.

"Oh, I'm sorry, I forgot," he said, recalling Donna's inability to speak without her brother speaking first. "Well if you have something to say, where's Blanton?"

She gave him a sarcastic look, first folding her arms in frustration and then lifting her palms upward as she shrugged her shoulders.

"So…you can't find him?"

Donna dramatically reared an arm back behind her. Gregory was confused by this and worried she might punch him again, but like a rocket, she shot a thumb up right in front of his nose. It was as if somehow this girl thought it was obvious what she wanted, even though she didn't speak a word. Being around the children in the Keagan Mansion did at least ease Gregory's despair about no longer having a child of his own.

"Well, why didn't you say so?" he joked to get back at her. Her expression went completely blank and irritated.

"Oh, don't get upset. I was only kidding. Let's go find your brother." As he went to sit up in his chair, Donna let out a friendly smile. Another punch landed sharply in his arm again.

"Ah—stop doing that, damn it!" he bellowed. He got up from his spot, and Donna merrily skipped to the door. "Once William comes back, and your brother Walter, too, I swear—"

Donna stopped in her tracks and turned to face him, raising her eyebrows.

"Forget it," Gregory said, moving past her into the hallway.

With Donna at his back, Gregory marched through the mansion, searching and calling for her brother, Blanton, who was nowhere to be found. They went to his room first, the library next, then through the living rooms and dining room, but they could not find him anywhere. When they went to check outside, Gregory spotted Maria Abigale, the mother of William's wife, Judith, gardening as her younger children played. He took note of Francis, Henrietta, and Florence, but still no Blanton.

"Excuse me, Mrs. Abigale, have you seen Blanton anywhere?" Gregory called out.

Maria put down her tools. "Gregory, by now you should be calling me Maria. I don't look old to you, do I?"

"No not at all, ma'am!" Gregory embarrassingly stuttered as he approached her. "You're a perfectly beautiful lady."

Maria smiled at him, and Gregory felt relieved. "I'm only teasing, but thank you for the compliment," Maria chirped as she rose off her knees and to her feet. "Now what's this business with Blanton?"

As much as he was trying to be polite, Gregory also meant the words he'd said to Maria. Though the color in her hair was beginning to fade, she wore her beauty well, and there was an infectious charm about her. Besides, she wasn't too much older than him.

"I'm looking for Blanton on behalf of Donna here, who's got something to say, and I'd prefer for her to say so without punching me in the arm again—as she's insisted on doing." He shot a look at Donna, who stuck her tongue out at him.

"No need to fret, darling. If there's one thing we women can do better than any man, it's finding things that are hidden away—well, now that I think of it, things that aren't hidden too for that matter!"

Gregory chuckled and followed her as she marched inside with purpose. Once again, they walked through all of the same rooms, with Maria scanning every corner. Still, Gregory saw nothing and was beginning to worry that the boy was not in the mansion at all.

"Donna, could you please check Francis's, Henrietta's, and Florence's rooms for me please?" Maria asked. Donna nodded and darted off, clearly desperate.

Once she was gone, Maria leaned close to Gregory. "Blanton is in the dining room, underneath the table, hiding behind the table cloth. I didn't want to alert Donna because I think he wants some alone time, but maybe you could go talk him out of it while she's distracted?"

It wasn't entirely surprising that Maria was so sharp, but Gregory was still taken aback. "I will, thanks for your help," he smiled. Maria winked back, and Gregory returned again to the dining room.

When he arrived, he eased his way over to the table. "Blanton, I know you're under there," he called. "I'm not going to pull up the cloth, but I just want to talk to you. It's just us, okay? I promise."

"Are you sure?" Blanton murmured. Gregory felt relief overcome him that Blanton was safe, but it almost simultaneously sunk to the ground as Donna came barging into the room.

"Blanton!" she shrieked, only now able to speak after hearing Blanton. "I heard you. I know you're there. Come out now."

"No, Donna, ple—," Gregory started, but it was too late. Blanton popped out of his hiding place and ran for the door. It seemed to Gregory that as Donna had gained weight, Blanton had lost weight, and seeing him in this state, running and hiding for some privacy, Gregory felt terrible for the boy.

"You lied to me," Blanton cried as he turned to Gregory. "I hate you!"

"Blanton stop it, calm down!" Donna reached a hand onto his arm.

"But I didn't mean to . . ." Gregory started. Before he could finish though, Blanton was out of the dining room, with Donna racing after him.

As they left, in came Maria, looking upset. "I'm so sorry Gregory," she said. "She got away. And I know he didn't mean what he said."

"It's okay," Gregory mumbled, not necessarily believing it would be and feeling like a failure. "William will be back soon enough."

*

42

"A time will come when you'll have to make a choice, William, between the relentless pursuit of your burning passions and your dedication to those who you love the most. Only then will you understand how difficult it is, no matter which path you might choose. Only then will you understand my choice."

The words of his father, Leonard, had echoed in his mind since the day William had left New Berkeley for the Murrieta. Now, as his posse traveled toward Prayer's Passage on their way back east, the statement seemed to ring even louder.

His only relief from the stress of his desire for his father's elusive approval were two beauties: the Murrieta landscape and his wife, Judith.

After leaving Fayette, William was pleased to see each sunrise reveal more magnificence than the last. As the spring set in, blue bonnets came to line the open, hilly fields they passed through, and the scent of the flowers filled the air. Smelling sweet, they reminded him of Judith, prompting him to look at her, as she slept in the wagon, and thought about how she'd been his comfort and support through this entire venture. Following the successful upheaval of the Riverlands, their travels east had been delayed by particularly harsh winter conditions. When the day had finally come to leave, William's nerves had begun to set in, but Judith had pulled him through it. The memory was crisp and clear in his mind as he looked back out to the field of blue bonnets.

With his necessities all packed and ready to go, William had felt paralyzed. Hands on his knees, eyes closed, and head bowed, he sat on the edge of the bed wondering whether he could do this. An arm softly placed around him broke his concentration.

"Everything's going to be alright, William."

Judith's hushed tone had rung through his whole body as if it were ice-pressed against his fevered skin. Her touch and the rosy punch of her perfume had brought him a welcomed tranquility, as it always had from the moment he'd met his gorgeous, powerful wife. With each passing day since their wedding, William had become more familiar with her, especially in the days of their delayed travels. The two would have loud, passionate sex multiple times a day, which for William had been as much a matter of passing the time and relieving stress as it was an indication of his desire for Judith. Yet while her touch had soothed, it hadn't removed his fear.

"Now that you're here, my love, I know it is." William wanted to appease her.

"Don't you lie to me," she'd said. "I know you, and I can see you don't truly believe it, but you need to. You need to not just for me but for both of us. This is your moment, William. I know it, my father knows it, and your brothers know it, too. If you don't, though, all that support and all your work will be for nothing. Leonard *will* see the man you've become, he has to, and my father's connections with him will help solidify that. But even if he ends up being a fool and resisting the truth, this is our world, baby."

"This is and always will be our world, I promise you." William had meant it too.

Still feeling energized by the way his wife had spoken to him that day, he smiled down at her as she continued to doze in the wagon. He knew that together the world would be theirs.

Admiring the landscape, William noticed the hills had begun to grow taller, and the grassy fields were substituted for dry, dirt-covered paths up ahead. Cassius indicated to William and the others they should now be on high alert, as the shallow canyon-like environment was an indication they had entered Prayer's Passage. The last time Cassius had been in the Passage, he had been leading the Abigales to William.

The landscape of the Passage was somewhat familiar from William's first time venturing into the Murrieta, but it had been some time since. He'd recalled the atmosphere being unnerving at the time, but it was possibly even more haunting now in the spring. Given the eerie feeling permeating the valley, the seasonal beauty only offered a disconcerting illusion.

With the thieves known as the "Highlanders" and a population of coyotes, venomous reptiles, and other dangerous forms of wildlife, nothing was safe about this place. Now as William scanned in all directions, he thought the path felt too calm. To William's left was a shallow tributary of the Chorisma, no wider than fifty feet across, with the occasional run-down home popping up on the other side, every half mile or so. To his right were canyon-like cliffs raised high overhead. He wondered first how anyone could live in those homes across the waterway. Could conditions here have somehow improved since his last visit? Yet it also, in some way, felt intentional that the river separated the two sides. It was as if the residents knew something no one else did.

Henry, Judith's father, pointed toward the base of the canyon wall. "What is that?" he called, squinting. Henry's leg was tapping rapidly, and his eyes darted in every direction. He was nervous.

Just off in the distance, William could spot two massive boars with powerful tusks. While they seemed to be grazing peacefully, they seemed to be aware of the wagon's presence and trotted along in the same direction as it.

"Those would be hogs," Cassius told Henry. "We'll keep an eye on them and take action should they get any closer. For now, they're far enough off that they shouldn't be bothered by us and so won't bother us in turn."

Over the next few hours, the ride through the Passage was relatively quiet. A larger-than-average house soon appeared in the distance on the other side of the river. It was still less than half the size of the Keagan Mansion, William thought, but it was noticeably different from the others. It had shutters painted a dark red around windows that were all either cracked or had outright holes in them. As they moved closer, William noted the holes were in fact bullet holes, which were littered across the wooden walls. Between the house and the stream was a field with high stalks. Standing in the center, well above those stalks was a tall, disfigured scarecrow. The patchwork of the thing suggested to William it had been made and remade. Though the house appeared abandoned, the scarecrow seemed to have been stitched together recently. The hogs, which had been steadily moving alongside their party but keeping their distance, began snorting, catching William's attention.

They seem agitated, he thought, *but by what?*

A crackling sounded from the house, and, in an instant, the scarecrow by the abandoned house went up in flames. The two horses leading the front of the wagon became startled, but Cassius was able to bring them to ease.

"What the hell's going on?" Judith murmured, just as a shot burst through the air and ripped straight through the cover of the wagon.

Judith screamed as William and Henry shielded her, pushing her down to the floor to safety.

"Highlanders!" Cassius cried as he jostled the reins and called for the horses to pick up speed. William looked out the front but ducked back down as three outlaws on horseback burst out from behind the house, slowing as they crossed the stream but continuing to fire their weapons. Each of the riders wore a cowboy hat and bandana that rested just below their eyes. Cassius dodged the first array of bullets from his left and fired back, hitting one of the Highlanders' horses. It fell screaming into the water.

"They'll be at our backs in a second!" Cassius screamed as they ran along the stream and passed the house on their left. "Grab weapons and fire out the back once they're in sight!"

The others, Judith included, followed his command. As soon as they passed, each of the three fired. Every click of the trigger intensified William's high with the intensity of the moment. There were no hits, but, as they reloaded, Cassius turned the wagon toward the stream.

The move seemed insane to William. "Are you nuts? What are you doing?"

"We won't lose them in this wagon. Our only choice is to shoot our way out of this. We'll take the house."

As their horses dashed into the stream, water splashed up into the wagon. The rocky river floor caused the wagon to jolt violently in crossing, which made aiming at those in pursuit even more difficult. Judith, William, and Henry continued to fire sporadically for cover and continued to miss. By William's count there were still at least four Highlanders after them: the two remaining on their horses, the one who fired the first shot and was likely holed up in the house, and the one whose horse had fallen but who had survived the fall and was running back toward the house, as well. He laughed hysterically and cheered at the riders' misfortune to have to double back and cross the stream yet again in the opposite direction—how clever Cassius was after all. There still could have been more in the home, but by his counting of their gunshot progression, it didn't seem likely.

They soon emerged from the edge of the narrow, shallow stream, and Cassius rushed the horses toward the house. However, as they moved closer two shots came from within it, one of which smashed through a spoke of one of the wheels, causing the wagon to collapse straight onto its side. Cassius was thrown off his perch, while William, Judith, and Henry were tossed around inside the wagon cover. William hit his head on the way down and was left dazed as he tried to right himself. He realized there must be two men in the house after all.

As he made it onto his knees, he spotted a frantic Cassius running over to him. "Come on! We have to get to the side of the house for cover—now! Grab the weapons, and let's go!"

William nodded, but first he needed to ensure Judith was all right. She was crouched beside him. He brushed her hair away from her face and was surprised to see a smile alongside her already-forming bruises. With a nod, she confirmed she was ready to run, and so they did.

Just as William and Judith made it to cover behind a corner of the house, the Highlanders shot their pistols again. William's group was now at an angle that placed them out of the line of sight of the two Highlanders in the house, but the ones on horseback were not far behind them. They were just making their way back across the water now. As much as William liked to lead, being in the action was something he felt he could never grow out of—his blood was singing with the joy of it.

William heard a gunshot and saw Henry, who had been sprinting toward them, fall to his knees just feet from the side of the house. Judith screamed as her father clutched the side of his head and struggled to get up.

"Daddy!" Judith bellowed.

William saw blood beginning to seep through Henry's fingers. He hastily analyzed his surroundings, knowing he needed to act.

"Give me your gun now, Judith, and stay here! Cassius, can you take care of the men inside?"

Cassius nodded and was off. William snatched the gun out of Judith's outstretched hand and ran directly toward Henry. With the revolver in his left hand, he fired upon the approaching riders as he slid to Henry's side. Luckily, he hit one of the Highlanders straight through the chest, knocking him off his horse and startling the other rider who circled back for his comrade. A bullet whizzed right past William, close enough that his ear began to ring. Once he realized he was still alive, he jolted around and emptied the revolver in his right hand at the house for cover.

When it was emptied he lifted Henry's pistol up off the floor. "Where are you hit!?"

"I think they took a piece off my ear!" Henry cried.

Realizing he had only a few seconds before the second horseman returned and hearing no more movement from inside the house, William called for Judith's help.

"Judith," he called. "Come here and get your father back to the house. Be quick about it!"

Judith rushed over as requested and lifted her father's arm over her shoulder. Once she had him, William darted behind the fallen wagon. The final Highlander on horseback soon made his return, barreling toward Judith and Henry at full speed. He fired, and William thought his heart might stop in his chest, but Judith and Henry reached the cover of the house just in time. When William felt the attacker was close enough to him, he jumped out of hiding and unloaded as rapidly as his pistol would fire. The smoke was thick and intoxicating as the bullets flew. When the air cleared, he realized that while he didn't hit the attacker directly, the horse had been struck multiple times and now lay collapsed on top of its rider.

The Highlander wailed in pain as William marched over triumphantly. He was surprised to note this was a woman by the pitch of voice. Creeping into view of her exposed upper torso, he spotted a gun pointed up at him. Almost simultaneously, he dove out of sight as the pinned woman screamed, fired two shots, and kept clicking the trigger even after the weapon was emptied. William jumped up to his feet, furious, and stormed around the horse to kick her pistol away. He placed his knee atop her neck and ripped the bandana off her face.

The first thought that struck him was the woman was fairly attractive despite her aggressiveness. She appeared to be slightly younger than him, with jet-black hair and green-blue eyes that reminded him of the oceans of the far-east. He felt somewhat guilty for strangling her. When a helpless look crossed her face, it hit him. That, combined with a lack of resistance, led William to ease up off her neck.

As he stood up though, Judith came running over and kicked the woman in the face.

"You stupid bitch!" she shrieked. She kicked the Highlander one more time and ran over to the discarded gun. Lifting it up, she stormed back over and pointed it at the defenseless woman's head. Her finger clicked the trigger two times, and when she realized it was out of ammo, she threw the weapon to the ground. At this point, her face was similar in color to her red-brown hair, which she had to push out of her face.

As much as William appreciated this side of his wife, he knew if they wanted to make it out of the Passage without further interruption, they needed to stop this ruckus now. He wrapped Judith in his arms.

"Baby, please."

"She can't get away with this. They can't do this to the Keagans! They have to know who we are and respect our authority."

William pointed down at the woman, who was bloodied and breathing heavily. "Look at her. Does it look like they've gotten away with this?" Judith glared back at him in response. "I know it's hard to accept, but taking this territory will need to happen one step at a time and will take the army of men we're building. We can't have all the respect we deserve right now. Believe me, I'm just as impatient about it, but it's just the way it is."

"Looks like you missed a spot!" The voice that sounded behind them was deep and raspy.

William turned in horror to see what must have been the last Highlander limping toward them, his pistol aimed straight at William's chest. Two shots cracked through the sky. William instinctively braced himself and shut his eyes.

When he opened them again, he was surprised to see the gunman shot dead. Looking toward the house, he spotted Cassius in the window with a rifle. Judith threw herself on him in tears.

"I am alive, right?" he gasped.

"You're damn right you are!" Judith shrieked.

"Must've missed thanks to Cassius," Henry chimed in, walking toward them.

Cassius exited the house in short order and was approaching them with his rifle in one hand and a revolver in the other, the latter of which he tossed to William.

"Was that the last of them?" Henry asked.

William looked at Cassius, who nodded.

"I think so," William answered. "At least I hope so. Either way, we need to get out of here as soon as possible. We've got three horses, two of ours and one of the Highlanders'. We'll have to ride swiftly and make it the rest of the way to the Doreshire port without the wagon. Judith, you'll ride with—" As he turned to address her, he found Judith several feet away from him, near the edge of the field of green stalks. She knelt over the dead man's body, lifting his revolver out of his hand. There was no more use in trying to keep her from killing the Highlander woman, William supposed.

"William!" he heard Cassius call. William looked up in time to see the two lumbering hogs that had been following them were now thundering toward him. Cassius fired the rifle, and luckily, the bullet struck one of the hogs straight through the rib cage. The hog squealed relentlessly as blood spewed from it, but the second one only gained speed.

With it upon him, William had no time to shoot before it tackled him to the ground, knocking the gun from his hand. As it swung its head to dig its tremendous tusks into him, he used both hands to grab them and hold it back. Recognizing his precarious position, he decided he'd need to make a move for a blade he had at his waist. With all his might, he held back the beast with his stronger right hand while reaching for his belt with the other. As he grabbed the handle of his weapon, though, he heard Cassius yelp in pain before firing off a second shot, presumably finishing the other hog, which must have managed to do some damage even with a bullet in its ribs. William's distraction caused his right hand to slip, and one of the tusks nicked the side of his face. Even as he screamed in pain, he began to stab at its stomach with his knife. William continued thrusting his blade furiously into the hog above him until he was able to land a fatal last blow into its throat.

For a moment, there was silence. Judith shouted though to break the calm. Drenched in the hog's blood, he prayed for the madness to end, recognizing the irony of it even as he begged whatever god there might or might not be for mercy. Prayer's Passage, indeed. Heaving the hog off him, he noticed Cassius standing across from him, a wound in his leg bleeding heavily. Even so, his rifle was aimed at a stranger, one who was holding Judith at gunpoint.

CHAPTER 4

TO GET HER APART

In the days following the alley attack, Latera was constantly looking over her shoulder, worrying she'd be exposed for stealing the pistol. Each day, she visited the Square, memorizing every corner of it in preparation. If they didn't catch her before Clovis's speech, she knew what she was going to do. She had to kill Clovis. With him gone, his men would be leaderless and disorganized. They did not worship Walter Keagan the way they did Clovis. And even if the Tokali took up arms to help the Keagans, the V'ahani would be sure to at least have a much safer, less depraved life with the deranged Clovis gone. Once the V'ahani of the North came to liberate them, the lack of leadership would greatly favor her people in a fight. She also expected it to be the last thing she ever did. But she was ready for that fate now more than ever. All she'd been through had built up to this. Killing Clovis Keagan and freeing her people would be her legacy.

When the day arrived, she tied the pistol to her thigh with a lengthy hair ribbon. All morning she was stone faced, trying to set her mind right until the announcement came as expected.

The sky was clear as she marched with the crowds of people toward the Square. She pushed her way through until she was as close to the balcony as possible. When she reached a point she felt she could make the shot from, she waited, her gaze fixed firmly upon the spot he would stand. She took a deep breath, and she knew she was truly ready.

For some time, Latera waited there, tuning out the chattering voices around her. The crowd openly speculated about what the news would be, but none of them knew of the reckoning that was to come.

Soon, they will be liberated, she thought. *Soon, they will all be liberated.*

After what felt to her like an eternity, he approached.

The majority of the audience cheered like the good little pets Clovis wanted them to be as he reached the front of the balcony with a dark grin on his face. He raised his hands in the air to silence them. Latera was now sliding her hand down the outside of her mid-length dress to her thigh.

"I suppose it's kinda nice to see y'all again," he shrieked. They applauded again, but his expression turned. "No, no, no. This won't do."

Latera made sure to be quick as she reached under her dress and grabbed the handle of her gun, but as she did Clovis turned back and walked out of sight. The crowd once again began yelling, but this time in confusion.

Latera felt something small press up against her back.

"Take your hand off the gun slowly—do it right now," a voice uttered behind her. She recognized that voice—it belonged to the man who had saved her during the attempted assault.

Of course he's a Keagan, she thought in despair. She began to turn around, but his hand clamped on her upper arm.

"Turn your head, and I'll blow a hole straight through you right here, do you understand me?" he said.

The crowd continued to roar as Clovis came back out to the balcony. "Just kidding! We have far too much to discuss!"

"You're going to very slowly and discreetly hand me the pistol you took, and then you're going to turn to your left and walk straight until we've left the Square. Nod to show me you understand," the man behind Latera demanded as she stood perfectly still.

There was no other option at this point but to nod, so she did. Anything else would have been suicide. She felt so defeated. Again, she was helpless, caught in the latest of a string of misfortunes. Following orders, Latera handed him the weapon before turning left and exiting the crowd with the man following right behind. As they exited the Square, she had to endure the wretched sound of Clovis merrily giving his speech. All she could think was she should have shot sooner.

Once out of sight of the Square, she stopped, preparing to hear the gunshot she was sure was to come.

"Just get it over with," she said, trying to remain stern and removed, but on the inside feeling the shock and horror beginning to sink in. In response to her command, several hands from behind wrapped a gag around her mouth and threw a burlap sack over her head a second later. As Latera was forcefully dragged through the streets, she prayed. Though her words were silent, Latera hoped the Mother could still hear her.

With the sack still over her head, she was forced into a chair and held down as her hands and feet were bound to the legs and arms. Latera heard footsteps which suggested they left her there. She waited at first, listening for any sign of movement. When there was none, she began to test her binds.

The first time she managed to tip over the chair and begin to crawl, someone in the room lifted her back up and put her in place. It shocked her—this still, utterly silent person, whom she'd heard not even a breath from, let alone a peep of frustration or anger at her attempted escape. After a moment or two to digest it, she stopped caring about whether there was someone there. She wasn't willing to wait patiently for her slaughter. She tried again, but her attempt was stopped a second time.

After some time of carrying on like this, she gave up. As tired as Latera was of feeling helpless, she knew she needed to stop resisting now or she'd exhaust herself too much to escape if there ever was an opportune time. She was exhausting herself—not only physically in her escape attempts but also mentally. Her nerves were frayed, which was evidenced by how she shook in her binds. Though her gag had been removed, the sack over her head remained in place as did the ropes tying down her limbs. She knew screaming would do no good and might even result in her getting shot. The more she thought about how helpless she was, how restricted, how controlled, the more the tremors shook her. Being so trapped after she'd had a glimmer of hope for freedom from the Hold opened a new and fresh fear inside her. With increasing frustration, she tried to keep her body still, but she simply couldn't. She wasn't happy her fear would reveal itself so visibly to her captors, either.

"Look," she said, hoping to get through to whoever was in the room. "I apologize for being so difficult in my escape attempts. But please...if you could just release all my limbs but one, I swear I will not resist any more. With no control of my arms or legs, I can hardly breathe. I have a feeling if you wanted me dead, I would be already. You also would not want me to ruin whatever you have planned for me by me dying, would you?"

Latera waited, still shaking involuntarily, but no reply came. Somehow, she thought she'd be able to squash the tremors when it counted—like now—but she couldn't. She was beginning to realize learning to control her fears, let alone overcoming them, would not be so easy.

"Please. I apologize again. And I would prefer chains if you had them. You could put them around one of my legs and I would have even less chance of escape." She was angered by the desperation that had crept into her tone, but she didn't know how much longer she could stand it.

Still, no response came.

Latera sat there for what felt like an hour or so more. She remained quiet, other than her jitters, and tried to distract herself from her ever-growing nerves. Tapping her fingers, she felt the wood of the chair's arm. She began to stroke a finger along the grain, but it was rough, and she jumped when a splinter dug in. Irritated at the sharp pain, she soon decided to try and fall asleep. It might help, she thought, to calm her down. Closing her eyes, she tried to think of the Riverlands and the soothing flow of the River White in the afternoons. She was brought back to the days when Hanzah and she would play with the rocks by the water.

"I accept your apology," the faintest of voices said in her ear.

She could have jumped right out of her binds from the fright. It was the same man from the alley.

Once again, she was shaking and breathing heavily—which only served to irritate her.

"For the sake of the Mother! You sick, twisted…! It was *you* standing there for all these hours, and you said nothing? Who are you, and what do you want from me?"

"Sometimes silence is the most magnificent sound the world has to offer, you know." This time the man was directly in front of her. He had moved without an audible step.

"Stop that!" It became silent again. Though her crown-braided hair was sweaty and damp against her forehead, she still felt an icy chill through her arms and neck. "Enough with this game—just answer me."

"What I want is for you to be silent." The man was now at her right. "Now you might be thinking, 'Well that's a simple request. Too simple in fact. He must be trying to trick me.' That is what you're thinking, is it not?"

"I do not—"

"Aha! I knew you couldn't do it, I just knew it! You don't know what silence even is. Nor do you know how to listen. But you're going to learn. Oh yes, you're going to have to learn—and learn fast."

Latera followed the order, listening as the man loudly, and rather dramatically, stamped his feet as he marched away from her to the right. A door ripped open and he let out a sharp, blaring whistle. Within a few seconds, she could hear cries for mercy and panting as others were brought into the room.

"Who is that?" Latera cried. "Do not hurt them!"

"Latera?" Winona shrieked. "Latera!"

"Winnie? Mika?" Latera called, hearing them both grunt as if they were shoved to the floor, followed by the clicking of pistols. "No, stop! Are you both all right? What have they done to you?"

"Quit your fuckin' whining!" another man said at the sound of Latera's quivering friends. They both obeyed as much as they probably could.

Latera's fingers now began to dig into the wooden armrests of her seat once again despite her previous splinter. At this point she could care less about the pain—she was furious and this needed to stop.

"What do you want from us?" she spat.

"I understand you can't see what's happening right now, so let me paint a picture for you, Latera." The voice of her tormentor came once again from behind and once again made her jump. "I've been watching you very closely. Because of this I know who your friends are, I know how you spend your time, and I know what it is you want."

"You have no idea what I want!" Latera exclaimed.

"Whether that's true or not, you know what *I* want is for you to be *silent* and to *listen*. Now let me finish describing the scene to you ...." At this point, he began circling her as he talked. "There are two men, two of your close friends, and two guns. And those two guns are being pointed at two heads, and those two heads are the two heads of your two close friends. That's pretty much it. So I believe that should provide you with the incentive to give me what I want, would you agree?"

Understanding the gravity of the situation, Latera nodded as she continued to shake.

"Good. So why are we here? We're here because you've been up to no good—sure. But given our forgiving nature, we're not going to punish you in the way you might be thinking, judging by your frenzied shaking."

Latera was angered that he would think she was quaking because of him, but she remained silent, since he did have the upper hand.

"Now, Mika and Winona," he said, only now sounding like he wasn't right on top of her. "May I call you Winnie, too, by the way? I like the sound of that name."

Latera could hear Winona panting fearfully while Mika did not make a sound. This monster's odd tangent was starting to make her nervous.

"So Mika, Winnie, I'm not gonna tell you what your courageous friend here tried to do, but I will say it was a catalyst for change. She wanted to do whatever it'd take to end the suffering you V'ahani have been experiencing, even at the risk of her own life, and guess what? Her goal was achieved. This martyr of yours might have potentially ended your pain."

Confusion swept over Latera. What did he mean? And more important, who was this man to the Keagans? She kept asking herself this, but the importance of the answer didn't strike her until this moment.

She heard the once again exaggerated, pounding footsteps as he marched back to her, but this time they were accompanied by his loud sniffing.

"Is that...is that hope I smell?" he said, continuing to sniff.

"Good, maybe now you see I do know what it is you're after, and I am willing to give it to you. You want your people to be safe. You want their suffering and mistreatment to end. Most nobly, you'd be willing to take it all away for them even at cost to yourself, but I'm here to tell you that you won't have to. What you will need to do is simple. You've been doing a much better job of it so far. Do you know what it is? You guessed it! Listen!"

Latera felt lost, but there was hope inside her, nonetheless. Whatever he meant by his words, the prospect of safety for the V'ahani was too enticing to ignore. By now, they both knew she'd do anything to achieve that end. Beginning to feel light-headed from sweating in the burlap sack for so long, Latera forced herself to focus.

"The V'ahani of the Riverlands are weak and dejected. Your leaders are gone, and there's nothing your people in the Mountainlands will be able to do but surrender if they want you to live. To keep your people alive, you, too, will do what I say— that we've established. The Tokali on the other hand...they've been under our control for some time, and though they've proven quite a bit by bringing you here, we would be fools if we weren't to keep a watchful eye on them. After all, that Tokali boy killed your V'ahani chieftain before Clovis finished having his fun with him, which he did not like *at all*. And considering the love-sick one, Elan, has shown nothing but defensiveness for you, we do have reason to be doubtful. Love, as much as it provides a reason to live, will likely also be the death of us all."

"There is no love between Elan and I," Latera snarled, unable to resist breaking the rule. She hated to even hear the suggestion.

"Well you made it pretty far, I suppose," the man chuckled. "You must continue to listen, though. Listen not just to me but to *them*. In return for the safety and assimilation of your people here at the Hold, you'll get close to that Elan fellow who loves you so dearly. You will learn the secrets he, his family, and any Tokali he's associated with are hiding. When you receive those secrets, you will bring them to me. Unfortunately, you'll have to be escorted to me similarly to the way you were today, and for now you can't know who I am. Given your most recent act of defiance, I can't chance you getting ideas. Just know I will be watching you at all times. You'll never see me, so make no attempt to look—it's a waste of both our times. You'll accept these terms because, like I've said, I know what you want, Latera. I know you still feel the burn of betrayal for what the Tokali have done. How could it ever go away? Even if your people didn't get along before, what they did was inexcusable, and this is your chance to get them back for it. Besides that though, we both also know what you don't want. Isn't that right, Winnie?"

Winnie said nothing.

Latera decided to take her stand. "I will do it."

The man clapped his hands at a slow pace. "A wise, necessary decision. We'll be in touch, princess."

Latera heard her friends being taken out, and silence came over the room again. Breathing deeply, she reveled in the freedom she felt when they finally cut her binds, and her body's return to stillness.

*

There was no more time to pretend. There was no arguing with Varek. Now, an opportunity had presented itself. It would be a risk for certain. It would be a risk that could get him killed, as a matter of fact. But he didn't care anymore. There seemed no hope at this point. They'd never believe him, and they'd kill him before Hanzah could think to come look for him here. And why would Hanzah come? They'd not told him he was here. They'd painted Dominic as another Eastern threat.

A sad turn of events for certain, but he had to lie when they'd asked if he traveled alone. After what happened to Hanzah's father, Dominic had to make sure the Morrells would be safe with *these* V'ahani. How could he have known the Morrells had immunity still—or that Varek and the V'ahani of the Mountainlands would hate men of Eastern descent so much?

Now, after months, Dominic had a stroke of luck that would allow him to make his attempted escape and use all the capabilities of survival he'd learned. When the guard had bound his hands behind the pole in the cell, Dominic had attempted to act cooperatively. With the guard's attention reduced, Dominic had kept his hands close to his back, with his wrists separated as much as possible before being bound. This provided him slack in the rope he could use to work his thumbs between it in the time he spent alone in the cell. The darkness was very much beneficial in this purpose. He twisted his wrists furiously, stretching the rope as much as possible and working up a profuse sweat with each attempt until his binds were loose enough to rip off.

Once he was freed, he crept over to the door leading into his cell. Carefully, he crouched down to peep through the crack at the bottom of the door. Through the thin gap, he saw another wall about five feet beyond the door. Dominic had no idea what to do now. Having been led into his cell always blindfolded, he had no concept of the layout of the Great Fortress.

In the middle of considering his options, he heard easy footsteps coming from the right, which broke the light as they passed in front of the door and continued down the hallway. Dominic noted the tanned feet had been in open-toed shoes, sprinkled with dark hair. A guard, he presumed, for no man coming in and out of the early-spring chill would be wearing sandals. So this man was stationed inside for a long period, meaning he was likely a guard on rotation. This might make things difficult. He also realized he may not have much time, and if he was found to have escaped his binds, he would be doomed.

He waited for the feet to return with his ear against the door. When he could hear them approaching, Dominic swept dirt through the crack, hoping the guard would rush in unthinkingly. Instead, the guard stopped walking and appeared to hesitate, before running off and disappearing. Dominic was horrified. Had the guard just run for reinforcements?

A crinkling sounded at the door, which began to creak open.

Another guard! Of course! There must have been a stationary one next to his door. Dominic hid behind the hinges and scooped up two handfuls of dirt this time, as a spear led the guard's way into the cell. When he saw the sentry's mouth drop at the sight of the empty pole, he jumped out and unloaded the handful of dirt in his eyes. The guard let out a yelp and fell to a knee, furiously wiping at his face. Dominic seized his opportunity and ripped the spear from the hands of the V'ahani. Flipping it around, he slapped the blunt side across the guard's temple. The guard dropped, unconscious.

Dominic heard steps running toward the cell, echoing through the halls. Panicking, he ripped the white, hooded coat off the guard and whipped out the binds he had escaped from. As quickly as he could, he slid into the coat and threw the hood over his head. As the steps neared the door, Dominic could tell it was only one person arriving. He lifted the spear to keep it by his side, then he ducked his head down and began to tie the unconscious V'ahani to the pole with their backs to the door as another guard entered the dark room, spear at the ready.

"What happened here?" the man asked.

Dominic said nothing at first as he tried to think through how to proceed, his heart racing. He was glad, for once, of the darkness, because it further hid the unconscious guard's face. "He tried to escape—his binds must have been too loose. I can handle it from here, thank you."

Dominic had never been so happy he'd learned the V'ahani language in his life. He wasn't sure about his accent, but he prayed it would be enough. He'd practiced it heavily with Hanzah on their journey in moments of boredom, so perhaps he'd improved.

"I heard a scream, though, what was that about?" the guard followed.

"It was nothing. We grappled, and I dropped my spear. He went for it, but I blinded him with some dirt and knocked him out."

"Well then," the guard sounded impressed. "Did the Mother make you resourceful or what? I suppose you needed to be though—nearly getting bested by an Easterner like this one."

"This worthless Eastern scum didn't even come close to... *besting* me." Realizing his lack of fluency with the language and knowing he couldn't hide his face by pretending to tie the man up much longer, Dominic decided he needed to end the conversation as soon as possible.

"I am fine to finish up here, though, so you may return to your post now. Thank you again for checking on me."

The V'ahani paused for a moment, turning his head sideways. Something had made this man uneasy. "Come see me at the quarters as soon as you are finished up. I will send someone else for cell duty for the rest of the night and will go summon the Masters now, so you can tell them about what he has done. I think this might be the last straw for this one."

Dominic nodded, fearful and feeling the urgency of his escape all the more. "Very well," he said before the guard left the cell.

There was no telling when this guard would come around, so now that Dominic was alone, he ripped off his socks, tied them together, and used them as a gag, which he wrapped around the pole. As disgusting and salty as they'd taste in the poor fellow's mouth, Dominic felt no pity following months of mistreatment. Though he knew the gag wouldn't completely silence the guard, whatever time he could buy would be precious to his escape.

Peering left and right through the doorway of the cell, Dominic was careful to only narrowly peek through his hood. The corridor was also very dark and was filled with the cries of Eastern men. Though he'd heard them for some time, they were clearer outside the cell. The newer captives tended to be louder and angrier, while the rest were exhausted and begging. No matter the tone, though, none could hide the desperation that inspired their cries.

Through openings along the walls, Dominic could tell it was night. The hall was lit only by dim candle fire crackling by the doors. Despite how accustomed his eyes had become to the darkness, there was no seeing down the entirety of the long pathway of the lined cells. He was only relieved there were no other guards in sight. He supposed two were enough to watch helpless men. As he edged out of his cell, Dominic pulled the door shut. Sweat poured out of him and soaked the thick V'ahani jacket he wore as he stared down the darkness before him. *Why was the tunnel so long with such few prisoners, and where could it possibly lead,* he wondered?

He wished for a moment his magic was real, not illusion, and a trap door would open to take him right back to Harran, to a time before any of this mess had begun, to the time when he had felt for once in his life he'd found his place in the world. Then he let the wish go, knowing no amount of wishing would help him now, and began down the hallway.

The whining of the Eastern prisoners grew louder in the halls as he went deeper and deeper, or at least he felt like he was hearing more of them. A large, wooden door at the end of the way came into his view. When he realized there was no one by it, he darted over and took a deep breath. Though he heard nothing on the other side, it was thick, and he was nervous. Whether the inside of the Great Fortress was bustling at this hour or empty, Dominic's escape would need to be calculated.

"And from your pain, your fortunes will be awoken," Dominic said under his breath, recalling the speech he'd always give at his shows—it had become his own inspirational credo. With that, he shoved open the heavy door and walked out onto the streets of the Great Fortress, hood still up. The late hour was noticeable by the sheer sparseness of people. Dominic walked briskly through the streets, his head down but turning in every direction. All he knew was he needed to find the southern gate of the Fortress fast, so he could have some idea of where he was escaping to. From what he'd heard, there was only ocean to the north, and at this point, he either needed to find Hanzah or head back through the Passage and to the East. Either way, he'd first need to travel south and get far away from the Fortress.

"Because what you are about to behold here isn't…it isn't beyond your own reach or ability."

Continuing on through the streets, he saw the occasional V'ahani walking by, but fortunately none paid him too much mind. The general design of the Fortress seemed to be a winding hill with the structures increasing in scale as it went up. As such, Dominic assumed his best course was to go down, and so he went until he came upon an open market looking area, which was empty. Looking down, he noticed the center of the marketplace floor broke away from the uniform stone path to form the design of an eye. The sight shocked him for a moment before he looked back up and saw an open archway that led out of the Fortress before him. Next to it, a young woman exited a huge building. Behind the door she emerged from, Dominic could see a stable. He froze at the sight of such an opportunity, which prompted the woman to look his way.

"This 'magic' as you will see it, it's drawn only from the magic you provide back to the world."

At first, Dominic took a slow step back, noting the woman

would be able to see his face. Deciding not to jump to conclusions, he raised a single hand slowly in the air to wave. His stomach dropped when she did not follow suite. Lowering his hand back down, he began to walk briskly toward her. He couldn't risk her alerting everyone until he was far away. She turned and rushed back toward the stable. Dominic darted toward her at full speed. The young V'ahani woman momentarily struggled with the barn door, which allowed him to catch up to her. Dominic grabbed onto her arm, prompting her to scream, but he easily overpowered her and put his hand over her mouth. He wondered in a panic what he'd do with her as he wrestled her into submission. Her scream was loud and long enough to be heard by anyone nearby.

"Please…stop this…I'm not going to hurt you," he grunted as she struggled and let out a muffled wail into his hand. There was still a respect somewhere inside him for the V'ahani, and hurting a woman was against his moral code. As the lights and voices of the awoken V'ahani began to flare in the Fortress, Dominic rushed her to the horses in the first stable. There were three in the first stable alone and too many to count in the remainder of the barn. When he opened the gate, he cheered the other two out, knowing it wouldn't slow his pursuers down much at all, but figuring it couldn't hurt.

"Get on," he ordered the woman, throwing her up onto the final horse. He decided he'd need a hostage to protect himself from being killed on the spot if they caught up to him, which now, they likely would. Of course, he would never hurt this woman, but they didn't know that—they wouldn't even believe it if he said so.

The horse whinnied as she hopped up onto it. Dominic climbed on behind her and kicked the steed onward. The horse darted out of the barn and through the grand arches of the Fortress. He could tell the V'ahani woman was scared enough of him now to listen to his orders, because she didn't even scream as they left the Fortress.

They rode on with great haste for some time on the same trail. Dominic knew the horse couldn't go on forever, but he was also ever aware that there would be an army at his back. He could only hope this beaten path would somehow lead somewhere he could get his bearings to find the trail back to the Riverlands. He'd leave the woman on the trail to find her way home as soon as he found a place to re-center himself. The Morrells and he had their struggles for weeks trying to find any familiar path.

"Where does this lead?" he asked.

"Please do not kill me," the woman pleaded to Dominic as they charged on, her home vanishing in the distance. "The Mother has blessed me with a loving family, and I do not want to leave them so soon."

It wasn't surprising to Dominic she was scared, and he did pity the girl. Of course, it wasn't her fault her people had put him through so much pain.

"Like I said, I'm not going to hurt you," he called out over the wind gusting past them. "Now tell me, where are we headed? I just want to get clear of this place, and then I promise I'll set you free."

"I am not a child. There is no need to lie to me. I have heard of the way you people are."

"We're not all the same—just as I have found that your people are not all the same." Dominic sighed in frustration. "If only your *Grand* Chieftain would believe that."

"Do not talk ill of our leader! If you are so good, why would they be chasing after you?"

"Look I don't want to…just please, this will be over sooner if you tell me where we're—"

The girl placed her hands on the horse and began to whisper. Dominic was horrified as the horse began to slow despite his kicking. He couldn't believe he didn't remember Hanzah's explanation that their people could control horses, too. "The grizzlies, horses, and birds," the boy had said.

"No, stop!" he cried, moving his hand over the woman's mouth and starting to kick again. He began to hear the faint calls of her people, charging through the trees at his back. He kicked harder, and the horse began to pick up speed. They raced on, the young woman continuing to struggle. The voices behind them grew louder and louder. Dominic could feel the flames of their torches at his back and was preparing to stop in surrender when the woman delivered an unexpected elbow into his gut. With his grip now released, she was once again able to speak to the horse, which came to such an abrupt halt Dominic went flying forward off it. He fell face first and scraped his cheek across the dirt. In great pain, he struggled to get up, looking back to see the girl and horse were gone.

Dominic began to crawl desperately forward toward the trees to hide, until he saw torchlight down the path in front of him. *But how were they also coming from the south?* He glimpsed their white garb and realized he was completely surrounded. A contingent of horses circled him with spears before he could react, and behind them he could see there was a whole herd more including women and children.

The spears soon opened up to allow in a man with a winter hat and thick, gray beard. Dominic was about ready to beg for mercy when a second group of V'ahani coming from the northern path descended on the circle.

"Where is that Eastern maggot?" Dominic heard Varek shout. "Orrin, back your men away this instant. You may all make your way to the Fortress now while we deal with this prisoner."

"Orrin?! Are you Uncle Orrin?" Dominic started to crawl toward the bearded Chieftain until the spears were once again aimed up and in his face.

Varek flared. "Silence. I have had enough of your lies. Bring him to me now so I may rid the Mother of one more of these filthy heathens."

One of Varek's guards stormed over, grabbing Dominic by the hair and shirt and dragging him over to the Grand Chieftain. He writhed in pain at the force in which they yanked his hair and began to beg.

"Please…ah, no…Orrin, please."

As Varek whipped out his blade, Orrin turned his head to the side, crookedly.

"The Chieftain Orrin is a name known by but a few Eastern men," he said, referencing himself. "Varek, hold your blade a minute while I analyze."

Orrin dismounted his horse and came right up close to Dominic's face, scanning him up and down. When he'd seemingly seen him from each angle, he turned his head once again. "No, I cannot say I have seen this one before…*however*…there is one word you said to me that only two people in this world have *ever* said to me. One word that can save your life right now if you can say it to me again. Now what is it? What might it be? And be quick about it, or it will be off with your head!"

Dominic struggled to answer. His mind raced too fast in panic and fear to follow what Orrin wanted him to say.

"Orrin, there is no need for this foolishness," Varek said.

Orrin looked at Dominic intently, waiting. When Dominic provided no response, he said, "Well then, I guess it is off with his—"

"Uncle!" From the crowd, Hanzah emerged.

"Yes that would most definitely be the word," Orrin said, as if it were Dominic whose mouth it came from.

"Hanzah!" Dominic managed to shout before his captor shook him to silence. He felt he could have fainted in relief at the sight of the boy.

"Uncle, this is Dominic Turner," Hanzah repeated. "This is the man who saved me."

Behind Hanzah, Dominic saw Harrison and Jeannie also emerge from the crowd. Only Jeannie smiled at the sight of him.

"Let us get back to the Fortress," Varek snarled in the silence following Hanzah's validation. His cold eyes sliced through Dominic. "There is much for us to discuss."

CHAPTER 5

CARTOMANCY

Though the man used Judith for cover, William could make out a thick, brown beard and long, unruly hair protruding behind her. This man didn't look or dress like the other Highlanders, which made William think he wasn't one. Those thieves had their own kind of brand to them. But whoever this man was, he'd won as far as William was concerned. William would do whatever it took to get the barrel of that gun off Judith's temple. He was filled with rage at the sight of it there, threatening his wife.

"I don't want to hurt her, but I'll do what I have to do!"

"Well that's good to hear because if you lay a harmful finger on her, I don't care what your intentions were, I'll skin you alive, and I will not hesitate. You hear me?" William stood, wiped the blood from his eyes, and grabbed his pistol off the ground. He gestured for Cassius to lower his weapon. Cassius followed his instruction on command. "What is it you're after? We've got a wagon over there full of goods, and we've fought off enough Highlanders already, so we don't want any more unnecessary trouble. You can take all of it. You can take your woman over there under that horse, too, if she's yours. She seems to be alive still, for now."

"That ain't my woman," the man said, confirming William's

suspicions. The man backed further away, dragging Judith with him. "I ain't one of them thieves neither. I don't even live this side of the stream, but I was watching y'all like I watch all outsiders. When I see trouble being caused, I stop it only to defend my home. Then y'all went and killed my damn hogs."

"Your hogs?" William asked, partly trying to stall, but also curious. "What do you train them or something?"

"That ain't none of your business what I do. All's you got to know is they was mine, and you killed them."

"Look, friend, we're sorry about your pigs, but they attacked us, so we did what we needed to do to defend ourselves," Cassius said. "I think it's only reasonable of us to want to preserve our own lives. But please, tell us your name, and let's talk this out like men."

"My name's Bronson, Bronson Mathis. Now, I'll be reasonable, but I'm afraid one of y'all will have to pay for what you've done. It's only fair. Which one of y'all's in charge here?"

William stepped forward with his hands up. He didn't agree with Bronson's definition of fair, but he'd pay what the man wanted to get Judith back by his side.

"My name's William Keagan, and I'm in charge. We Keagans have a lot of power here in the Murrieta, and we can get you whatever it is you want. There are plenty more hogs in the lands we control back west we could provide you with. We could also give you the goods we have with us in the meantime."

"That sounds like a start, but I'm also going to need the guarantee y'all will get out of my home here, and leave your weapons behind with me."

"Well now, Bronson, we'd be defensele—"

"Y'all will leave them and go, or this lady will die!" Bronson jerked the gun against Judith's temple, which made the others jump.

With a cringe, William waved his hands. "No! Just take the gun off her, please."

Out of the corner of William's eye, he spotted a rustling in the stalks. He looked to Cassius who nodded. He'd seen it, too. Were they about to suffer another ambush or was whatever was in the stalks what Bronson wanted to protect?

"All right then, drop your weapon." Bronson gestured for William to come toward him with his revolver. William followed his command, throwing down his pistol and creeping forward with the attacker's gun now trained on William but his arm still holding Judith to his side.

"You next," Bronson said, indicating Cassius drop his weapon.

But instead, Cassius aimed his rifle at the field of stalks. Bronson trembled as he pointed his weapon back at Judith.

Cassius pulled back the bar, taking things a step further. "I don't know you, Bronson Mathis. If I'm not mistaken, though, which I'm usually not, I read you to be a sensible man. And I can also read that whatever is shaking those stalks is what you really care about, ain't it? That, or you've got a plan to ambush us. So which is it?"

"I don't know what you think is going on, but you better not take another step, you bastard!" Bronson jerked Judith closer to him.

William was beginning to get nervous and frustrated with the risk it seemed Cassius was taking. William was just as concerned with an ambush, but that was no reason to put Judith at risk. It might never come to be, if they cooperated. If Cassius's gamble resulted in harm to Judith he'd kill both men.

"All right, now, let's just hold on a God-damned second," William said. "Cassius, don't take another step." Cassius nodded but kept his eyes on Bronson.

"Now, Bronson, hear this." William locked eyes with Judith, communicating for her to trust him. "I don't think any of these threats of violence are necessary. Now, we're sorry for being involved with some trouble on your land, but if you live 'round here, you're aware the Highlanders are the true source of that trouble. We were just making our way through and defending ourselves. Look, the value you place on keeping your home safe, I respect it. You thought we might be a threat, so you attacked us first. Any man would do the same."

William paused, taking a breath, and laid out his offer. "And I understand we went and killed those hogs of yours, which I'm thinking are your main line of defense, and now you need recompense to survive in this dangerous land, here. So, let's settle this. We'll repay you the hogs as soon as we can get a message west, and, in the meantime, we'll leave you our goods and two of our weapons. But we'll take the rest to defend ourselves, as we aren't out of Prayer's Passage yet. In exchange, you let my wife go and let us on our way, and we'll leave you alone."

"All your weapons."

William grinded his teeth at the man's obstinacy. "You're a stubborn man, Bronson, but there's one thing you aren't taking into account."

"What's that?"

"Cassius?"

"The fact that if you don't settle this peacefully, you will die, Bronson Mathis. And if you die, so do the folks you're hiding in those stalks over there. I may not hit them right this minute, but if you harm Judith or William just to try to get everything you want, you can bet Henry, who's got a gun trained on you, will kill you, and then I'll burn that field to the ground with them inside it."

Both William and Bronson shifted their attention to Henry, who'd been quiet throughout this whole exchange, to see that Henry did indeed have a gun aimed at Bronson from beside the house.

"So, what'll it be, Bronson? Are you going to be reasonable and take William's generous offer?" Cassius had a different brand of intensity than William's brother, Clovis. Unlike Clovis, Cassius did not smile or perk up in any way with his threats. Instead, his face was stern, and he seemed to sulk as his words got darker. There was a kind of resentment and accepted necessity in them.

Bronson froze and sighed. He glanced dejectedly toward the stalks and then down at the ground, cursing under his breath. "All right, all right. But you don't hurt me or mine."

"You've got my word no one will be harmed," William interjected, now feeling some hope for the safety of his wife, who also was beginning to calm herself. "Cassius will throw his weapons down at the same time as you, and we'll talk this out. Isn't that right, Cassius?"

Cassius nodded at both men. "Of course," he agreed. "I'll count down from three and throw them down if you agree to do the same."

"Yes, yes," Bronson uttered. "I agree."

"Three," Cassius started. "Two." William looked reassuringly into Judith's eyes as she began to shake. "One, now!" Cassius called. Both men threw away their weapons and William breathed a massive sigh of relief as an emotional Judith came running into his embrace.

Bronson whistled and a woman and a young boy emerged from their hiding place in the field. The woman walked into Bronson's arms. When he let her go and she turned to face the Keagans, William noted her bandana-covered hair was also messy. Both she and her son were dressed in light tan outfits which were as ragged as Bronson's. Yet, there was something very different about this woman, even beyond a youthful glow that made her appear to be somewhere in her twenties.

"If you don't mind my asking, is this your wife and son?" William asked.

"That's right," Bronson said. "My wife, Nova, and my son, Kai."

"Now that we're past trying to kill each other, it's a pleasure to meet y'all," William joked, growing curious about who these people were. "Do y'all live here?"

As they talked, Cassius went off to fetch the horses and recover only some basic provisions from their wagon. As promised, they'd be leaving the goods with Bronson.

"These abandoned homes along the waterway are about as far north as we go when the Highlanders are off, and we can use them for shelter," Bronson answered William. "Anything further is their territory, and we don't want no part of them. We spend the rest of our time south beyond the cliffs. It's a place they tend to stay away from since the wildlife is a little more...wild. But we patrol all of the Passage as we've had a fair few coming in to try to take what's ours by starting here first. We've been following your group to make sure you were just passing through, but once y'all didn't run from the Highlanders and fought them instead, we worried you'd come for us next. Those Highlanders are already enough of a burden for us. They're what truly makes Prayer's Passage what it is."

"I never understood the Highlanders," William said glancing over at the woman pinned beneath her horse. She was wheezing heavily, and he almost pitied her helplessness. "They claim to be free since they have no authority or organization, yet they identify as a group and obviously live in groups. They are no different than the gangs, other than the fact that they have no loyalty, even to each other."

Bronson tilted his head and frowned. "I take it you folks are part of the gangs, then?"

"That's right, I'm the leader of the Keagan gang." William was proud to say it. "We aren't like the other gangs, though. It's my intention to unite the Murrieta and connect it with the East in trade and prosperity. Of course, it would be under our leadership, but sometimes a kind, yet forceful leader is needed to tame such a wild place. I intend to take care of the Passage, too, y'all better believe that."

"Forgive me, but you are no different than the others, Mr. Keagan," Nova chimed in.

"Excuse me?" Judith snarled.

William, whose lip curled into a grin, lifted a calming hand to his wife. The wound on his face stung, and he almost grabbed at it as his cheeks perked up. "No, that's fine. No need to be alarmed,

Judith," he insisted. "Honesty's only ever a good thing—especially in a place where it would otherwise remain hidden. Speaking of which, there's something familiar about you, Nova, but I can't seem to place it. I don't know if it'll help much with all the types of people there are back east, but which city are you from?"

Nova's eyes widened as she looked to Bronson.

"Nova isn't from the cities. She's from here."

"Well no one's *from here* unless . . ." William started as the truth hit him. "The hogs—your son and you were the ones controlling them, weren't y'all? Y'all are natives."

Nova's expression went icily stern. "That is right," she affirmed. "We are natives."

Another painful smile overtook William's face at the news, but he was too intrigued to try and hold it back. "Fascinating you two are together," he said. "But I suppose it's not my place to judge. So y'all just live off the land out here and patrol the Passage?"

"That's also right," Bronson said. "Nova and I met and fell in love a little less than ten years ago. I came to the Murrieta at a time no other Easterners dared to. When I realized how freely I could live here, I decided to stay. A while later, I came across this beautiful creature and we bonded in that common interest. It's the only way we know how to live now—free. In a way, we've become a part of this place, so we feel it's our duty to keep our eyes peeled whenever people come in or out of the Passage. It's a bit easier too thanks to Nova's and Kai's abilities."

Cassius returned with the horses, which he set up for riding. "Bronson, a deal's a deal, as you made it with William. So, if you're wanting the provisions and goods we have, I'd suggest you hide them in that field now for later, or load them on your horses if you got some hidden away somewhere. Whatever you like, but now's your chance."

Bronson turned to Nova, who nodded and let out a tremendous, yet soothing, whistle. It felt supernatural and musical in its pitch, as if it were beckoning to its target, rather than calling. Two horses appeared in the distance out of an opening in the canyon and ran over at an astounding pace. The family got right to work once the stallions arrived.

Cassius pulled three bottles of alcohol from the wagon, and strolled into the house. William stood watching Bronson's family, and an idea came to him. He was ever the strategist, after all.

"I'll tell you what," William said, approaching Bronson, who was securing his saddle bags. "My gang's growing fast, and we won't stop growing any time soon. I know y'all probably aren't fond of that, but if y'all can help see us the rest of the way through the Passage now, and do so again on our return a week after, I'll personally ensure this lifestyle you're currently enjoying is maintained when we move in here to control the Highlanders. You don't need to travel with us, either. If you could monitor our surroundings and have our back if there's any more trouble, I'd be forever in y'all's debt."

Bronson looked at Nova and ran his fingers through his messy beard. "Like I've said, the Highlanders are a plague on the Passage," he scorned. "So I see no harm in making an ally with their enemy. I suppose you have a deal—if Nova permits it."

Turning to Nova in anticipation, William clenched his fists. "No man can tame this place, William Keagan," she started to William's despair. "It would best suit you to remember when considering the steps of this journey of yours. That being said, we will help you."

As William went to shake their hands, Cassius emerged from the house, which was erupting with flames. "We should be going now," he informed them. "The fire will draw the attention of the Highlanders and should distract them long enough for us to make our escape to Doreshire if we ride fast."

"Before we leave, I need to know," William said turning to Nova and Kai. "I'm familiar with the native clans, especially the Tokali. But they don't seem to have much of a grip on their abilities at all. Does that make you V'ahani, then?"

"Our son and I do not identify ourselves with either clan distinctly," Nova posited, mysteriously.

"Okay..." William scratched his head. "One more thing, though. You said 'our' son. Does that make Bronson Kai's true father?"

Bronson nodded. "Yes, it does. I know what you're wondering. Since Kai has native blood in him, he, too, has the abilities of his mother. It's not needed for both parents to be native if faith in the Mother deity is practiced and training maintained. Don't get the wrong idea and think there to be any way around Her place here."

William was speechless. Never had he considered the possibility of mixing the bloodlines of natives with Easterners. In a way, he was slightly repulsed by the idea. However, this revelation would change some things.

"Thanks again for your help," he relayed to Nova, who nodded. William lifted two pistols and handed them over to Bronson. Another two were slipped into his own holsters as he dashed over to his horse and climbed up. Guiding it over to Judith, who would be riding with him, he extended one of the pistols to her. "If you still want to kill the Highlander, you can," he offered kindly.

"Thanks, but no thanks. I think that woman's some kind of demon with my first two attempts each failing so bad. I'll pass for now. I'm content with her as is."

The different layers of his wife never ceased to amaze William. He pulled her up onto his horse, and she wrapped her arms around him from behind. Reveling in every minute of her embrace, he was overcome with joy she was safe. In his world, her safety had the highest of importance, well before his own. Having been presented with the possibility of losing her just minutes before, William felt he would happily give his life for this woman if it were to ever come to it again.

As Cassius and Henry rode off like lightning, she gave him a gentle kiss on the cheek. Once again, he beamed despite the pain of the cut nearby her peck. With that, they stormed off for Doreshire.

*

Things were not getting any easier for Gregory. He shook his head as he walked through the halls to meet with Collin McCormack and Frankie Covington. The two drove him crazy. He knew William wanted to keep them here rather than sending them back to Daniel or Clovis, but he found the two men rather annoying. They bickered constantly, as Collin, with his heavily scarred face, seemed to consider Frankie a youthful nuisance and Frankie was beginning to grow into his own enough to not appreciate it. Maybe it was something about having a role in the Keagan house that boosted Frankie's confidence. Gregory tended to side with him over Collin, who was extremely impatient and obsessed with getting back to the north. After William ordered the not-so-dynamic duo to remain at the mansion and do whatever Gregory asked, he tasked them with providing him updates on how things were progressing outside the Keagan mansion, as well as overseeing the communication of any orders he gave. The pair was already sitting in the study when he came in and, unsurprisingly, were bickering.

"Ah Gregory, perfect, perhaps you can end this debate and enlighten this idiot boy," Collin said as Gregory took a seat with a sigh.

"What'd I tell you about calling me a boy? Why can't you quit it already?"

"Look, I'm not getting in the middle of whatever garbage you two are throwing at each other." Gregory was in no mood, scratching furiously at his head. It felt to him at times like there were tiny bugs running through what was left of his hair, but he knew it wasn't true. He had someone look. There were no bugs. It was just a thing he felt.

"What news do you have for me?" Gregory asked.

"First, please tell the boy my green is the same as your green."

"What?" Gregory was lost.

"I just think it's possible the green you see, that you've seen your whole life, might be different from the one I do," Frankie defensively chimed. "I mean, reds and blues, too—really any color, I mean."

Collin's shoulders shrugged, and he lifted his hands before pointing to Frankie. "See what I have to deal with?" he asked. "The hash this twit spews out of his mouth sometimes . . ."

"I guess it's—wait, no," Gregory caught himself from getting wrapped up in their spat, even though he thought the question was an interesting one. "Just tell me what I need to know. I'm growing wrinkles, and my hair's graying by the day. The last thing I need right now is the stress you two consistently provide me."

"Daniel sent news of a murder in Harran. He's investigating it, but he says he needs Clovis soon, since he fears there might be some rebellious types afoot," Frankie answered. "Also, Clovis says he isn't ready yet and he's—and the messenger made a point these were Clovis' exact words—he's, 'having too much fun right now but will be ready soon probably.'"

"I could go up to Harran if you send me with some—" Collin started.

"No," Gregory shot back with a sigh. He leaned back in his chair and rubbed his eyes, at a loss of why things always had to be so difficult. "Stop asking me to go up there. You ask me all the goddamn time, and my answer is always the same, so just stop it. Just tell Daniel he'll have to wait for Clovis, but send him what loyal bodies we have left here so he has what he needs to try and lock the place down. We should be okay with a scarcity of followers in Fayette for now, I think. Also, ask Clovis *politely* to provide us a timeframe. It's mind boggling to me you didn't already have one for me, but I guess I shouldn't be surprised since you're spending your days worrying about colors."

"I'm not worried about them at all—it's this moron that's worried," Collin said.

"Good God, I'm leaving," Gregory groaned as he got up to leave the room. "Do what I asked."

"Why can't you understand it's a possibility?" he heard Frankie ask as he left. Though Gregory rolled his eyes, he did think about it some more.

Now feeling somewhat hungry, Gregory made his way to the kitchen. Already there was Maria, who was chewing on something.

"Hello there," she said after she'd scarfed it down. "I just made some soup. Would you like some?"

"Hi, yes please, that'd be great," he said as he found a place to sit. "I wanted to talk to you, too. I've been doing my best to keep things in order around here on my own. I'm just not used to it—running things. But I do want to at least make the spirit of this mansion better, if nowhere else. At the same time, I can see Blanton struggling, and I feel for him. I want to help him, but I don't know how."

"I take it you've never had kids?" Maria asked as she brought him a bowl and sat with him.

"Well I actually did have a son back East, but he was taken from me too soon," Gregory somberly told her. "My boy died far too young, and I never even got to say goodbye."

"Gregory," Maria gasped, putting her hand on his arm.

He paused, taking a deep breath and patting Maria's hand. Even now, fourteen years, three months, and seventeen days later, it was difficult to speak about it. "He was only four, and, at the time, I was working while his mother, my wife at the time, stayed home with him. One day when I was at work, my wife took him on a ferry ride along the Chorisma for what was supposed to be a fun outing. Apparently, he fell into the river while playing with some other children, and the current was unexpectedly rough. They couldn't save him and never found his body."

Maria huffed out a breath. "That's terrible. I'm so sorry to hear it. I didn't mean to—"

"No, no," Gregory reassured her. "You didn't know, so no worries. But that's my story."

"Whatever happened to your wife, if you don't mind my asking?" Maria followed.

"I was a miner back East," Gregory started. "I worked long days, and it was hard, dangerous work, but I did it to support my family and didn't mind it one bit. Because of it, though, I wasn't home a whole lot, and I suppose life became kind of monotonous—which again, at the time, I also didn't mind or even notice to be honest. She could be testy before, but after our son died, the change in her was clear. She started living a much different type of life and after a while told me she was bored with me and wanted to leave me."

"Goodness, what a terrible thing," Maria gasped. "There can be no greater pain for any parent than the loss of a child. For her to abandon you in times like that though…and for what?"

"I don't pretend to understand it, but it definitely broke me for a while. I guess she needed a complete change while I was just trying to hold onto what was left. In any case, after we split, going to work every day in the same place that had supported our family became too much to handle for me, so I had to quit, and that's when I decided to change things up. That's when I came here."

"Well look at you now." Maria's compliment made him smile for what felt like the first time in weeks. "How far you've come, Gregory Calloway."

"Thank you," he said.

"All right, so you want to know how to help Blanton," Maria

said after a brief silence. "The thing about children is their ability to dream is much more available to them than ours is. For a child, there are no limits. If they want to be a star or a leader—or in Blanton's case from what I know, a strong man—they don't yet have the wall we build at some point that tells us we *probably* can't do it."

"Wow, that's a…very well thought out point," Gregory responded in awe.

"Yeah, I ain't just some dumb old lady," Maria joked. "I used to be a school teacher in New Berkeley when I was a bit younger. But basically, the point is Blanton has lofty aspirations of some kind, so if you can satisfy his young mind's hunger to dream, he'll love you forever for it. It's the same reason a good teacher changes a life."

"Okay, that makes sense. And I think it gives me an idea. Thank you so much for this, Maria. And for the soup, it was delicious." He approached her and they gave each other a hug with their bodies kept far apart, which he kicked himself for.

"Anytime, and anytime you need to talk, just ask," Maria said. "I know things can get hard, but there's too much good inside of you to ever lose sight of the bigger picture."

Gregory basked in Maria's validation for the next few days and thought hard, planning out how he could impact Blanton the way she suggested. He was nervous about his ability to impress and relate to the boy, but one morning he worked up the courage to go and try. While Donna was asleep, he snuck into their room and gently shook him.

"Hey Blanton." Gregory held a finger to his mouth for him to be quiet. "Come with me, there's something I want to show you."

Blanton hesitated for a minute. "I promise it'll just be you and me, buddy."

Blanton nodded and together they snuck out of the room. Once Blanton was dressed, they went outside, and Gregory readied two horses.

"We'll have to head into town," Gregory said. "I hope you're ready for a big surprise."

"What is it? Where are we going?" Blanton asked as they rode off.

"Wouldn't be a surprise if I told you," Gregory answered, naturally feeling the fatherly traits he'd thought he'd lost being dug back out of him.

"You don't have to do this just because of what happened, you know," Blanton said after they had reached the town. "I don't want you to feel bad for me or anything."

"It's not that at all, Blanton," Gregory assured him, the circus tents now coming into sight. "I want to teach you something I learned much later in life—something that changed the way I see things."

"I don't know what that means."

"Not yet," Gregory said as their horses marched through the grounds. They soon turned a corner, and ahead of them stood a tremendous man with a moustache and folded arms standing in front of an old, red tent. Gregory watched as Blanton's mouth dropped at the sight of the strong man waiting for them.

"Do you see that fellow we are approaching?"

"Yes," Blanton answered, visibly excited.

"That could be you one day," Gregory said in a low tone. "People will tell you otherwise. They'll say you couldn't reach that goal, but they're wrong. Only you can decide what you can or cannot do, Blanton. Only you can keep yourself from the things you want most or from getting yourself to them. Don't you ever forget that."

Gregory swung off his horse and grabbed the reins of Blanton's. Helping Blanton down, he tied the horses together and kept ahold of a bridle.

"Hello Blanton," the strong man from the circus greeted as they approached him. "I hear you want to be strong like me?"

"Y-yes, sir," Blanton nodded.

"Well then how about you train with me, and I can show you how? What do you say?" the man asked.

Blanton nodded again with a huge smile and turned to hug Gregory. The hug was what Gregory needed—an affirmation he could be the man he wanted to be. It also made him think of what once was and he felt a tear form in his eye. He wiped it away as soon as he felt it though.

"So he's agreed to train with you once a week for now," Gregory said. "It'll be your time to work hard, and in those times, there'll be no Donna, I promise. However, because of that, I'm gonna need you to come out when we call for you at home, all right? I understand if you want to be alone sometimes, but don't hide for too long please?"

"I won't," Blanton affirmed, rushing into the tent.

Gregory nodded to the strong man, who nodded back but looked past him as a man on a horse came from behind. It was Frankie.

"Gregory, I'm sorry to interrupt, but Collin is gone," Frankie said, panting. "He must have snuck off in the night."

It was obvious to Gregory good fortune wasn't meant to last for him, but he still felt better about how things went with Blanton. He took a deep breath and looked up at the sky.

"We both know where he went, Frankie," he said. "Go after him, and if you can come back as soon as possible, do so. For now, make sure I have someone here to backfill you."

"Will do, sir."

"Oh, and Frankie? You're doing well," Gregory said, trying to keep things positive. "I'll make sure William knows when he returns."

Frankie nodded with a grin and headed off with haste.

The strong man took hold of both horses' reins so Gregory could swing back up on his. "You can leave him here for now, just make sure someone comes to pick him up in an hour or so.

"Yeah, thanks again for this. Maybe one day I'll join you two for a little break. I could use one."

"We all could sometimes," the strong man said.

As Gregory took the reins back from the strong man, he thought he hadn't heard truer words in a while.

*

The jail in Harran was a rickety building and had only two cells. As Daniel walked up to its porch, he realized that since the Keagans had first moved into the town, he hadn't met a sheriff of any kind.

How could there be a jail with no sheriff to oversee it?

Recalling the image of his man, who was murdered and covered in a wolf skin, seemingly without obvious cause, Daniel realized that law in the Murrieta wasn't likely established yet. Still, there had to be some story behind this makeshift prison.

He entered the doors to speak to another murderer, the imbecile Charles Langston, because he was desperate for information at this point. With the Hold having now been captured for a couple months, he could use Clovis's help and was frustrated by the denials his requests received.

Despite his frustration though, he was somewhat relieved as well. When he thought on his brother's arrival in any place, he always came back to the memory of how Fayette was taken. It was a scar on his mind that would sting him until the day he died. Though there was a battle in resistance staged by the people of that town, the things done to them once the place was taken were nothing short of brutal. Examples were made of the leaders and those who remained would know better than to do anything but kneel. The most difficult part of it all to deal with though was there seemed nothing Daniel could do to stop it once it began. By the time William and him were both involved, the damage had been done. Whether he wanted to risk that damage here in Harran was a creeping doubt he couldn't part with.

At the same time, while Gregory was able to send some men from Fayette, Daniel remained the highest-ranking gang member in the town, and he did worry for his safety. As such, he cut his days much shorter than usual and made his key appointments very early in the mornings. It was clear, though, he'd need to take matters into his own hands.

It was only the crack of dawn, so Daniel expected he'd have to wake Charles up, but jumped a bit when he saw him sitting straight up and staring ahead.

"Charles," Daniel greeted.

"What do you want?" Charles remained stone faced and frozen in an almost meditative position.

"Uh, I just have a question or two I was hoping you could help me with, possibly in exchange for a nice steak dinner tonight?" Daniel offered.

Charles finally reacted, turning his head with a smile and clapping his hands loudly together. "That's...wow. I don't know what to say to that. It's...priceless. Do you take me for some kind of puppy dog? You think I'll help you—you who cut off my balls, you who took that which made me whole—and for no more than a treat?"

There was something very different about Charles in his exile. Somehow, Daniel felt for the first time like he was in a conversation where he didn't have the upper-hand. The discovery of the recent murder had shaken him up. He knew that, and he was worried he was losing his confidence. He loathed the thought.

"There's uh—there's been another murder and...I was wondering if you might know anything?"

"Hmm, let's see, do I know anything? Hmm. Hmm. HMM!" Charles erratically began to yell. "I know I used to know everything, and now I'm stuck here in this hellhole, and I hardly even exist. I know you pieces of shit are blind and walking without a stick."

"Ok I'm just gonna—" Daniel started while walking toward the door to leave.

"I know I'm a government man and shouldn't be treated so

unlawfully." Charles had not paused from before and was getting louder. He was also sweating profusely now and breathing heavily.

"There's no government in the Murrieta, you delusional ass," Daniel retorted. "Even the cell you sit in is a prop, just like your *position*. It's all a charade."

"I know your f—"

Daniel slammed the door shut and could hear only muffled wails from there. Standing outside the jail, he felt panic flood through his system. No one had any information. No one he interviewed knew a thing. And he kept seeing the grisly scene of the murder over and over again in his head. He was fighting a threat without any information—without any way to negotiate. That's what Daniel did, after all. He talked his way out of things. How could he talk his way out if no one was talking to him?

His breathing became quick and shallow. He couldn't be seen like this. He didn't know where to go or what to do, but with no one in the streets, he just ran. His legs carried him to the Kennedale home, where he banged loudly on the door. When Cassie answered with a yawn, he begged her for water. Cassie looked scared and hurried Daniel over to the kitchen table as Debra came down the stairs. Cassie handed him a glass, and as he drank, he realized this was not a good look for him at all. He needed to settle down.

"I need y'all's help," Daniel told them, deciding he would open himself up. He needed friends somehow—real friends. Even with more of his men in the town and the fling he had with Johanna, he still felt so alone. The men were pawns on a board, and, as nice as the barmaid was to share his bed with, he did not feel she actually heard a single word he said.

Cassie exchanged a glance with her sister. "I'm not sure what we'd be able to help you with."

"Tell me my fortune," Daniel said as he slicked back his hair that had fallen out of place.

"What?" Debra followed.

"You heard me." Daniel looked up and, seeing the fearful reactions on the Kennedales' freckled faces, realized he needed to correct himself. He wasn't even sure why he'd answered so forcefully. It was possible he'd gotten too used to the power of his name. "I'm...I didn't mean it that way. I just need to know what's to become of me. I feel I've maybe...that maybe I've done some kind of wrong, and I wonder if it'll consume me—if it's already consumed me. If y'all don't want to help me, I get it. I understand if y'all feel like I'm a villain. But I'm trying my best to make this situation right, I really am."

"No, we'll help you," Debra jumped. He was glad to see compassion in each of their eyes.

"Yeah, of course, we'll tell you your fortune," Cassie was quick to say, exchanging glances with her sister. From the moment he met them, Daniel was impressed by the sisters' ability to communicate silently. It was secretive, but he knew all families had secrets.

"Did something happen?" Cassie asked. "You always seem so calm and collected. Why the sudden change?"

"There's been another murder," Daniel informed them, partly to see their reaction and partly to continue on the trend of honesty. "It was a gruesome one, and I thought we'd have rid ourselves of that by now, but I guess not. I also haven't the slightest idea of where to begin with it, and, like I said, I worry about my responsibility in all this."

"In all of what exactly?" Cassie asked.

"What's become of this whole place, you know?" Daniel pondered. "Harran and the Riverlands and the Murrieta in general. And not even just in what's passed, but also my role in what's to come. I'm hoping it isn't too late for me to do some good for this world—if I haven't ruined that chance already. I thought...I thought I was doing my part for the greater good, but lately, lately I wonder. I just don't know anymore."

"Within that fear you have of hurting others is a caring heart, Daniel," Debra assured him. "The lack of that's what makes a person evil, and that isn't you."

"Let's get you to the Tomorrow Room, and we can tell you what we see, okay?" Cassie said.

For the first time that day, Daniel felt more like himself. He was taking action, at least.

The sisters led him up the stairs and into a somewhat-cheaply decorated room with colorful curtains hanging to cover the walls. It was all very purple, and there were many odd shapes and symbols. Daniel would normally roll his eyes at the spectacle of places like this, but he tried to be respectful and more understanding. Debra pulled out a seat, which she motioned for him to sit on, and the Kennedales took their places on the other side of the table, facing him.

"We always like to begin with some information before we work with our clients," Debra said.

Daniel didn't like the idea of being considered a "client," as he had always been skeptical of this type of thing. But again, he forced himself to be open-minded.

"Just so you're comfortable with how we're going to do things here. It won't be nothing too crazy or dangerous, don't worry," Debra said.

"Our sessions involve a combination of cartomancy and precognition," Cassie explained as she placed a deck of strange cards on the table. "As Debra said, you shouldn't expect any pain or a fearful experience of any kind. Our readings have stirred emotions in the past, though."

"Carto-what now?" Daniel asked, not following much of what was said.

"Basically we use cards to tell us things about your past, present, and future," Debra explained as the pace of her words became faster.

"What the cards tell us will provide reactions and information from you that then lead us to have premonitions of the future," Cassie further elaborated.

"To be honest, y'all's little spiel about all this is only making me more on edge," Daniel half-joked.

Cassie stuck the deck of cards out in front of Daniel. "You asked for this, didn't you?" she said coyly. "Just shuffle these cards and spread them out face down on the table."

Daniel shuffled and did as directed.

"I see you're a big card player, huh?" Debra grinned with a wink. "I wouldn't sit down at a table with you."

"But you haven't even flipped the cards over yet," Daniel exclaimed. "How did you . . .?"

"Oh no, that wasn't a reading," Debra said, as she and Cassie laughed. Cassie brought the cards back into a deck and gave half to Debra. "It was only a presumption."

The Kennedales turned six cards over each, arranged on the

table very specifically but in no way Daniel could figure out the pattern. They did it so quickly and even placed some cards in front of the other sister's set, rather than with their own six. Once the cards were placed, they each crocked their heads sideways at the exact same moment. Daniel squinted his eyes, trying to look closely to see if there was some kind of tiny words on the cards or tablecloth but there was nothing he could discern. Cassie and Debra continued to observe, their faces changing expressions at the same moments. It was as if the same story were playing out in front of each of them. The flickering of expressions soon stopped, and they both frowned.

"What is it?" Daniel asked nervously. "Y'all don't look too thrilled."

"We feel . . ." Cassie started. Resentful doubt crept in to Daniel's mind.

"We feel there is hope for you yet, Daniel," Debra followed. Both sisters' eyes were closed. Relief swept over Daniel.

"Yes…yes!" Cassie sat up straight, with Debra following in sync. "Hope there is. But there can be no change without change. There can be no good without good."

"I want there to be good. I can change," Daniel said enthusiastically. "How do I need to change?"

The Kennedales opened their eyes for a brief moment and looked toward one another. They closed them again soon after, and their expressions went sour.

"You'll be tested," Debra said.

"Tested by forces that come from behind. Will you look in the mirror in time to see them? Hmm."

"What does—? Are you saying—are you saying I'll be betrayed?" Daniel asked. "By who? And a mirror? So…will I betray myself? Tell me, please!"

The Kennedales became very relaxed. Daniel read their faces as neither negative nor positive. "Look to the sky and you will find the answers," Debra said.

"Look to the sky and you will find the truth." After Cassie finished, their eyes opened, and they appeared as if they had returned to their normal selves.

"I think I am leaving with more questions than answers, but I need to be going now." Daniel stood up now without the same panic as he had felt earlier, but he needed to prepare for whatever was coming.

"If you feel that way, then you heard what we've said loud and clear," Cassie said, both sisters still sitting as he moved toward the door. "Reflect on it further, and you'll discover what it is you need to do."

"If you ever need to talk to us again, feel free to come on over," Debra called. Daniel sensed an almost flirtatious tone, and though she wasn't particularly attractive, he somehow still appreciated it.

"Thank you for this," he said sincerely as he walked out of the strange room and onward out of the Kennedale house altogether.

For the first time he could remember, besides in times when he was physically ill, Daniel spent the entire afternoon inside the walls of his hotel room. He was not sulking but contemplating fiercely. What did it all mean? How did he need to change? What was he missing? How would he find it? And if he did, how would he react in turn?

When one of his men came to his door to check on him, Daniel told him to round up all the Keagan men and all the townspeople of Harran for a speech he would give at sunset. He didn't yet know what he'd say, but he knew he needed to say something.

CHAPTER 6

A FACE THAT LOOKS LIKE MINE

For days, talk of an assembly between the Grand Chieftain, his Masters, and the Councilmen of the Mountainlands spread like wildfire through the Great Fortress. As the V'ahani with the most knowledge of the situation to the south, Hanzah was proud to be included in this meeting. The exclusivity of it excited him even more when he heard others talk of how they wished they'd be able to hear what was said. It'd make him puff out his chest, and sometimes he would even note to them he would be there.

Unfortunately, however, his Easterner friends would not be permitted to attend. Hanzah had spoken to Dominic about it, who understood and preferred not to be in the same room as Varek. Dominic was not ashamed to admit his fear of the Grand Chieftain and said at this point, he was just happy to no longer be locked in a dark cell. But Hanzah worried about the Morrells, who he felt wouldn't understand quite as easily—especially with the way Harrison had been acting. When the Morrells had been reunited with Dominic, Jeannie had seemed excited initially, but the colder and more distant Harrison was to Dominic throughout the exchange, the quieter Jeannie had become. Harrison seemed focused only on returning his family's status and name to its previous power. He seemed unforgiving of Dominic leaving them in the woods—no matter the reason. And Dominic, after trying to explain to no avail, withdrew from them. It had pained Hanzah to witness such a reunion. For his part, he'd been happy to see Dominic, but given all he had to balance already, he'd let them be, hoping they would reconcile on their own. So, Hanzah waited until the morning of the meeting to inform them they would not be joining in the proceedings.

"Hello, my friends," he said as he entered their assigned dwelling. It was apart from Dominic's at Harrison's request.

"Hey! Is it time for the Grand Chieftain's meeting?" Harrison asked, as he pulled a shirt over his head.

"That is what I have come here to talk to you both about. I regret to inform you that neither of you will be able to attend this meeting—by the orders of the Grand Chieftain himself."

"But why not?" Jeannie spoke up from her cot.

"You're the son of the former Chieftain of the Riverlands," Harrison said. "If anyone should be able to get us into this meeting it should be you."

"Yes, well I am sorry, because I did try to speak to my uncle about it, but the Grand Chieftain's word is final. It is always final, you see."

"Did you even ask Varek, though?" Harrison asked. "I mean, this is our livelihood. Our family's done so much for your people, and we deserve the opportunity to continue on that tradition. I've been talked down to by your leaders for some time now, but I can't accept that anymore. I—*we* could and should be an asset to the V'ahani."

"What Harrison's trying to say is we also know more about the situation than even you do, Hanzah," Jeannie said. "Surely that must be valuable to them."

"We are going to discuss what the next steps will be, and then I will fill you in." Hanzah tried to stand his ground. His eyes began to wander, and he found it hard to look at them. He also instinctively kept fidgeting with his messy hair. "I promise I will fill you in."

"At least tell us what they're planning, so we can voice our concerns," Harrison pleaded. Hanzah noticed Harrison's use of hand gestures tended to increase dramatically as he became more flustered.

"Listen to me please—I cannot tell you how much I appreciate all you have both done for me," Hanzah said, while readying to leave them. "We have been through so much together, and I will never forget that. But this is a turning point for my people, and it is bigger than me. I have not had too many dealings with the Grand Chieftain. He is the leader of our people, and I am just the young, inexperienced son of a dead Chieftain. I wonder daily if I will ever even develop fully into the man my father envisioned me to become, while also fearing constantly for the safety of my sister, who is held hostage by the Keagans and surrounded by danger. At this point, I need to contribute however I can to saving her, which means I must do as my leaders tell me. It is what my father would have wished."

"But Hanzah, you at least have your uncle," Harrison said with a sigh.

"Who do we have?"

Jeannie's words and twinkling eyes broke Hanzah's heart, but there was nothing he felt he could do. "I am sorry," he said. "I mean that. In time, you will show Varek your worth, too, and the Morrell name will be restored in the Riverlands. You need to believe me when I say it is what I want for you. But as of right now, it would take magic the likes of which only Dominic could conjure to get you into that room—and it seems to me you no longer care much for him. I must be going now, my friends, but I will see you both shortly."

Hanzah stared them down for a few moments more, hoping they would understand the message he was trying to send. After leaving, he went to the stable to find a horse to take him to the Grand Chieftain's Hall at the highest point of the Fortress grounds. With a whispered order Hanzah gave into its ear, the white steed prodded on with as much haste as it could. The power of the beast was evident, as its muscles flared on each gallop. It was always a difficult trek up the steep mountainous pathway, but when Hanzah made it he spotted his uncle. He thanked his horse softly as he dismounted, and it whinnied back as he tied it up outside the Hall.

"Oh, hello there, Hanzah," Orrin greeted, rocking on the balls of his feet as he stood in a trance-like state. This is how his uncle always looked when deep in thought. Oddly, he appeared more relaxed and content during the process than at any other time.

"Hello." The lack of bustle around the Hall distracted and confused Hanzah. From what he heard, it was typical for those in the Fortress to wait outside patiently for these meetings to end so they could hear the news. As exciting as Hanzah knew this meeting was, he found the custom surprising considering the difficulty of climbing the hilly streets of the Fortress. "Where is everyone?"

"Well, first of all, you are early. Terribly early," Orrin said.

"But you said the meeting would take place around noon," Hanzah said, disheartened by the news.

"Noon? No, not at all," Orrin shook his head. He appeared almost shocked Hanzah would suggest it. "Let this be a lesson to you, my boy. Sometimes you need to fetch a shovel and—"

"Wait, a shovel?" Hanzah interrupted. "How is that at all—"

"Yes, a shovel," Orrin sang over him, fixing the position of his hat on his head. "Sometimes you need to go find yourself a shovel, open up your ears as wide as possible, and scoop out all of the wax that builds up in there." Hanzah's expression went flat, and he rolled his eyes. "The look on your face would suggest you need a shovel right now as well. Shovels come in handy especially when speaking to your elders because—as a young person—it is important wax not fill your ears to the point you miss the lessons we try to teach. Or misinterpret those lessons. That could have even more catastrophic results, you know. I am convinced many Easterners do not take good enough advantage of the great benefit provided by shovels—a tool one of them actually invented! And I know you might say, of course, some of what us older folks spew is filled with the most silly and unnecessary of insights, too. But even then, it is polite to listen closely. You know what, let me go find you a shovel. Yeah, I will go get you a—"

"You said I could meet you here at noon…oh for the Mother's sake, why did I not ask you to elaborate before?" Hanzah said, trying to get back to the point while Orrin huffed and puffed following his speech. As much as he tried to show respect, at times it greatly irritated Hanzah this was the man he was to follow now.

Especially after his father's straightforward way of teaching him lessons, his uncle's tangents were very difficult to adjust to.

"Precisely! You did hear me. Of course, just because I come here at a certain time does not mean the thing starts at that time. I like to be early rather than late. In that, I do not think I am alone either. You might find this very surprising, Hanzah, but my mind tends to race before meetings such as these. Being here now helps me to get my thoughts in order and to visualize what I am going to say…Oh by the way, did you still want me to get you a shovel though—you know, for future use?"

Hanzah laughed. He couldn't do anything else at this point. Orrin was either being serious and therefore a fool, or he was joking, and his dedication to the joke was admittedly pretty funny. "No, I should be all right, I think," Hanzah said. "So when *will* the meeting begin?"

Moving to the steps of the Hall, Orrin took a seat in an almost meditative position. "In the future. Until then, relax and visualize with me."

Though he followed his uncle's lead and found the quiet somewhat peaceful for a period of time, the wait for the gathering droned on. Hanzah traced the sun's position in the sky as he fidgeted in his spot on the steps. The spring air felt nice, but there was no way to get comfortable sitting this way. His back began to ache, which prompted him to lay sideways for periods. As much as he wanted to ask the whole time for an update, any update, he couldn't do it. Arkouda always taught him not to be a pest, and anything he had learned from his father was now of the utmost importance to put into practice. As he sat and his eyes grew heavy, though, he couldn't keep from dozing off.

Hanzah was awoken by his uncle to see Varek, his three Masters, and Orrin's three councilmen were marching up the stairs into the Hall.

"Tired, Hanzah?" Varek quipped as he passed. "If I had been invited to such a meeting at your age, I would have been standing at attention since the night before."

"No, Grand Chieftain," Hanzah straightened himself out. He felt his cheeks grow warm and rosy in his shame. "I was—"

"He was learning for the first time about how to use a shovel for the wax," Orrin interrupted, beaming ear to ear. Hanzah couldn't tell if this was in his defense or not.

"A shovel . . .?" Varek started with a sideways glance at Orrin. "Well, never mind."

Orrin smiled at Hanzah and put an arm around his shoulder as Varek led everyone through the doors and into the Hall. The first room Hanzah saw as he entered was vast and extravagant. The cobble designs on the walkways of the Fortress continued into the room. On first arrival, Hanzah had been in awe of the designs and structures. The cobble walkways were paved in the shape of animals and mountains, while white banners were draped from building to building. For a moment, he thought it kind of all looked similar to the images he'd seen in the Maiden's Canvas, but the mastery just wasn't on the same level here. Still, it left him in awe. Hanzah's favorite design was of a snake so long it extended from outside the Hall, up the entryway to below his feet, and onto the walls down the hallway. There were also several V'ahani lounging around, who began whispering as the leaders walked past toward another doorway with several guards standing in front of it.

"We could have been in here the whole time?" Hanzah tilted his head back as the guards parted to let them all into a smaller, empty room.

"Well, of course," Orrin said. "The Hall is open to all V'ahani, only these chambers of the Masters' are off limits. I never said it was not open, did I?"

As much as it irritated him, he remembered the shovel. "No, I suppose you did not," Hanzah sighed as he followed his uncle and the other leaders in coming down to his knees in a circle.

Orrin tapped the side of his forehead with a grin and made a digging motion, which made Hanzah chuckle just as Varek opened his mouth to begin.

"Is something funny, Hanzah?" Varek snarled.

Hanzah's heart sunk straight through his stomach and he froze. "Um—no Ch—Grand Chieftain," he stuttered.

Why couldn't he do anything right? he wondered as he fought back tears.

"That was bad timing on my part, Grand Chieftain," Orrin said in a dramatically more stern voice than Hanzah had been used to from his uncle. "Hanzah is very excited to hear what you have to say and is nothing but grateful to have been included here."

Varek gave Orrin a look—with his good eye at least—and Hanzah stared at Orrin, dumbfounded but impressed by the sudden shift once the doors were closed.

"You all know the reason for this gathering. We are here because of the unfortunate decisions of the councilmen of the Riverlands. Now, Arkouda's daughter, Latera, has accepted the role as the apparent caretaker of our brothers and sisters captured at the Tokali Hold. In our few communications with her since their capture, she describes a dire situation. It is a situation we must find a way to resolve, and so here we are. Orrin should have some more information to share on this gang, who is now our greatest enemy."

"On the contrary, Varek, Hanzah is best suited to discuss the Keagans," Orrin said without as much as a blink.

The whole weight of the room shifted to Hanzah's shoulders. Even with Orrin's resounding support, it didn't get any easier for him to shake his nerves.

"Well, I would not know where to begin when it comes to the Keagans," Hanzah said.

"Let me go!" he heard Jeannie's yelling voice outside. Two guards came barging into the room, one restraining Harrison and the other restraining Jeannie.

"We can help! Let us help!" Harrison exclaimed as he resisted. "Please, we know more about what you're discussing than any of you, and we want to help!"

"And how do you know what we are discussing?" Orrin asked, switching back into the common tongue so Harrison could understand him.

Despite his initial fear to speak, Hanzah was now furious at having been interrupted. He saw this now as his opportunity to show his worth, and it was interrupted selfishly by the Morrells. It was clear to him they didn't take his advice either about utilizing Dominic to make the entrance without a scene. Whether it was mostly Harrison or not, they could be so petty at times, and now, as his guests, their behavior was reflecting badly on him, as well. At least if Dominic had snuck them in, Hanzah could have passed them all off as having a valuable skillset. Now, they were just interruptions, barging into a sacred space where they were not welcome.

"I am sorry for the interruption Grand Chieftain, Masters, and Councilmen," the guard exhaled. "These two tried to create a diversion in the Hall to sneak in, but they failed."

"Then throw them both in a cell," one of Varek's Masters demanded. "This room is reserved for only the leaders of the V'ahani. If our own people cannot be here, these two should be killed for entering, quite frankly."

"May I be blunt, Grand Chieftain?" Orrin followed and was given a nod of assent. "My sincerest apologies as I do not mean to offend, but what was just said was an absurdity and for the love of the Mother should not be repeated by one with a sane mind."

"How dare you," the same Master retorted.

"Watch your step, Chieftain," Varek warned.

"Excuse me for getting emotional, but perhaps I can word it better," Orrin back-peddled. Hanzah appreciated his uncle sticking-up for the Morrells, despite his frustration at losing his platform and his anger with them at the moment. He was also pleased to avoid having to defend them himself and further risking Varek's disfavor.

"To get right to the point…hatred and motivation are ignited in the same way a fire is: by disruption, by disturbance. Once the spark has been made, though, the difference between hatred and motivation is the way in which their flames are spread. Grand Chieftain, would you say our defensiveness against the Easterners is a result of a hatred toward them, or a motivation to keep our people safe?"

"The latter, of course," Varek scoffed. "It is the Easterners who are filled with hatred."

"Maybe so," Orrin agreed. "Either way, we also have a certain desperation. The Morrells share that same desperation. The question is: will they use it to motivate them or only for vengeful ends?"

Before Harrison and Jeannie could answer, Orrin continued, "I think their behavior would suggest they are not so different from us. It seems to me they want to restore the legacy of their family above all. In that, I see motivation."

"Those Keagans burned down our home and chased me through the woods," Jeannie spoke up. "I can't imagine the position your people must be in, but Harrison and I know Harran. We've met the Keagan brother, Daniel, who inhabits it now and have spoken to him. He seemed like someone you'd much rather talk to than the men who attacked our home."

"With your protection, Jeannie and I would be willing to sneak into Harran and talk to him. We'd do our best to negotiate the safe return of your people. We'll do whatever it takes to earn your trust in us. We do not want revenge; we want to restore the Murrieta to the place it was." Jeannie shot Harrison a look of surprise.

At this point, Varek and the Masters were listening and pondering, so Hanzah decided not to let his moment be completely stolen. "No, our people should be front and center in whatever discussion is had," he said firmly, purposefully playing into Varek's more aggressive personality and looking to him for affirmation.

The pace of Varek's blinking increased as he nodded. "Yes, this is a very good point, Hanzah. You will not go alone and you will not speak, either. I understand your desires and can appreciate them to an extent, but these are our people, so we will do the negotiating if there is any opportunity at all to do so."

"Any opportunity? Negotiating? You aren't considering giving in to the Keagans, are you?" Jeannie questioned, to no response. "No, you can't do that! You can't let them win."

"The enemy of my enemy is my friend, Orrin. As much as that is true, she's only a child who doesn't understand the greater ways of the world. You Morrells may join us and will have our protection as our allies, but you will not speak, as I have said. There is too much at stake for you to risk the lives of our people, who are being held hostage by a mad man, with a badly-timed outburst of anger. The only question is how do we get this Daniel's attention in Harran without making them suspicious of a fight?"

There was silence for a few moments after Varek's remark. Jeannie bit her tongue in frustration until Harrison lifted his head. "The field before the bridge to the Mountainlands would be the perfect place for a negotiation. It's a wide open space you all know better than anyone, so there won't be any option for trickery on their end."

"And an abundance of grizzlies there, as well, should they even try," one of Orrin's councilmen added.

"Uncle, you told me about the message you all sent to the Keagan stronghold in Fayette using the storm of crows. What if we send another message, only this time let it be a directional one. They will likely be wanting to speak to us."

"That might work, Hanzah," Orrin said, with a look Varek's way, who nodded himself.

"And if it fails, we will have no choice but to meet them in Harran. But for now, we will prepare our warriors and send the crows as suggested. Let us make haste, our people have been in need of our assistance for too long."

They soon stood and departed, at which point Hanzah walked away next to his uncle.

"You were so impressive in there," Hanzah lauded Orrin.

"Was I? I blacked out."

As they laughed together, Hanzah was glad he could now tell when his uncle was joking.

*

"What's your name?" the old harbormaster of Doreshire asked William, squinting at him dramatically through thick glasses.

The man's hair was long and wiry, and his teeth were rotting. This didn't seem to keep him from smiling though, much to William's dismay. William also wondered what must be on the clipboard the old fellow clenched so tightly his hands turned white.

"My name is William Keagan. This is my wife, father-in-law, and our guide is in the john doing his business. The four of us made our way through the Passage and into Doreshire and now need to get on the next ferry to New Berkeley, please."

"Piss off," the harbormaster blurted out, leaning even closer to William now and looking him up and down.

"Um…beg your pardon?" William said with a chuckle as he looked to the others to make sure he heard the man right.

"Yeah, I bet you think you're real funny, huh?"

"Sir, I—"

"A fellow with the last name Keagan in Doreshire…my arse," he interrupted. "Leonard Keagan would have no interest in a trip through the Passage. For that matter, he wouldn't even cross the Chorisma himself, so I wouldn't expect him to let his blood."

This angered William, partly because the harbormaster on the Murrieta side of the Chorisma still didn't know about the presence of his gang there, but also because he'd suggested Leonard might actually care to protect his family. This man would know of William soon enough.

"Leonard has no interest yet, but he will once he receives word of what his son has achieved here," William said as Cassius returned to join them. "When that day comes though, and I tell him you gave me a hard time, it surely will be your arse."

The old man kept squinting as his expression turned doubtful, but also fearful.

"Is there a problem here? I thought I took a while in there. Figured we'd be looking around for a place to relax by now."

"Cassius…hello," the old man said with a swift bow of his head before he turned back to William. "No—no problem at all! I'm sorry, Mr. Keagan; it was a misunderstanding. Just that we get some people trying to pass off as important to get on our boats fairly regularly around here. It's not every day you meet someone who has your name, either."

William gave a tiny smirk to Cassius. In reality, it once again bothered him the respect he was given wasn't entirely his own. He decided, though, he would take advantage of this opportunity it offered him.

"Don't ever apologize," he said to the harbormaster. "Apologies are for the weak, and they're almost never truly sincere. What you were doing, sir, is your job and the Highlanders ain't far enough out of Doreshire for you or anyone else in y'all's town to be slacking on their job."

"Of course not, I would never."

"Well, that's good to hear," William said, wagging a finger in the man's direction and now purposely squinting the same way the man had been squinting at him. "You know something, you and me, we're gonna be friends. I can just tell. Wouldn't you agree?"

William abruptly approached the harbormaster and put his arm around his shoulder, guiding him up the pier near the ship. The air reeked of salt and fish, and the lamplights lining the town were dim, as the sun was beginning to set.

"It would be my privilege to befriend such a dignified figure," the man answered. William could feel the harbormaster's shoulders tense up beneath his arm.

"Wow—to think, the harbormaster of a key port town calling *me* a dignified figure!" William gave a look back to his comrades behind them. "Sir, the honor is all mine. But let me ask you, what does it mean to you?"

"What does what mean?"

"Friendship," William clenched his fist behind his back. "What would a friendship with me mean to you?"

"A whole hell of a lot, that's what."

"Well...sure," William rolled his eyes. "But look, what I'm

trying to get at is I know y'all got a problem with thieves here, and I need reliable transport over the Chorisma. So, what do you say I make you the friendly promise that when the time's right, we strike up a deal? Once my gang has a hold on the Murrieta, I'll ensure y'all don't have a single Highlander to worry about here. And, in exchange, whenever you see this here lion's paw pin I got on my chest, you know not to ask questions."

"You really think you'll be able to handle those bastards, huh?"

Since he seemed less scared now and more intrigued, William moved his hand to the man's shoulder and reached the other out to shake. "Like I said, once we're all set up, there won't be a place in this Territory for folks like them no more. So what do you say?"

"I'd say that sounds pretty good," the man shook William's hand. "Next ship to New Berkeley leaves first thing in the morning. Your friends and you will have a place aboard and no qualms from me, Mr. Keagan."

William had spotted a small boat earlier that was now beginning to take off, which he was hoping they would have been able to make it onto. "Don't suppose you could hold that fancy little one up for us?" he asked.

The harbormaster looked out at it and shook his head. "I'm sor—" he began before catching himself. "*Unfortunately*, that is a private vessel—one of your father's, in fact. Common folk in this town just don't get access to beauties like that without his direct word. Despite the arrangement we discussed, and despite that you ain't common folk by any means, I hope you'd understand I need to respect his wishes."

As the boat began to pull away, William's gaze was fixed on a lone figure aboard it, standing still and appearing to stare directly at him.

"Of course," William acknowledged, still looking out at the ship with growing curiosity. "Your allegiance to him will be one and the same with the deal we've made—soon enough anyway. We're going to turn in for now though. You have a nice night, and I look forward to our partnership." They shook once again, and, with that, William and his group were off.

As they walked off the pier and into Doreshire, the rotten smell did not go away. There was an eeriness about the place as it became darker. Its inhabitants appeared to be as lowdown as their storefronts and homes suggested. Like the port town they lived in, they had a look of being mostly passed over as they plodded through the muddy streets in filthy, worn-out clothes. As William walked past one mother and toddler in particular, he noticed these people did not necessarily seem depressed by all this. They weren't a smiling bunch, but the looks on their faces just seemed somewhat indifferent to it all. He felt Judith cling to his arm and lean her head on his shoulder.

"That little girl was *so* adorable. Cuteness on such a level doesn't belong in a place like this."

"She was a precious one, and you're right, it doesn't." William kissed her cheek.

"Once we begin to clear the Passage and get a hold here in Doreshire, do you think I could do my part to spruce this place up?" she asked with batted lashes. "Doreshire is the first stop people will see in our Murrieta, and it should be a grand entrance. There should be arches and attractions, and all the homes should be repainted, and traveling Easterners should feel welcome."

"I'm thrilled with what we did in Fayette, and I'd love to see that done here, too," William said, thinking out loud. "I want to help these people and bring everyone together. It eats away at me sometimes the things we have to do to make that happen, but sometimes they just give us no choice—don't they? I mean...I want what my father has, but I want to get it in a better way than he did. Do you think we're doing that?"

As they approached the inn they would stay at for the night, Judith stopped him. He turned to face her, and she put her hands on his shoulders.

"Are you not turning in?" Henry called out from ahead, holding open the door. Cassius had already gone inside.

"Go ahead, Daddy, we'll just be a second." Judith's head was turned toward Henry until he disappeared inside, and then was back to William. "You have to promise me this place can be my project, baby, please. It'll be a great way for me to bond with my sisters and brother, as well."

"Well, of course, you know I'd never tell you no. But did you even hear me on the rest?"

"Yes, yes, of course I did!" Her voice was sweet before smashing her lips into his and pulling away with a huge smile. William could see it within her—she was making all the plans for Doreshire right this minute, as if this whole town were a part of their house. "You *are* doing the right thing. You're doing more than the right thing and I'm so proud of you for it. I mean, look at what your father's grip has done to this place. It's so dingy it's as if he has no care for the message it sends. We can and will do better, baby. Together we will give these people hope and a home they can be proud of."

"That little girl got me thinking," William said, after taking a pause of appreciation for her enthusiasm. "I've always wanted a child. I can prove I'm not my father."

"Oh, please don't bring *that* up. Not now."

"Why not?" William shot back.

"I don't have a problem with it, baby, but there's so much we still need to accomplish first. And do you think this place is even safe enough yet?"

"I know, I know. It's just…first, I'd never let anything happen to them." William had been eager for an opportunity to convince her of this and figured this might be it. "But I've also always wanted to be a father. Maybe it's because of how my own was to my brothers and me. All I want is to give my children the love I was constantly wishing I had. And I would take a boy or a girl, too—hopefully one of each. But if it was just a girl, I'd be fine. I'd dedicate my life to showing her the beauty that exists in this world, because y'all would be all the beauty I could hope for in mine. If we had a son, he would receive nothing but love from his father. And though I'd be sure he'd learn what it takes to be a man, he would always be guided in that pursuit, never kicked to the side to figure out on his own how cruel people can be."

Judith's smile grew as he spoke, and it inflated him more and more. When he finished, she put her hand around his head, running her fingers through his hair. It felt so soothing to William—he loved the way her nails grazed the back of his scalp.

"You will be a father, and you'll be a great one," she said. "I'm sure of it. Let's go inside though and get to bed. We got a long day on the river ahead of us tomorrow."

With a nod, William followed her into the inn and to their room. Finally, having some privacy, they got right back to passionately and sweetly making love that night. They carried on this way until William simply had no energy left, which didn't take as long as other times, given their exhausting ride through the Passage, and he swiftly passed out.

William woke in the morning to a slightly busier Doreshire. People were out and about, some walking toward the pier and others walked away from it. Out in front of the inn, he spotted Henry sitting out on the porch and joined him.

"Morning," William chimed.

"Oh, good morning, William. How are you doing?"

"I'm good, you?"

"Can't complain. Ready to see how my city's changed."

"Oh, I know, me too. I'm excited about it. Can I ask you something about that, by the way?"

"Of course, what is it?" Henry tilted his head.

"Why did you come here to the Murrieta? I know personally what's attainable here. From your perspective though, to leave my father's side when you could have retired and had your family provided for in New Berkley…it seems like it would have been a risk, especially considering the nature of this place."

Henry nodded and shrugged his shoulders with a grin. "I can't tell you it didn't involve a degree of risk." He ran his fingers through his dark, graying hair. "The things that got Leonard and me to the top in New Berkeley though, those always involved risk. It's a funny thing. If you have none of it, you can't succeed; if you have any of it, you can fail; and if you have too much of it, you will fail. I'd say as the Eastern cities have grown, and governing forces have started to sprout—or attempted to sprout—there's started to become too much risk in Leonard's business for me to feel comfortable with the long-term future of my family."

"So, you think his business will be cracked down upon?" William gasped as his heart sunk. "If that's the case, why didn't you tell me before?"

"Goodness, no! I'm sorry, I didn't mean to worry you. But no, he should be fine for years to come. Plus, even if those powers did rise, there isn't a man your father couldn't buy or provide whatever incentive needed to leave him be. It's more that I became more of a family man, and the more I did, the harder time I had living with the stress of being a gangster in New Berkeley. As much as I did love the thrill for a long time, a growing moral conscience does not thrive when one's involved in the kind of activities we were there. That conscience tends to grow when you have a beautiful wife, who changes the way you see the world."

William chuckled at a wink from Henry. "I got you. Well, you know we all gotta get our hands dirty sometimes."

"Yes, of course—I'm no fool. I'd be some kind of hypocrite, as well, to criticize you for it. No, for me I just couldn't stand to be involved anymore. I took a gamble on you for sure, but at least with you I had a way out. Also, don't worry about Maria either, she understands, too."

"Glad to hear it, Henry," William said as Judith and Cassius came out of the inn to join them.

With all of them awake and gathered, they went for a quick breakfast before joining those walking toward the boats. Once they reached the pier, William spotted the ship departing for the East that morning. It was bigger than he thought it would be, with tall masts and what looked like a statue of an angel on the front. There was a decent line of about forty people waiting to board, one which Cassius pointed them toward.

As they waited for the line to creep forward, William spotted the harbormaster, clipboard firmly in hand. Almost as soon as he did, the man looked up at them. Shaking his head back and forth, he rushed over.

"No, no, no," he called out. "Mr. Keagan, you don't have to wait in this line. Please follow me to the front."

There was an emphasis the harbormaster placed on William's last name. It was likely so the others waiting in line would hear who it was and understand, which it seemed to William like they did. None looked angry or even upset. Like the day before, they just appeared accustomed and indifferent to the special treatment he got and they lacked.

"No, that's okay," William said, loud enough for those in line to hear. Judith had been mid-step to cut out of the line but paused sharply and stood up properly at William's words. "We will wait like everyone else."

The harbormaster looked utterly confused, maybe even a bit upset, but shrugged his shoulders and was soon back at his clipboard. As for the others waiting, their faces began to show some form of life. While in line, several expressed their respect for what he'd done. William basked in the praise the whole time it took the line to clear. Judith, on the other hand, professed her impatience several times, and Henry did his best to calm her down. It didn't work well, but there seemed nothing Henry wouldn't endure for his family.

When they were a few people back in line to enter the ship, an argument between a man and woman could be heard from behind them on the pier. The woman screamed bloody murder, as the man carried away a young girl who was crying, kicking, and screaming herself.

"Come back with my daughter, goddammit!" The woman punched and slapped his back.

"There you go again with that 'your daughter' bullshit. There you go making a scene like some kind of crazy bitch thinking I ain't got no right to my own child."

"Some people . . ." Henry said as he turned back toward the boat.

Still on the high of his previous good deed and recognizing the girl as the one he had seen the night before, William decided to act. Somehow, it felt like any misfortune he witnessed from here on in his journey would be the direct responsibility of Leonard, and he wanted to correct each one. He stormed back down the pier away from the others.

"Where are you going? We're next to board," Judith said to no avail.

The mother of the child delivered one more blow, which caused the man to shout in rage. He dropped the girl to the ground and pushed the woman back. With the girl still crying, William rushed over to her.

"Are you all right, sweetheart?" he asked. She shook her head in tears. A sadness came over him as he lifted her up and sat her down on the wooden planks of the pier. "Well, you're gonna be, okay? I know it doesn't feel like it right now, but you aren't alone. Your pain shall pass, and you will be loved, little bird." That made a smile pop across her cute little face, which warmed William's heart.

"Can you do something for me?" He asked again, waiting for her to nod in response. "Can you trust me? Cover your ears and close your eyes until I come back okay? When I do, everything will be back to normal." She nodded one last time and followed his instruction.

"You should've known better than to try and hide my daughter away from me," the man growled at the woman. "That ain't fair."

"You can't see why? What other choice did I have? You're a monster!"

"Doesn't matter what I've done, you ain't got no right. I tried living in this Territory, and I'm done with it. I'm taking her back East now, and you can stay here alone. You'll always be alone."

William rushed the man, who must not have even noticed him, and tackled him to the ground. When he tried to fight back, reaching for William's throat, William punched the man across the face and restrained him with an arm over his chest.

"This is none of your business, mister," the man gasped.

"A fellow hurting a child is something I would aim to make my business."

"Whatever. There ain't no sheriffs here."

The word, "sheriff," struck William as funny. It was a title he never considered, but he kind of liked the ring that came with it. Though he did have bigger dreams than becoming a sheriff, maybe it could become something of a nickname one day. It made him grin.

"Not officially, but I am most definitely a sheriff of sorts here in the Murrieta," he said. "If you ain't heard of Sheriff William Keagan yet, you just might soon. Now I tell you what, you're gonna get on that boat with me and leave these ladies be or you and me are gonna have a—"

"You're William Keagan?" the man interrupted icily.

"Yes, I—"

"Your brother is Clovis Keagan?" he followed again.

This question made William's heart sink, because he knew there was only one place it could go. Without an answer, he looked away toward his family.

"You are, ain't you? Do you even realize the...the devastation that demon has caused me? You can't. You couldn't possibly."

William could see the fear and panic welling up in the man's eyes. Still, he could say nothing.

"He killed my friends. But he didn't just kill them. I...I've seen murder before, and while I ain't no killer, I at least understand human nature. Sometimes people kill to get something they want, and that's a part of life I suppose. But what your brother did...it wasn't even killing. It was something else entirely. And what could I do besides watch helplessly as he enjoyed every minute of it? Nothing!"

There were no words William could offer because he knew it was true. What could he do though? Daniel and he loved their brother, and there wasn't a thing they wouldn't do for him. They just wanted Clovis to be happy, and they thought after all this time they had found that for him here. Guilt always sat in the back of his mind for looking the other way, but Clovis had never received the love he deserved, and William was convinced his actions weren't his brother's fault. The same way it wouldn't have been this little girl's fault if she were to become half of what Clovis was because of her father's behavior. Whether he was right or wrong in his sentiment, and as much as he did at times struggle with it, he had long past accepted it as the only way.

"I'm as ruined by the things I've seen, but he is my brother and protecting him has always been my purpose."

"Well, then. Who's the true devil? The hellhound? Or the man who releases it?" the man asked.

William was stunned but tried desperately to remain steadfast.

"Look, just get off me and let me say bye to my daughter. You were right to stop me. I've caused both of them too much pain. Somewhere along the way, maybe when your brother came along or maybe some other time, I progressively started losing my ability to care anymore. So I'll get on the boat as you say and leave them be. Hell, maybe I'll go even further than its destination. But all I know is, I better not see you even once while I'm on it, because if I do, I'll pull you into the river and drown us both."

William nodded and released the man. He stumbled, feeling dizzy, but headed back toward the pier. By now, the young girl had opened her eyes and ran up to him to give him a hug. William put an arm around her but could only grimace back.

Once on the ship, he went straight to the front deck. For the entirety of the ride, he stood with his arms crossed atop the railing, watching as the boat split through the waves before it.

What life beneath the water might the boat be disrupting? What lives might be split in two the same way the current was?

There was no going back now, but by the time New Berkeley

came into sight, William considered there might be a better way to go forward. Maybe it was time for him to change the way things were.

William looked out over New Berkley. Smoke billowed in the air from multiple locations. Tall buildings littered the landscape, and though he had seen factories before, the degree of expansion in the years since he left this place was staggering. With the harbor now coming into view, he began to worry that perhaps he wasn't equipped to conquer this place. The city looked like a monster ready to swallow him whole if he approached it the wrong way. But when he recalled how he'd already begun to tame the untamable beast of the Murrieta, he stood a little taller.

The figures of people bustling on the shore came closer and closer into William's view. He scanned the crowd, going through face after face and noticing how different they each were. New Berkeley had seemingly grown more than just physically, he thought. Still scanning, his gaze snapped to one man in particular, who was dressed very well and flanked by two other men. William realized there, waiting on the pier, was his father, Leonard Keagan.

CHAPTER 7

SIGNED AND SEALED

"I keep them eating off these filthy fucking streets—and right out of the palm of my hand," Leonard Keagan said with a smirk.

William had been surprised when his father had met their party at the docks, but less so when Leonard showed them an ostentatious display of power instead of a sincere welcome. He continued his casual lecture on his city now as he led them away from the shipyard and through New Berkeley. William noted his father, now in his upper fifties, had the same pep in his step he had had when William was a child. His perfectly tailored suit was complete, with a red, folded handkerchief in the chest pocket, a fancy bow tie always matching the color of his handkerchief, and a ribbon-wrapped fedora hat with a small red feather sticking out. As William had heard many times when he was younger, the feather belonged to a cardinal that used to fly up to Leonard's window as a child. Leonard would always keep bread by it to feed the bird when it came around, until one morning he was awoken to a shotgun blast. Unfortunately, that cardinal had been crapping on the roof, and Leonard's father had grown sick of it. When Leonard told the story, he'd frequently referred to it as the, "day he was introduced to the world."

Two of Leonard's associates, whom William remembered from his youth, had also accompanied his father to the docks. The first was Jackson "Forrest" Hayes. Uncle Forrest, as William called him, despite their lack of blood or in-law relation, was Leonard's closest friend and business partner. To William, Clovis, and Daniel, Forrest was even more of a scoundrel than their father. The problem with the immaculately clean-cut man was he didn't trust a soul other than Leonard. Maybe it was the nature of their business or their childhood bond, but William couldn't know for sure because Forrest wouldn't trust him enough to open up about it. Leonard always said Forrest's careful nature was what allowed them to stay under the radar in a lot of cases.

The other associate was Myrna Hendrix. Myrna was closer in age to William and took on a bigger role in Leonard's business at about the same time William left New Berkeley. Starting out as a waitress at one of Leonard's speakeasies, Myrna's popularity was quick to grow thanks to her sharp wit and beauty. But underneath both, or perhaps because of both, she was a true predator. She'd made sure every man had wanted her, and she'd been able to take advantage of the lot of them without any being able to turn the tables back on her. With so many suckers coming through Leonard's casinos, Myrna had free reign to pickpocket and con to her heart's content, even while working at the bar. Of course, she was unaware Leonard knew of her activities from the beginning. William's father let it go on for some time until he decided her talents could be very useful to him on a larger scale. Though William wasn't around long enough to know what that had included, he'd be sure to always check his pockets around her.

William looked around, making note of how filthy the streets were. There was soot everywhere and, unlike in Doreshire, a general look of dejection on the faces of those around him. They looked tired and hopeless. Once again, William hoped the connection to the West might alleviate their struggles through combined prosperity, which reminded him of what his father had just said. "Who do you mean when you say 'them'? Who's eating off the streets? Oh, and where's Uncle Jimmy? Was he too busy to come greet us?"

"I mean all of them," Leonard said, gesturing toward the city as if this alone answered the question. "The workers, the politicians, the entertainers, the poor, the 'middle' class, the ones who *think* they're wealthy, the young, the old, the healthy, and the sick…they all eat because I allow them to. New Berkeley is my beautiful jungle, and it'll keep growing thanks to the rain I pour into its concrete roots. As for Jimmy's whereabouts, your guess is as good as mine."

"Interesting metaphor." His head pivoting around to behold the city, William wondered about this mysterious note on his uncle— Walter Keagan's father—Jimmy. He thought it might have meant Jimmy had fallen out of favor with Leonard. At the same time though, William had more pressing issues to worry about on this trip than their drama.

"I guess beauty is in the eye of the beholder," Judith said, looking around in disgust. Growing up in the more rural outskirts of town like many of New Berkeley's wealthy, she would have been sheltered from the laborers who built the city high. William knew his father was one of the only well-off people in the whole city to remain living in it.

Myrna tilted her head back into the air and inhaled deeply, and William wondered if she smelled something different than he did. He smelled only piss, smoke, and garbage.

"That is true," Myrna said to Judith. "As it is that some eyes also see more clearly than others."

"What did you say?" Judith snapped.

"Misunderstanding, I'm sure," Henry said, much to William's relief. "Some people like the city, while others like the countryside. Having spent a great deal of time in both, I've come to garner an appreciation for each."

"Is that all it was?" Judith squinted her eyes at Myrna. "A misunderstanding?"

Myrna glared back at Judith with a grin. "Sure."

William could tell it was going to be a nightmare between the two, and he hoped he could keep them separated at least until a deal with his father was made.

"But why keep the city this way?" William asked his father, trying to change the subject. "If you gave your subjects more, wouldn't they have more love for you?"

"Hell, I've grown this city for them more than they could've dreamed, but I give when the time's right to give, and I do it in small amounts," Leonard snorted. "If everything were peachy all the time, they'd stop appreciating the strength of my hand. Gold is much more valuable to someone without any than it is to a wealthy man."

William deeply disagreed with his father on this front, so he decided not to continue the conversation at the risk of offending Leonard so early in their trip.

"Cassius, how's your time in the wilderness been?" Forrest asked as they walked through streets lined with old apartment buildings and factories.

"Enlightening."

"Hmm, a one word answer," Forrest said, staring right at Cassius as he spoke. William had wondered how Forrest managed to walk this way without ever stumbling or running into things. His peripheral vision must have been remarkable. "One word answers provide the fewest details, yet you could dig more meaning out of them than a ten-page letter. We'll have to talk more once we get to the office."

The office was where Leonard ran his operation, but was also where he and his closest confidants lived. All business was conducted on the first floor, which, if it was the same as when William left New Berkeley, would be littered with papers, books, whiteboards, and lower-level bookkeepers who were all, "really good," at their jobs. It was also where most of his father's henchmen would hold their meetings before hitting the streets of New Berkeley. In the past the upper floors were made up of the massive penthouses William and his brothers were raised in—that is again, if nothing had changed.

William noticed Judith gesturing to him with wide eyes, and he was sure to be casual as he fell behind the group with her.

"Are we almost there yet? This wasn't at all a 'brisk walk.' Why would your father not prepare us a carriage or something?"

"You didn't have to deal much with my father despite your father's association with him, did you?"

"No, but if he's usually half as unreasonable as this, I'm glad I didn't. Oh and who does that bitch of his think she is talking to me like that? We're guests here, and we're their equals, so they should treat us accordingly. All of them. Heck, if anything I'm her damn superior."

"He's doing this on purpose." William intentionally ignored Judith's gripe with Myrna. "He wanted us to see what's become of *his* city. This is what he does, and it's the way he is. I would know."

"Well, you'd better not let him get to you, William. Like I said, we're their equals. This deal you aim to make needs to be fair and nothing less. You've worked too hard for him to intimidate you with his mirage of superiority. I mean look at this place…this is no kingdom. Even with its height and bustle, there's no hiding this is the true image of a wasteland painted in masterful strokes by a miserable artist who signs in your father's name."

William grabbed her by the arm. "Don't you speak of him that way. He might be a menace, but he's my father and quite possibly *the* most powerful man in all of Duresia. If we're to make this deal with him, I need your cooperation, not your agitation of an already tense scenario. Do you understand?"

"Uh-huh," Judith said with an eye roll.

William noticed they were now within a few blocks of the office. "You're not convincing me I'm being heard."

"Well, if I were being listened to, perhaps I'd be more inclined to listen," Judith said before turning to him with a sigh. "Look, I'm impatient, William. That's a part of me. I'm impatient, and I'm frustrated, and my god-damned feet hurt."

"Yeah, I know. But trust me, okay? We'll be there soon. And this trip won't take too long in general. Before you know it, we'll be back home."

Judith nodded. "Carry me?" she said with a cute grin. "Piggy-back?"

William laughed, as he hunched over his back. "Your chariot awaits, m'lady."

His wife abruptly gave him a forceful smooch, and he tried desperately not to let it end. Her kisses were always so invigorating, even in a place like New Berkeley where William felt small.

"I love you, William Keagan." She looked him straight in the eye. "And I trust you."

"I'm so glad to h—" he started, but she jumped up onto his back. In no way did he think she had meant it when he'd jokingly hunched over. "Good lord, darling, you're too much."

"Just enough?" she asked from behind.

"Just the perfect amount," he confirmed as he leveled her out in his grip and carried her on. With her arms around his shoulders and her legs wrapped around his waist, he felt powerful. Like he could carry her forever, no matter what anyone said. He was suddenly a kid again—the kid before his childhood troubles. Now, as he trotted through the bleak streets with Judith on his back, all those difficulties felt so far behind him. With her by his side, he was now exactly the man he wanted to be.

A short while later, the office came into sight and, with his legs getting tired, he let her down. Leonard held the door open for his guests ahead of them. Everyone filed in one-by-one to the same first floor operating room William remembered. Young guns were wandering busily about, chattering loudly and calling out to the others.

"My apologies for the noise," Leonard addressed the guests.

"Gentlemen," he said somewhat louder, but not nearly loud enough to be heard over the bustling. Yet, somehow, the entire room fell silent, and all movement stopped. "Thank you. I need one of y'all to lead Mr. Abigale and his lovely daughter to their rooms. Provide them with whatever they need—Abigales, please think no request too grand. Cassius, you know where to go, but all the same— whatever you may need. William, if you'd join me for a bit, I'd like to catch up with my son. It's been far too long."

Not without skepticism, William followed his father's orders and allowed Myrna to lead him to a private room. He knew Judith might be bothered by being ushered off, but hoped she'd understand after their conversation. William marched in, followed by Leonard. Forrest had seemingly wandered off.

"So, right off the bat, I need to ask you a frank question, son," Leonard said. "What's up with the fancy get-up and the paw pin? What kind of funny business you getting into in that place?"

"Well, I needed to establish my own brand, the same way you did," William began, feeling embarrassed as much as bothered. "It's part of the reason I'm here actually—to talk business with you."

"Brand, eh? All right, but I don't want to talk business right now," Leonard dismissed. "All I do is talk business, and I haven't seen you in years. Why don't we go out on the town and have some fun first?"

William felt a small bubbling of excitement at the prospect of truly re-connecting with his father. Maybe at his age, his father had seen the light and acquired some perspective on their relationship. At the same time, he didn't want to display that excitement or deviate too much from his course. They'd always had a tough relationship and he had a hard time trusting this sudden change, especially before Leonard had even heard of his progress in the Murrieta. He needed to keep things on even ground and not appear like an eager son.

"After the journey I've had, I'd like some fun myself, so I'll take you up on the offer. But we will talk business another time, won't we? Or am I missing something here?"

"About a father trying to bond with his son?" Myrna intruded into the conversation. "I don't think—"

"No," Leonard interrupted. "William, you're um…you're right, let me be more direct. I get you came here for a reason. But it's been, what, fifteen years since you left?"

"Almost twelve and a half years now—give or take," William corrected.

"Well, shit…but still, all that's in the past, and look at you now. You've changed—as have things around here. When your brothers and you were young, we were just a group of organized thieves. You might even remember after your mom died when Forrest and I founded our Harrowed Sons gang, as we called it back when we organized and moved into protection rackets."

"I remember it all," William said.

"Well there's plenty you missed, too," Leonard followed. "Around the time you boys left was when we started expanding into casinos and whore houses. We were making so much money by that point we were running out of places to put it. Honestly, I even stopped caring about making more of it because once you get to the point you can't count it, power becomes the only object. That's when the factories started to sprout. So we threw as much cash as we had into them and now? Now we control markets; we control labor. Hell, we control the whole damn economy of this city. Point I'm trying to make is, for better or worse, I'm not the man you remember, and I'm sure you ain't the boy I remember either. If I'm gonna even consider going into business with you, I need to figure out who— and what—you've become."

"Well I'll show you the man I've become—I swear on it," William promised. "I just want to be clear I did come here to talk important business with you, and I want to be sure we have our time for it at some point. I want to make sure we're on the same page. We never used to be on the same page, Dad, but I've learned a lot in my time away, and I want to be now more than ever. There's a lot I have to say and I think you'll want to hear it all."

"Of course," Leonard remarked. "We'll talk, William, okay? Like I said, I need to get to know you first. You'll be very much aware of my intentions as the days go by, but tonight I just want to spend some time re-connecting. Does that work for you?"

It worked for William, so he nodded. Besides, his father wasn't the only one who had some sizing up to do. William needed to study his father and assess his sincerity. But a thought nudged his mind.

"But if you don't want to talk business now, what'd you need to speak to me privately about? We could've planned this catching-up outing in the hallway," William said.

"Oh, yeah…well the reason I wanted to talk apart from your friends, the Abigales—"

"You mean my *family* the Abigales? As in my wife and my father-in-law? And aren't they your friends, too?"

Leonard paused. "Sure they are. Henry was useful though and I ain't ever ready for someone useful to go soft and retire. Don't you worry we're fine, we're just not the best of pals no more. Besides that though, I wanted to tell you apart from them I'm happy you're here and to extend an invitation—to just you—to join me tonight at one of my casinos."

William raised his brows. "I see," he chided. "Just me?"

"I know you have your own family now, son, but they'll only distract us from the catching up we need to do. Let tonight be about us."

"Yeah, I can agree to that. But you'll make sure everyone shows them respect, generally speaking, won't you?"

"They are my guests and your relatives. Of course, they'll be given respect."

"All right, then. Until tonight."

Myrna led William out the door and to his room to prepare for the evening. He was feeling enthused about his father's apparent attempt to get to know him and, in so doing, consider going into business with him. He'd have to convince Judith to stay in for the night, but it would be worth it to finally get time with his dad and move closer to the arrangement that would ensure wealth beyond Judith's imagination. What would Daniel and Clovis think if they could see the way their father was behaving? For years Daniel had told him not to worry about Leonard, and now, after all this time, William's persistence in restoring their ties felt validated. It could be the beginning not only of a hugely beneficial business partnership, but of restoring their personal relationship, too.

And that is what William reflected on hours later, as he made his way to the casino.

Myrna was accompanying him in the carriage and carried an impressive amount of firepower on her. Across her back was a massive shotgun and in two holsters on either side of her waist were revolvers. William also spotted a lengthy blade strapped to her ankle.

"Are you going to war?" William asked jokingly.

"That's so funny." There wasn't a hint of sarcasm in Myrna's voice, but she also didn't laugh or change expression at all either, which put William off. "Leonard has a great sense of humor, too."

He hadn't been very familiar with Myrna before leaving New Berkeley, but he was kind of glad about it as he was beginning to share Judith's disdain for her.

"Yeah . . ." William said as the carriage turned a corner. "So, have you had to use all those things recently or . . .? When I left, most of my father's rivals had backed down. Are there any new threats I should know about?"

The carriage ground to a halt.

"Looks like we're here," Myrna said. "Your father's waiting for you inside. Please, don't hesitate on my account. I'll meet you all in there shortly."

William stepped down from his ride. "I wasn't going to hes—," the clacking of horse hooves drowned out his reply as Myrna rode off.

Turning in grumpily toward the alleyway leading to the casino doors, he scanned the entrance. The doors were guarded by two massive men, who stared down a line of people waiting outside.

After reviewing the antsy, gambling-obsessed characters waiting, William stared down at the ground and took a deep breath, trying to clear his mind. He felt deeply irritated for some reason—rubbed wrong by the entire city. His gaze became fixed on a piece of pigeon shit and stayed there for a minute until he snapped out of it and realized he'd spaced out again. Well, at least his irritation was gone. He looked up and made his way past the line and toward the doors.

One or two of those in line yelled out with fists balled, but once the guards announced it was a guest of Leonard's, the line fell silent. As William marched into the casino, he was taken aback by all the colors and noise and excitement. Ravenous men and women alike yelled at the craps tables, while others crowded around roulette wheels in tense anticipation. The most intimidating looking of all the guests sat silently around poker tables, gazing intensely at the cards or their opponents. It was like another world totally apart from the bleak city—an escape.

"William!" he heard Leonard shout. As he spotted his father beckoning him over, William saw Leonard was sitting around a poker table with Myrna, Forrest, and some other shady-looking figures. Cassius stood next to one final open seat he pulled out for William. Even without her shotgun, Myrna was still armed to the teeth. Maybe it was an intimidating poker tactic.

"Join us, son," Leonard said as William took his seat. "These clowns have been practically handing me their money all night."

Poker was a game William liked to think he was good at, though he assumed anyone who played the game thought the same. Nonetheless, this was a prime opportunity to prove his mettle to his father. Through the first few early hands, he folded frequently and observed the other players as best he could. Like his father had suggested, many at the table were somewhat sheepish. One young man in particular was practically shaking, especially when it came down to him and another player head-to-head. Myrna seemed to play mostly stronger hands, but was not as conservative a player as Forrest, who was losing chips little-by-little through the game because of it. Last there was Leonard, who made a habit of bullying the others out of hands with his sizable stack. After his analysis, William began playing in earnest, he was able to win a couple hands and make some money.

A few more hands came and went, the most recent featuring a win for Forrest who had been holding pocket aces. He was thrilled, and William wasted no time in folding as he read it on his face from the start. One other player, a middle-aged man in a non-descript suit, wasn't as aware and ended up losing his entire stack because of it. He dejectedly left the table after the loss.

"About time I got a hand," Forrest said.

"About time you played a damn hand," William shot back, catching Leonard's grin.

Ah, so he respects the moxie, William thought.

"Quite the bark on your son, huh?" Forrest called to Leonard. "Didn't you ever teach him the long game?"

"I don't think so," William said coyly, not intending whatsoever to back down even when facing Leonard's closest confidante. "At least, not if the long game is to bleed slowly but surely till your stack is empty. Is that the long game? Guess I learned something new today."

"You hear something?" Forrest said, still looking at Leonard.

William rolled his eyes, but felt he'd came out on top of the exchange.

The next hand came for William—five and eight, both diamonds. Leonard made a small bet, which was enough to get the others to fold, but William felt confident and ready to show his father what he was worth. "Call."

"Finally, someone who wants to play a game," Leonard said.

"Easy money," Forrest said, ever obnoxious and overconfident.

Fuck him, William thought, but decided to have some kind of filter for now so didn't express the sentiment out loud.

The flop came eight-ace-four, club-diamond-club, respectively. William was sure to hide his excitement as he hit the pair and saw Leonard was quick to check.

"You like hog?" William asked his father as he raised.

"Hog?" Leonard asked. He took a moment before doubling William's bet. "Like…roasted or sausage or what?"

Perhaps his father had an Ace, straight draw, or clubs, then. It was the minimum raise though, so William called.

"Roasted." A king of spades came on the turn. "They're all over the place near Fayette. And my chefs know how to prepare those suckers better than any other. Sometime when you come to the Murrieta, I'll have them make us some."

Leonard made the same bet as previous, to which William wasted no time in calling. It was time to show his dominance, and he wasn't buying Leonard having a king.

"Maybe if I make the trip sometime, sure," Leonard said. William imagined his shortness was due to frustration with the quick call. The river came next—two of clubs. A moment or two passed as they both considered the cards on the table. William considered the odds of Leonard hitting a straight.

Leonard looked William right in the eye with a grin. "All-in." His stack was double William's, so a bad call would be the end of the line for him.

"Good lord, you play fast, huh?" William chuckled.

"Like I said, son, I don't know you, but I intend to see who you've become since you left," Leonard said, still eyeballing him intensely. "Guess we're gonna see what you're made of tonight after all. What's it gonna be?"

William breathed deeply as his mind raced. Leonard might be bluffing. His ego had always been inflated, and he probably had too much fun baiting William. But if he wasn't bluffing, William would lose it all. This game was about more than winning, though. Whatever the outcome, William needed to show his father above all else he was willing to play and play fiercely.

"Call," he boldly announced, though his stomach was tied in a knot. "What do you have?"

"Twos," Leonard scoffed.

"Really? Hell yeah!" William couldn't help but shake his fists in the air.

"What a call . . ." the nervous young man at the table mumbled.

"Sure, good call," Leonard sighed with a nod. The victory was about much more than winning money for William. It was what he needed to get his father's respect. He'd taken a step toward being seen as a man to be respected in Leonard's world. Even beyond his greater plans, spending the time with his father and playing the game felt good, too. It felt simple, and it was a joy William hadn't imagined he'd find in his return to New Berkeley.

He watched as Leonard simply shrugged off the dealer passing just under half his stack William's way. Another few hands passed, and William remained exhilarated by the big win, though he was determined to keep calm.

"I ain't seen you around here, so pardon my bluntness, but you're a little flounder you know that?" Leonard remarked to the young man as he took about a quarter of his stack on a big win.

"Oh—I know. But I try my best." No one at the table joined the young man in his laughter.

"What did a mother name someone who swims so deep only to flop out the way you do, flounder?"

"My name is Leroy Calloway, sir."

"Leroy Calloway, hmm . . ."

William was in awe of the speed in which the dealer was throwing out the cards and was only half-absorbing the conversation. He tried to focus again.

"Well I don't know how you got a seat at my table, but I ain't one to complain about robbing a boy like you blind," Leonard said.

"You know it's funny you should say that sir, because that's what brought me to your table."

William, now the big blind, looked down at a two-four off suit. Leonard started with a small raise, to which there were calls all around the table. Since it was his father who started the betting, William decided to play ball.

"So what're you saying?" Leonard said, picking up the conversation with Leroy again. "That you wanted to get robbed blind?" He chuckled.

The dealer, so quick and precise in her movements, delivered two more twos and a ten on the flop—William was in with a three-of-a-kind. He decided to check and see if he could bait the others. Leonard took it, betting a third the pot.

"No sir, I don't reckon there's a soul in the world who'd want to be robbed blind, particularly me," Leroy said, as he folded his hand away. "You see, my mother was robbed and beaten by your men, and it left a bit of an impression on me."

Everyone at the table, including the dealer, went quiet and looked up at Leroy.

"Now, I don't know who you are, but you should know who I am and that you shouldn't be sneaking into my table making unfounded accusations. My men don't steal from innocent old ladies, so what did she do wrong?"

Two folds led to Myrna, who William was surprised to see bet the previous pot plus Leonard's additional third—they must have both had high pairs. William decided to call for now once he saw it would be down to the three of them, and Leonard followed suit.

"Now sir, don't get me wrong, I ain't accusing you of nothing." A seven came on the turn—all cards of different suits. "You see, I was of the impression it was a misunderstanding. My mother is just a worker though, like myself, and we foot the bills for my three young half-siblings and me. I saved up as much as I could on the side to make this meeting happen. She likes to have her fun for sure, but she ain't put no hurting on nobody in her life. Matter of fact she's the only one whose been hurt by folks—my daddy even."

"Look son, I got plenty of rivals who are more violent than me; it was probably one of them." Leonard called this time around. William stared his father down, beginning to wonder whether there was something to the boy's accusation. His father never did explain himself. "Now if your daddy's violent to your mother, maybe he arranged something. If that is the case, and you'd like me to take care of him, I can do so because I respect the balls on you to come face me."

"No sir, my daddy up and left us when I was too young to remember much of him. He went to go out West to the Murrieta," Leroy said. William's gaze snapped to the boy at the mention of the Murrieta. The young man couldn't have been much older than eighteen, yet there was something about him William couldn't put his finger on.

Leroy sighed. "But my mother was sure it was your men, and I believe her. I'm not entirely certain how to go about it, but I just want this to be made right."

"All in," Myrna said. William's attention was ripped away from Leroy, as he was befuddled by this move. Considering how she played to that point, he thought it was possible she could have a two with a higher second card than his four.

"Come on," Leonard moaned.

"Sir, about my mother . . ." Leroy tried to continue.

"Who cares about her? No one." Leonard slumped with despair at Myrna's all-in. "We're playing a game here. This is a place of entertainment. Why should I have to ask for the courtesy to finish a hand before talks like these in my own establishment?"

"What in the hell do you have?" William asked Myrna, feeling for Leroy and trying to distract Leonard from him. Myrna's expression was like stone. "What the hell does she have?" he said again, this time to his father.

"Shit, I'd put her on a deuce, but hell if I know," Leonard said as a commotion began at the doors. It sounded like a tussle between the guards and some people outside. No one at the table seemed to pay it any mind, as they were probably used to it.

William stared down his father, then Myrna. How badly he wanted to be bold again, yet he knew with two players—and one he didn't trust at all in Myrna—it might be foolish.

"Fold," William said, living to fight another day.

Leonard took another peek at his cards. "Ha! Maybe you are wiser than I thought. This broad is not the one to be trifled with. I fold. What do you got Myrna? You better be showing me those cards."

After pulling the pot toward her, Myrna flipped her cards without a word. Queen-ten. What an epic bluff. William couldn't believe it, yet having heard of Myrna's ways, he kind of could. She played the true long game and won.

With the hand over, William looked at Leroy again, and he realized what it was he couldn't place before. He couldn't believe he'd been so distracted by the game when it was so obvious.

"Did you say your last name was Calloway?" William asked him. "Is your father's name Gregory?"

"You bitch," Leonard snickered with a grin at Myrna.

Leroy sat up in his seat, centering on William. "That's right. Do you know him?"

"Yes, I do. I know him very well. Look, I don't claim familiarity with your mother, but your father Gregory is a good man. I don't take him as one who would ever hurt your mother, despite what she's done to him."

"Done to him?" Leroy asked. "What are you talking about? He left us."

"Leroy, I don't know how to tell you this, but your father thought you dead for a long time…at least that's what your mother told him before she pushed him away. I have no idea how she could do this to such a softhearted man, but I'm glad I met you because now we can fix it. I can tell him I saw you, and we can arrange for you two to see each other." William couldn't imagine how hard it must be for Leroy to hear this about his own mother.

"There's no way that can be right…my mother loves—" Leroy stopped mid-sentence. "But if what you say is true—"

Two loud gunshots burst through the casino, followed by several more. Forrest dove over to Leonard and pulled him to the ground under the table. William followed suit and looked up to see Myrna and Cassius ducking for cover behind the bar and furiously returning fire. His ears rang, and he was stunned by the suddenness of the assault. He wondered what it could mean. Amid the shooting, he looked to the side of the table and saw Leroy laying on the ground, covered in blood. William did not hesitate as he darted out and came to his side.

"William, get back here!" He recognized Leonard's call behind him.

Ripping off a piece of Leroy's clothing, William used it as a rag to apply pressure to the wound. "You're gonna be all right, Leroy."

"I only wanted to help my mother! Please, don't leave me! Please don't let me die!"

"You're a good son, Leroy, and I'm not going anywhere, you hear me?" William promised, grabbing his hand and looking him in the eyes. "We're gonna get you home, and I'm gonna take you to see your daddy. You don't even know how happy he'll be to see you."

The gunshots had ended, but the casino was filled with people swarming and trampling each other in a frenzy. It was clear to William that Leroy was dying, but he couldn't accept it. It felt to him as if Gregory himself was the one fading away in front of him. He applied pressure to the wound, which was in Leroy's stomach, and his mind raced about what he could do. Should he reach in to get the bullet out? Was it too soon to make such a move?

"Someone get me some fucking salt water!" he screamed. He spotted Cassius and Myrna now returning. "Salt water! I need it now! God damn it, someone go get me salt water, please!"

"Is it true?" Leroy was beginning to wheeze as he was weakening. "Is it true what you said about my father?"

"Yes, of course," William looked up to see if anyone was doing anything to help, and then back down at Gregory's son. No one had appeared to be moving to meet his request. William made careful note Leonard in particular just stared indifferently at him. "He loved you Leroy, and he didn't want to leave you. He wanted you to come with him."

A smile expanded across Leroy's face. "Tell him I said . . ."

"You'll tell him," William cried, an intense ferocity overtaking him. "I'm gonna take you to him, and you're going to tell him."

"Tell him I said I hope I see him again one day," Leroy mumbled. His eyes were glassy and wide open as his grip was beginning to loosen in William's hand.

"No, no, no," William stuttered, tightening his own grip as Leroy took one last deep breath. "Stay with me, son. Stay with me."

Hunching over Leroy in utter pain and despair, William realized his best friend's son, who Gregory never even knew was alive, was gone. All those years with the worst heartbreak a person can feel, but he imagined it would be even worse to find out this way that it all wasn't even necessary. And for this to happen to a man as good as Gregory?

Why? What did a man this good ever do to deserve such a thing? To lose the person he loved most in the world...

At the very idea of Gregory, Judith, his brothers, and all those he loved, William began to weep, unable to bear the thought. And in that moment, he couldn't let go of this young man he'd only just met. He now understood perfectly, as Gregory's loss became his own, the pain of losing this young life all over again—and all he could think was no one deserved this feeling. When he found himself able to let go, he looked up from the body to see his father, still staring at him without expression.

*

When the time came for Daniel to address the people of Harran, the sun was on its way down and the shadows of the Murrieta stretched further and further across the land. Outside the hotel, the entire town gathered. There were about a hundred men, women, and children, surrounded by about fifty armed members of the Keagan gang.

As he was about to start talking, he scanned the quieting crowd. He spotted the Kennedales, whom he smiled at with a slight nod. He saw Donald, who'd been helped out with a seat by the other townsfolk. He saw Johanna, who gave him a wink. He saw a few families, couples young and old, and a few solo onlookers. Some looked angry—he carefully noted them—but overall what he saw was mostly fear. Still though, he felt tense. Armed with two pistols on either side of his hips, a knife at his ankle, and bullet-resistant padding both underneath his shirt and pants, Daniel was ready for anything. Whether it be a gunshot or an explosion or a riot, he figured it'd be best to draw the attackers out by giving them a clearer shot than they'd had since the murder. With that thought, he began.

"It's kind of funny, I didn't plan this gathering out at all, and I had no idea what I wanted to get out of it," Daniel admitted. The sun now peeked below the hotel's awning and into his face, restricting his view of the faces in the crowd. "But now that I'm here looking at each of y'all, I feel like I have it all figured out. This is why I came here. Because even though I want wealth—and I do want wealth very much, I'd be lying to y'all if I said otherwise—my desire for that is trivial compared to my desire to build something great here in the Murrieta."

"Since when was fire a tool of choice for building?" Cheers followed the outburst.

"I believe," Daniel said, trying to ignore the remark, "we, together, can build something great. I've seen y'all out there with your families, friends, husbands, and wives. I promise y'all I want nothing more than to provide a better life here for everyone. But to do so I need y'all to cooperate and to tell me what's needed from us when I come around and ask."

"Flames burned down the same people who'd already built something great here!" the same man called.

"We need *y'all* to leave!" another woman said. The cheering continued until several Keagan men began loading and lifting their rifles at the crowd. Children started to cry and scream, and while the anger became more even tempered, it still sat heavy as a fog in the air.

"Lower your weapons right now! Each goddamn one of y'all!" Daniel was furious with his men as he turned back to the people of Harran. "Look I'll open the floor to y'all right here and now so we can get on the same page, but please, I need civility. I'm telling y'all I'll work tirelessly to meet every request, no matter how small or large they might be. And as for your Morrells...I've expressed my condolences more times than I can count, but as I've said each time, my men were fired upon and had to defend themselves. I don't know what more y'all could ask of me than to try my best to give y'all the same they did. Who knows—maybe we could make this place even better." He took a deep breath, "But either way, y'all got y'all's blood, too. Whoever was the perpetrator of this recent act knows what I'm talking about. And it was awful what you did, but I'd understand if maybe you even felt like you needed to do it. So you know what? I'll tell y'all this right now, if y'all show me decency and work with me, I'm willing to completely look the other way on the murder of one of my men—as long as whoever did it steps up. Doesn't have to be now. Could just be to me in private. But I need to know, so I know what and who I'm working with going forward. Do we have a deal?"

The crowd was silent now, and Daniel felt he had their affirmation. Debra and Cassie even seemed to smile a bit. "Good. Now let's open the floor, so y'all can be heard."

Someone spoke up promptly, but Daniel was distracted by something coming overhead in their direction. His stomach dropped when he realized it was a flock of crows.

Not now, he thought. *Not when a distraction is the last thing I need.*

Unlike at William's wedding, where the crows were a tremendous mass, this time they flew in a "V" formation, with the formation seeming to repeat endlessly. Daniel counted each "V" as they passed over the hotel. By the time he got to the fiftieth and final one, he realized it must have been a sign. The birds were like arrows pointing north—the V'ahani, he figured. He turned back toward the crowd, and though almost every one of them stared straight up, the Kennedales simply stared at him. They'd told him to look to sky, hadn't they?

This was the sign.

"My apologies, but I'm afraid we must pick this conversation up another time," Daniel said to groans from the crowd. "I don't mean to cut y'all short, and y'all *will* be heard, but if y'all could please allow me to consider the meaning of what we've seen tonight, I'll be all ears as soon as possible."

The people of Harran wouldn't be pleased, and while Daniel did worry about it, he needed to inform his men of how they would respond to this sign from the V'ahani. He assembled them in the saloon, where he informed them that in a week's time he'd lead a contingent north up the River White to just before the Mountainlands. There they would camp for a week, which for him would be a much-needed week away from Harran, and await a sign from the V'ahani. He assumed they wanted to talk and needed to see if that was the case. This was the perfect time to do it, too, because although they'd likely be outnumbered, there'd be no hostility from the mountain men given their brothers and sisters, the V'ahani of the Riverlands, were still hostages at the Hold. They wouldn't risk the lives of their kin to shed his blood.

After briefing his men, he found Johanna and headed to bed. As iffy as the talk with the people of Harran was, he felt great about where things were now. Once he did get the opportunity to talk to the townspeople, the killer would hopefully step forward, and that'd be the end of it. If they didn't step forward after he delivered on his promise, he felt he'd have the justification to take action and find out who it was when the time came. For now, this stalling of the situation was good enough.

Things were looking up, and his enthusiasm showed in the bedroom that night. Over the past few days, Johanna and he had stopped talking outside of sex. It didn't bother him much—they had little to say—and at least in the bedroom, they connected well enough to make up for it. So he kept coming back.

When the deed was done, he was quick to pass out in sleep until a dream of being unable to breathe woke him—except it wasn't a dream at all. A pillow smothered his face and someone was on top of him holding it down with all his or her might. He resisted violently but his arms were pinned under the person's legs and his lungs were burning.

"I'm gonna miss these nights, hun," he heard Johanna say. With a shock, he realized *she* was the one trying to kill him. All he could do was mumble back in opposition.

She replied to his indecipherable mumble nonetheless. "I mean it, I will. But ain't none of us here are gonna miss you and your scum gang."

Beginning to feel the pressure building in his torso and faintness in his limbs, he noticed the weight had been lifted slightly from the left side of the pillow. As he was turning his head toward the loose end to attempt to steal some air, a knife tore through the pillow to the right of his neck. Realizing his opportunity, he used all the strength in his legs to knee Johanna in the back. Having used her weight to thrust the knife, the force pushed her forward into the bedframe, allowing Daniel to escape from being pinned. With the pillow off his head, he knocked the knife away from where she'd dropped it on the bed and overpowered Johanna. In a fury, he put his hands on her throat and squeezed. As shades of purple started spreading over her skin, he realized he'd never killed anyone before and became uneasy. It led him to ease up slightly, though he kept enough force on her neck to hold her down.

"Why did you do this? Why?"

"The fire you've ignited," Johanna said, struggling to speak but continuously resisting. "It didn't start with me. It won't end with me either."

"Who else? Who else, Johanna!?"

Johanna only clamped her jaw tight and resisted.

"Dammit! How many nights have we shared a bed?" Daniel shrieked as some of his men hurried into the room. When he turned his head toward them, Johanna spit in his face. In disgust, he furiously wiped it away and tightened his grip. "How many long nights have you been lying beside me in wait only to deceive me?"

"Welcome to Harran," Johanna said with a smirk as they grabbed her.

Daniel could only stare at her in disbelief as he let her go. He gave the order to have her taken to the other cell at the jail. Designating one of the men as the new town sheriff, he ordered him to oversee any conversation between Johanna and his other prisoner, Charles.

That night, for the first time in a while, Daniel lay in bed alone. Staring out his window, he wondered if he'd be able to sleep in the same bed with anyone ever again.

CHAPTER 8

AT THE DOORSTEP

Latera felt hope on the horizon in the days following her encounter with her mysterious Keagan overseer. As she wandered the grounds, always remaining out in the open and on alert for any chance to connect with Elan, she was pleased to note an almost immediate shift in the treatment of the V'ahani. There were no more assaults or bullying by the Keagans. In fact, it seemed as if her people were now on the same footing in their eyes as the Tokali—who did not take kindly to that fact.

Following the change of treatment, the bickering and the occasional skirmishes that broke out between the two clans increased. Though they remained minor incidents, it spoke to the frustration of the Tokali—which felt good to see. Even if the Tokali couldn't know a fraction of the pain and confusion the V'ahani had experienced after their betrayal, it was something. The bastards deserved worse.

"Latera!"

Latera spun around and saw Winona making her way toward her through the bustling crowd. Even in this particularly hot spring heat, her friend managed to look lovely. Latera couldn't recall the last time she'd made any true effort with her own appearance.

"Winnie!" Latera hugged her friend.

"He was not kidding, Latera," Winona said with her hands on Latera's shoulders and a smile which could've made Latera cry. She'd almost forgotten what joy looked like.

"What? Who do you mean?" Latera asked.

"The man who captured us," Winona said. "I do not know what you have done since, but thank you. You are our true savior."

As happy as Latera was to hear such kind words, she was wary of how loud Winona was speaking. She looked around anxiously and pulled her friend aside.

"I am so glad you are feeling better." Latera caught an upset-looking Elan out of the corner of her eye. She needed to end this conversation and get ahold of him. "I hope Mika is, as well. But you must listen to me when I say you cannot tell anyone about what happened. This stays between the three of us or it could put all the safety our people now enjoy in jeopardy. Do you understand me?"

"I understand, but . . ." Winona said hesitantly, looking worried, "I know I have said this before, but you should not have to suffer for us. You should not have to go through this alone."

"Do not worry yourself about me," Latera commanded, beginning to move away to shuffle after Elan. "I must go now, but I am fine."

"Maybe physically you are fine, but your tired eyes tell another story, Latera," Winona said. She wondered how much Winona saw of her pain, but there was no time to think about it and little to be accomplished by acknowledging it.

"I am fine, Winnie. Now excuse me."

Winona's worried eyes burned into her back as Latera ran to catch up with Elan.

"Elan! Elan, wait!" The second call had come when he didn't react to the first and was the one he heard, at which point he spun around. So did the group of young men surrounding him. They all seemed to be about her and Elan's age.

Ah, so they aren't just part of the crowd. Shame, Latera thought.

"Latera?" he said in a surprised tone.

She approached him and the others. "Yes, I wanted to speak to you."

"Is this the one you are always going on about?" the curly-haired young man standing next to Elan asked. Elan blushed and the others chuckled in response. "So the current color of his face means yes, correct?"

"Oh, leave him be," another said with a laugh. He was the tallest and most attractive of the bunch. "We have heard a lot about you, though. My name is Pharaoh."

"Hello, Pharaoh," Latera greeted him with a smile as she half-bowed and half-nodded her head.

"Hammond," the one who originally mocked Elan said.

"Warrick," a thinner one with slightly worse posture greeted her with a wave.

"Yeah, yeah, and I'm Shelton." The final member of the group did not even bother to look at her. Of them all, he was the shortest, and yet his hair was also in a bun like Elan's, Pharaoh's and Hammond's. Could he have possibly been a warrior, too, Latera wondered? And why was he so grumpy?

"Ah, so what did you want to talk about, Latera?"

"I just wanted to thank you for trusting me last week. I appreciated not being in the dark for once."

"Oh, well, I am sure you will no longer need me to tell you about such events, seeing as the Keagans have taken such a sudden shine to your people," Elan said with a sprinkle of jealousy. "Would you like to walk with us?"

"I'd be happy to. And it has been a very welcome change. We are thankful for it." Latera hoped to rub a little salt in the jealousy wound as she now followed them.

"It is strange, but I am glad to see the Keagans delivering on their word of peace," the one named Pharaoh said.

Great, Latera thought, *another brainwashed pretty-boy.*

"Of course, it is strange," Hammond snapped. "They are a cult, and their behavior is unpredictable. Now one of our own—Shelton's brother, for the sake of the Mother—is a prisoner, and we do not know a thing about his condition."

Latera looked carefully at Hammond and added him to a mental list of Tokali she'd known to show backbone or intelligence of any kind. In fact, he was the first.

"For someone who has such a problem with them, you have sure adapted to their slang quickly enough," Elan mocked.

"What have our parents said about this kind of talk in the open?" Pharaoh said to them both. "Save it for a safer place."

As Shelton hung his head and Hammond placed his arm around his shoulder, they continued on in silence for a bit. Latera's interest was now piqued beyond the mission she was assigned. She had no idea this discord existed within the Tokali about their decision—especially within a group of close friends. There was a tension there, and she knew she needed to get to the heart of it.

She bumped into the backs of Elan and Pharaoh, who both turned with a start. Latera realized she had been distracted by her thoughts, and now she'd entered the region of the Hold where the Tokali resided. The V'ahani tended to avoid this area, assuming they were not welcome. The group turned around to look at her expectantly, but she stood still and silent.

"We are just going to go talk to my parents now," Elan informed her, seeming to imply he was expecting her to leave. "I will come find you another time, and we can talk more then."

"I—I would very much like to meet them," Latera said desperately, knowing she did not have anything concrete to take to her stalker and worrying things would go back to the way they were if she failed him. "Healing begins with discussion, Elan. Healing can lead to unity. I know that is what your people want most of all."

Elan stared at her with his big, hazel eyes. They were beautifully vibrant, but they were always filled with so much uncertainty.

"She is right," Shelton blurted. "She is their representative, and we need our people to be on the same page. Plus, she might know more about our discovery than even we do."

"Discovery?" Latera asked.

"Damn it, Shelton!" Elan clapped his hands to his thighs. "All right, let us get inside before one of you idiots shouts your life story from the balcony of the Square."

Excitement filled Latera, even as her nerves caused her stomach to quake. She needed to be extra careful about what she said. She also needed to say the right things to get them to trust her and open up. Could she manage it?

163

When she entered Elan's home, his parents, Adila and Malik, approached her. It was at that time she noted Elan had his mother's eyes and father's thick, dark hair.

"We have heard so much of you, Latera," Adila said as they all knelt down in a living area after introductions. "It is funny, your eyes are so light blue—like the snow—and yet, I see a fire inside of them. I have heard it from our son, as well. I know this whole ordeal must have been…difficult. It is a shame we had no other choice in the matter."

Right off the bat Latera was fuming and could tell Adila was testing her. The old woman would do well not to underestimate her.

"'No other choice' is an interesting way to put it. After meeting these friends Elan has, it seems fairly evident there was not a consensus on your decision, or have I misinterpreted the tensions?" Latera said, letting her question linger only for a breath. "It is difficult to get a whole people to agree on such a hard decision, I suppose. In any case, what of this discovery you mentioned Shelton? How might I be able to help?"

"How dare you come into a Tokali home and question our alignment," Pharaoh cried.

Elan shook his head. "I knew this would be a mistake."

"Well, is she wrong? We do not agree!" Hammond questioned.

"I did not think it was the case before, but I can see now it is clear I was misguided," Shelton sided with Hammond.

"Clear only to you, Shelton. We all agreed on this course! Do not change your mind now. We do not even know Gannon is in any true danger!" Elan said next.

The volume in their voices increased as they kept snapping at each other.

"I should have brought something to document this," Warrick said to himself.

"Boys," Malik howled, and the young men fell silent. "I will talk to the Keagans again and demand information on Gannon. In the meantime, what have I said about a united front?"

"Yes, do not let anyone," Adila shot Latera a look, "cause you to fall apart in such a fashion. You are our warriors—our most prized sons. Remember that."

The young men grumbled but all nodded in agreement.

"The Keagans are treating the V'ahani better lately and so should we," Malik said. "Our people have not taken well to this shift, worrying it means we may have fallen out of favor and are beginning to suffer worse conditions, but there is no evidence to support this fear. So we need to lead by example. We should have from the beginning. The V'ahani should have been treated better from the beginning. Surely our guest here agrees. I imagine that is why she is here, to begin to build some understanding between our people."

Latera recognized the opportunity and forged ahead into her lies. "Yes, equal treatment is part of why I have come. As I told Elan, healing begins with discussion. I believe if we are all more at peace, the Keagans will opt to leave both our peoples be."

"As much as it seems the V'ahani want conflict to exist," Adila snipped, looking right at Latera, "I agree. Unity is what we wanted, after all, so we must be an example for the V'ahani."

Was Adila seriously suggesting the Tokali were the example

the V'ahani should follow? Latera's rage was boiling, but she kept a tight hold of it. No matter how impossible Elan's mother was making it, she could not lose her temper, because she'd lose any chance of learning about their "discovery" along with it.

"And in that spirit, I would like to be an example to my people by helping you how I can. What was it you were talking about earlier, Shelton?" she asked again.

Shelton looked at his friends, and Latera did not look away from him.

"What is it your people desire, Latera?" Adila interrupted.

Freedom.

But Latera dare not answer Adila. She could not lie well enough to hide the truth she knew burned in her eyes.

So instead, she looked only at Shelton. "I desire to help you."

"Can I tell her?" he asked.

"I think you should," Hammond said. "It has only just begun, and she could help us with it, do you not think so, Malik?"

Latera couldn't deny she was beginning to like Hammond. He seemed to be the only Tokali she had met with any sense. Shelton was a close second, but he was still too hesitant for her liking.

"Do the V'ahani want to be our enemies for all eternity at the expense of this great Territory?" Latera still refused to look Adila's way as she kept on.

There would be nothing left of the great Territory if Latera followed the Tokali's way. But again, she only answered Shelton. "I want to help you, Shelton."

He opened his mouth, but Pharaoh cut in.

"If her people are foolish enough to cross ours, I think it would be good to maintain the element of surprise for our defense."

"I am not sure," Elan said.

When was he ever? But for once Latera appreciated his attempt to win her favor by not directly disagreeing.

"Do your people want to spite us so much that when an opportunity for unity—for the survival of us all—presents itself on the doorstep of the Murrieta, you would still fight it?" Adila would not quit pestering her.

In that moment, Latera could not contain her rage or her disgust. She stood sharply. But Malik raised his hands in the air as she was about to storm out of the home.

"Not long ago we discovered our abilities extend beyond what we thought," he started to the horror of those in protest—including Adila. "I know she is a V'ahani, but Hammond is right. Despite his emotional opinion of the Keagans, he is right that she is more aware when it comes to these matters than we are. She is more in touch with the Mother and might be able to give us some hint as to what this means for us."

"What *what* means?" Latera asked. The question coming out sharper than she intended. He'd mentioned a connection to the Mother...

Could they control the grizzlies, too? Fear skittered down her spine.

"We were out on a hunt not too long ago and discovered we can speak to the hogs," Malik said.

Latera croaked, but tamped down her laughter just in time. "The hogs?" So it was the horses, birds, and *hogs* for the Tokali. Of course they had measly, fat pigs while the V'ahani were gifted the ferocious grizzlies—only the Mother could conjure such an appropriate thing. A sense of satisfaction ran through her.

"Yes," Malik answered. "The hogs of the south are great, fierce, and dangerous creatures and Hammond here came to stop one dead in its tracks on a hunt. We have tried to replicate it since but have had significant difficulties."

She wasn't surprised Hammond was the one to stop the pig. The Mother only bonded to the strong. She was surprised they were admitted out of the Hold, but it made sense. The Keagans were too lazy to hunt their own meat when someone else could do it for them.

Now how could she keep this in her favor?

"When next you go on your hunt, take me with you. It may take some time if I cannot also communicate with the hogs, but I should still be able to help if not. Each young V'ahani goes through an initiation, which trains our minds to be one with the Mother. I can teach you what I have learned to allow me to hone my skills."

"I am going on this hunt, as well," Adila said.

Adila was fiercely protective and deeply suspicious. If they were not on opposite sides of the truth, Latera might respect her.

"Fair enough," Malik followed. "I will have Elan find you in the coming days and we will see what you can do."

"Very well," Latera said, "You may find me when you are ready." Malik nodded to her.

"I should likely go now. I have been away from my people for too long," Latera said, as she started toward the door. "I look forward to seeing what your pigs can do."

"Hogs," Elan testily corrected her.

Latera stared at him for a moment, gave a fake "of course" and left.

Helping the Tokali was the last thing she wanted or intended to do, but it was what she needed them to think she would do for now. The encounter had not been a pleasant one. It would be a painful task for her to deal with this cowardly clan.

From Elan's home, Latera marched toward the V'ahani region of the Hold in case Adila had sent any of the Tokali to watch her. After making sure she was not followed, she veered toward the Keagan part of the Hold.

There were no natives there whatsoever when she arrived, and it reeked of alcohol. The men who were out and about were loud and obnoxious, though they were brought to silence when they beheld her marching purposefully through their streets. They looked equal parts confused, angry, and in awe. It was the last which filled her with the most courage.

When it was clear she had their full attention, she pulled a thick hair ribbon from her pocket and wrapped it around her head, covering her eyes.

"Take me to him," she demanded aloud. "I have what he is looking for."

*

The journey back toward Harran brought up bad memories for Jeannie, but she had to admit spring in the Mountainlands was a sight to see. The last remnants of snow were melting off the cliffs, and the lushness of the damp greenery had intensified. Walking along the path, the beauty often distracted her, and several times she failed to walk straight, grazing Harrison's shoulder. He would protest the more she did it, but once she started pointing out the sights that were distracting her—a rainbow stretching radiantly from the clouds here, an adorable white squirrel carefully staring them down from a tree there—he would back off. And how could he not with all the tranquility that surrounded them?

There was also a sense of physical safety with an army of V'ahani at their backs, though she still did worry about seeing the Keagans. As much as being away from Harran was a scary thing for her, traveling through the Mountainlands was preferable to being subject to her family's killers. Now she'd have to face them once again.

She hoped the V'ahani and the Keagans could come to some kind of peaceful resolution—preferably one that allowed her and Harrison to remain with Hanzah and his people, away from any place under full Keagan control. She knew there wasn't much likelihood to that hope, but she wished for it nonetheless. As difficult as the V'ahani could sometimes be, and as much as Harrison worried about Varek's hatred for all Easterners, she still considered the V'ahani to be the allies her father always told her they were. Concerns aside, they were more honorable than the Keagans any day.

For a while, Jeannie had been leading the natives down the trail, purely due to her rapt attention on the nature of the North. She consistently ran ahead to see how the next bend had changed from winter to spring. But even as she clamored at the front of the group, she was aware Dominic remained toward the back of the crowd, always keeping his head down. He'd been quiet and reserved since they found him, and Jeannie did wonder what he must be feeling. She wanted to speak to him, despite Harrison's distrust.

How could the son of the only man able to unite anyone in the Murrieta be so at odds with everyone around him? Surely there had to be some way she could help her brother become more like her father, but after days of traveling, she still wasn't sure how to alter his distrusting attitude.

As she worried over the issue yet again, an opening appeared through the trees in the trail before her, and she saw it: the V'ahani bridge over the River White. Trotting toward it, she could see it had been repaired since Dominic's horse Nala had fallen in months ago. Across the field on the other side of the bridge she saw a small fire rising into the air. Her stomach sunk at the sight, but she saw little else before she was yanked off the path and into cover.

"Jeannie, what the hell are you doing? They could've seen you."

"They're gonna have to see me eventually, Harrison," she said, despite the fact she'd prefer *not* to see the Keagans ever again.

Varek came for cover near them, along with one of his men, as well as Orrin and Hanzah. Varek held up a hand for his fighters to stay back.

"This is all they brought?" The lack of numbers for this group of Keagans was a fact Jeannie only now recognized as she turned back. The campsite on the other side of the field was very small, and from the figures walking around, it seemed there couldn't be more than thirty men in total.

"I do not suppose they would have needed much, considering our people are at their mercy," Orrin said. "At least we can assume they are not looking for a fight. Not for now, at least."

Varek shook his head. "We will make no such assumptions. I want their camp surrounded by the grizzlies—two for each man if possible. This lot needs to feel as captive and trapped in our lands as our people must feel in theirs. Give the order now. Once ready, we will meet them on the plain and see what they have to say."

The V'ahani fighter who had followed Varek nodded and ran back toward the others. Standing straight up, Varek walked with a kind of swagger out of the cover. Jeannie felt her nerves kicking in full force now with the confrontation about to begin. She turned to Harrison, who looked back at her only until Hanzah and Orrin followed Varek out of hiding. Harrison darted out next to catch up. With a sigh, Jeannie followed suit.

As she had thought, crossing the bridge was much easier this time, as it was much more heavily fortified. Once she had stepped off the last plank, the movement in the Keagan camp began. They looked like ants as they scurried back and forth, except ants were much more efficient. They were more like mosquitoes, actually—pests only here to suck the life out of everything around them.

Before long she saw *him* emerge. Tall and well-maintained in extravagant dress, Daniel Keagan still managed to appear more inappropriate in the setting than a clown at a burial. Something about his posture did seem different than before, but Jeannie couldn't give it much thought as she focused all her attention on what was about to unfold. Though she knew Daniel wasn't the devil himself—that title she reserved for Clovis—his words would be received with the same caution as the tail of a rattlesnake.

The V'ahani fighters filed across the bridge at Varek's orders and took position horizontally along the river banks. Some who crossed stood at attention with spears and shields, while a select few wielded rifles. Jeannie knew more remained under cover on the other side, ready should they need to order the grizzlies to descend upon the Keagans. From the trees of the Riverlands before them, Jeannie could see the barrels of rifles pointed their way.

Jeannie and Harrison remained behind the councilmen. Varek stood before all of them and marched about a quarter of the way across the open field before stopping dead in his tracks. Jeannie assumed Dominic stayed behind on the other side of the river, and she didn't blame him. As for Daniel, he walked out alone, about the same distance out of the woods from the other side.

Varek raised a hand Daniel's way. "No further or you all die!" Daniel's pace stopped on cue. The Grand Chieftain said nothing after that, and silence reigned for a few tense minutes.

Daniel became the first to act and shrugged his shoulders. "Well? Y'all are the ones who requested my presence up here in your own interesting little way of communicating. What is it y'all want?"

"You know very well what we want," Varek snarled. "I should not have to waste my breath to say it. The question is what do you want for their return?"

"Pretty sure y'all are aware of that as well, friend," Daniel quipped. "The V'ahani of the Riverlands will be free to go if y'all surrender to us right here and now. Otherwise, well, I don't need to waste the breath to tell you what my brother Clovis can do."

"He will not lay a finger on them!" Varek flared. "You and your men are surrounded, even if you do not see it. If I give the order— or if I am killed—my men will order our grizzlies upon you, and they will tear you limb from limb. We will not let you go until your brother lets them go. If he ever wants to see you again, those are our demands."

Jeannie felt empowered by the Grand Chieftain's response and hoped Harrison did as well. She could see this frustrated Daniel, however, as he rolled his eyes and slicked back his hair.

"Look, I'm gonna be frank with y'all, I don't want this. I don't want Clovis to hurt them, but he will."

"No, sir! He's lying!" Harrison stomped his foot. "You sent him straight to our doorstep with a wick and a flame and free range to kill. You have no reigns over him!"

"Silence!" Varek turned to Harrison.

"Nah, don't be silent, Harrison Morrell," Daniel demanded as he crept forward one step at a time. "You know, I've heard this idea tossed around more than once now, and if there's anything I've learned over the years it's that if it's green, and it's lumpy, and it ribbits, chances are it's a damned frog."

"But it could also be a toad," Orrin said, furrowing his brow and stroking his beard. Jeannie couldn't help but chuckle, and she heard Hanzah follow suit.

"What? I—well…whatever. You get what I'm trying to—"

"No, I do not have any clue the point you are trying to get across, because what you claim to have 'learned' is an entirely incorrect assumption," Orrin interrupted.

Daniel sighed. "Regardless, I'm just trying to say I've heard the story multiple times now from multiple sources, and I'm willing to look further into it is all."

"Liar!" Jeannie involuntarily blurted, as she couldn't help but doubt every word he said. "And it's not a story. It's the truth."

"Jeannie, if this version of events is true, I know what you saw there that day," Daniel crept forward some more. "I know because I've seen it, too, and it's ruined me. There's a hole in me six feet deep for every one of them people my brother's slaughtered—your family members included, if it's true. It eats away at me every day. I know my brother doesn't have a shred of decency in him, but you have to believe I thought William and I—I thought we had him under control. What I'm realizing is we only have an inkling of what's going on in Clovis's mind, and that's the dangerous part. Surrender is just about the only way to keep this chaos from carrying on though. It's the only thing that'll get William to for-sure give him the order to stand down for good and to get him away from those people. Chieftain, or whatever your title might be because I don't mean to show no disrespect, I…I need you to surrender here. If you don't, it won't matter."

"The jaws of my grizzlies biting into your flesh will matter very much I assure you."

Again, Jeannie appreciated Varek's strong response. Daniel could never be trusted, no matter how convincing he sounded.

"I'm not asking you because I'm afraid of those bears," Daniel pleaded. "For all I know, maybe I deserve a mauling like only they could give for all that's happened. But please, if you do that… the toll on your people will be ten-fold, and I'm not just talking about the V'ahani of the Riverlands. As much as we've done for Clovis, William and I might be the only people he feels anything for in this world. If you let us end this in the peaceful, prosperous arrangement we've planned, we can substitute his broken leash for chains. We can and will put an end to this, I promise you. I'll see to it with what power I do have."

Varek stared silently for a moment at Daniel before turning to huddle with Orrin and his councilmen. Jeannie and Harrison were very purposefully left out, and Jeannie felt her knees buckle—they couldn't be about to agree to the Keagans' terms, they just couldn't.

After a few moments of whispering, Varek turned back. "I should kill you now, Daniel Keagan, for the monster you and your brother unleashed, for the crimes he has committed. I should kill you now for daring to challenge the V'ahani."

Varek paused and Jeannie ceased to breathe.

"But as much pleasure as that may give me, I will not give your rabid dog reason to attack my people. Should we come to this agreement, we will need true evidence your monster will be stopped. Your word is not enough. Your words mean nothing, as they are lies the moment they leave your lips. It is the same with all of your kind. So, bring me proof, Daniel Keagan, that what you speak is true. Proof you will stop your monster. Reason for me to control my fury. If you fail, blood will soak these lands."

"Chieftain—"

"Nothing is decided. My people and I will retreat behind the river to discuss what our decision will be. Return to your camp for now and await my return to this spot in four days' time precisely. You will hear my answer at that time."

Daniel nodded and turned back as the V'ahani leaders did the same. But Jeannie could not move. An icy chill ran up her spine as she imagined a world where there was no safe place for her and Harrison—no place for them to run from the Keagans.

Harrison grabbed her arm and dragged her along until she turned and walked on her own back toward the mountains.

Dominic came from across the bridge and over to them. "Did you both hear what he said?"

"Yes, I did," Harrison sighed.

"What is it?" Jeannie asked them both, confused. "You mean how they're going to surrender?"

But both Dominic and Harrison ignored her.

"Whenever I think hope is lost and feel most ready to run . . ." Dominic said to Harrison.

"It might be a sign. But how can we know if it's true? What if he's lying?"

"We can investigate. And we must."

Jeannie felt lost, but glad to see Harrison and Dominic on the same page. "Investigate what?"

Harrison turned toward her. "I know our struggle with the V'ahani has mostly been my fault, Jeannie. I'm only now learning, thanks to your help, what it takes to form the bonds father was able to form. So far it's been a challenge to say the least. For that I'm sorry—sorry to you both. Dominic, if you can forgive me, we need your help."

"There is nothing to forgive."

"There is, though. I doubted you—even after all you've done for us. But I see now, if we want to restore the Morrell legacy, we'll have to start from the ground up. You are our closest ally, and you are the first stone. I promise you, I won't forget it again."

"Is Hanzah the second, then?" Jeannie asked.

Dominic stretched his fingers before him. "The V'ahani trusted

Adonis because he had something to give them, which he provided with consistency."

"Exactly," Harrison said. "And yes, Hanzah will always be our ally and friend. But he is finding his own way among his people, too, which is going to take time—the same time it takes us to find ours. And just like he starts with the people he finds most familiar …"

"We will start with ours—in Harran?" Jeannie blurted, Harrison's logic coming together in her head. "But how? Daniel still remains there, and the V'ahani are near ready to surrender?"

"By taking advantage of what it is we heard come out of his mouth today," Dominic lit up.

"What's that?" Jeannie asked.

"Doubt," Harrison enthusiastically answered.

"*True* doubt," Dominic reiterated.

"Doubt…you mean Daniel doubting Clovis?"

"Yes! See, if we can get one of the leaders of the gang to doubt another, to lose faith in another, to *turn* on another—"

"We can break them apart!" Jeannie exclaimed.

"Precisely."

Maybe this was how they would not just recover, but evolve. Jeannie was so proud of Harrison. It seemed he was beginning to adapt to their situation the way their father always told them they'd need to. But a worry crawled through her mind.

"But Harrison, we can't trust Daniel."

This time it was Dominic who answered her. "No, Jeannie, not on his words alone. But if we see it for ourselves, when he doesn't know we're there …"

Staring wide-eyed at Dominic and then at her brother, Jeannie couldn't believe what they were suggesting, but it was the only thing that seemed to make sense.

"Wait. You want to sneak back into Harran?"

*

Two mornings after Latera brought the news of the Tokali's newfound ability to her anonymous captor, she woke feeling energized. In one fell swoop she was able to spite the cowardly clan and bring more promises of well-being to her people. But as she sat up on her cot, she noticed others crowding around to whisper in the tight space.

Braiding her hair and throwing on her sandals with haste, she approached a group of V'ahani whispering nearby. "What is all this fuss about?" she asked. "Is everyone all right?"

"Latera, hello," one of the women in the group bowed.

Though she shook her head, Latera was grateful for the show of respect. "There is no need for such greetings. I am one of you."

"That is not true," a man in the group said. "You are not just another daughter of the Mother. We all know what you have given to save us from this evil, and we will not forget it. You will be the first Chieftess of the V'ahani, Latera."

"Your words are kind and do not fall on unappreciative ears," Latera said as she truly pondered the possibility. How far she'd come in such a short time for her people to think of her this way. Though she wasn't doing these things for any accolade, she reveled in their pride and gratitude nonetheless. "But please, tell me what is going on."

The group she had approached all exchanged glances, seemingly unsure of what to say. "There has been a, uh…well, we do not know what it means," the woman spoke up again.

"Go to the gates of the Hold and you will see," the man said as he shook his head and shrugged his shoulders. "Maybe you will have some idea. Our people have all been speculating, but speculation is all we have. You need to see it for yourself."

Latera nodded and darted off, now worried about the lack of a clear answer. All she knew was if the Keagans were lying to her and they planned to hurt her people, she'd take revenge or die trying. As she hustled through the streets toward the gates, the crowds grew in size. Some were returning in confusion from what they'd seen, some were just making their way toward it, and the rest were either up in the lookouts over the walls or out in the fields before the Hold, frozen in place. Latera decided there were too many out there to make her way through, so a bird's eye view over the walls would be better. Shifting through Keagans, Tokali, and V'ahani she worked her way up the stairs. Once she did, she made it to the walkway atop the walls and looked out onto the people below her. The crowd did not extend out far from the Hold into the field, but scattered before them was a tremendous mass of slaughtered hog carcasses.

What had she done?

The sight was so vile and the stench so bad Latera instantaneously backed away from the wall and hunched over with her hands on her knees to catch a clean breath of air. After she gathered her senses, she forced herself to look out again.

Surely the Tokali would guess this was her fault. How could her captor send such an obvious and immediate message? Didn't he know he'd painted a target on her back? She needed to find out who he was and she needed to do it now.

Having seen enough, she turned to head back down the stairwell and out into the streets. People began to clear again as she jogged away from the gates and back to the inner-Hold. Her only move now would be to make her way back to the Keagan camp before—

Her equilibrium spun as she was grabbed mid-run and yanked into an alley. She was thrown against the wall before she could even catch her breath.

"No, please, stop!" At first she resisted but she stopped struggling when she realized it was Elan and his friends. They backed away from her, looks of disgust and betrayal on their faces.

"We are not going to hurt you, as much as we should," Hammond said.

"I did not mean—"

"How could you do this, Latera?" Elan cried. "And do not dare deny it."

"No—I . . ." she panted in a hysteria.

"You judged me and hated me for making decisions to protect my people at the expense of your own and now, within days of us talking, you sell mine out." Elan's tied-back hair fell out of place in his ferocity. "Do you even *see* how much of a hypocrite you are?"

"Do not call me that." No matter how defensive she wanted to get though, she couldn't deny it. Now hearing it said out loud, she couldn't believe she had helped the Keagans—even to spite the Tokali. "*You* and your feeble clan dragged us into this mess. If you are all so loyal to them, why would you even want to keep your abilities a secret?"

"We would have told them. We just needed to understand it first," Pharaoh said.

"There is no way you can mean that," Shelton turned on Pharaoh to Latera's surprise.

"Of course I do—"

"To this day, Pharaoh?" Hammond asked. Latera heard the debate, but her mind was now racing. "Still? With one of our best friends continuing to rot in a cell?"

"I can fix this," Latera said to herself.

"What did you say?" Warrick, who'd been silent and writing to that point, asked her.

"You heard my father, Hammond. We will talk to them and get Gannon free." Elan tried to make an assurance Latera knew he couldn't make.

"How the hell can you know that?" Shelton said. "If it was your father or mother or anyone you loved in that cell, things would absolutely be different. With the words that came out of Clovis's mouth, with how he'd said Gannon would be 'dealt' with, how could you believe him to be safe?"

Pharaoh turned up his palms. "This is what we signed up for, Shelton! Gannon disobeyed the agreement!"

"I can fix this," Latera's eyes widened as she turned to Warrick, who was the only one apparently listening. The sparks were flying in her head now.

"That's right, this is what you signed up for," Elan said to Shelton. "Hammond was the only one of us who took issue with the unification from the beginning."

"Psh, unification," Hammond scoffed under his breath.

"Gannon knew the law here would be as the Keagans defined it and so did you. And now you are going to question it, because he chose to take mercy on a V'ahani Chieftain? Do you want to do so at the expense of unity?" Elan finished.

"I am going to leave now," Latera informed Warrick as the rest argued. "But Warrick, you must let them bicker. I need you to remember this, as well. Write it down if you must. I will not make you any promises I cannot keep, but if the solution to all this comes suddenly, it will be because of me. Do you understand?"

"Um…no, I do not think—"

"You will know when it comes," she said again, desperately trying to get through to him, but knowing she couldn't tell him anything of substance. She couldn't tell a soul if she wanted her plan to work. But if anyone would trust her out of this group, Warrick seemed to be the only viable option at this point. He was the only one listening. "This is only the beginning, but I will need you on my side if our people are ever truly to unite, okay? It will start with us, or it will not start at all."

"All right, go do what you must," Warrick waved her on. "I will write that down and all they say, too."

"This is not unity," Latera heard Shelton shout as she made off for the mouth of the alleyway.

"Enough of that word," Hammond said. "It is the opposite of what they want us to have because it is the thing we need most."

As Latera exited and ran for the Keagan camp, purposefully tearing her garb in different places along the way, she thought about the last thing Hammond said. Could he have been the only member of either clan to see it? The Tokali and V'ahani did need to unite, but each and every move the Keagans made thus far in the Hold was to get them to do the opposite. Despite the fact that this mystery person saved her and offered protection for her people, he was hurting them even more by having Latera achieve that protection at the expense of the Tokali. The clans were fellow prisoners now, and they would need to work together to escape this madness. But how could she possibly convince them to rebel in an alliance? Or maybe, that wasn't the answer at all—maybe she'd need to shatter the prospect of this false unity first. Would that get them to see, with all their emotions released, who the real enemy was? Her mind continued to bounce in different directions, but she knew where she was going to start once she reached the Keagans.

The process this time was much the same. Latera stood out in a crowd and was soon apprehended with a sack placed over her head. In a dark room with her hands tied to a chair, she sat again, awaiting the unknown man and hoping this time she might have true ground to gain.

CHAPTER 9

CONDUCTION

Hanzah had felt the tension during the meeting with Daniel Keagan. Yet the lack of escalation was encouraging, or at least that's what Varek, his Masters, and Orrin's council all agreed on. It was mostly Orrin alone who was still unsure—though it seemed he was more hung up on the frog-toad comment than anything else. Hanzah himself couldn't help but feel uncertain, though he also shared in the encouragement of his leaders. It pleased him to be on the same page. With a general consensus cemented, Varek decided they would accept the Keagans' terms, along with the assurance Clovis Keagan would be reined in. Given Clovis's violent instability, Varek begrudgingly agreed he could give the monster no reason to harm their people in the Hold. Kidnapping Daniel would cost V'ahani lives, and the V'ahani people always came first for Varek—no matter how badly he wished to put these Easterners in their place. As much as it pained Hanzah to think the Keagans might assume any kind of authority over his people, the relief he might soon be reunited with Latera overcame that qualm.

Hanzah had noticed, too, Dominic seemed to be back in the good graces of the Morrells. His friends had made their peace with one another, just as his people were about to broker their own.

Once his leaders' decision became official, he sought out his friends to share his excitement.

"It is so good to see you all together again," Hanzah said as he approached them. They were sitting huddled together and turned sharply when he spoke.

"Hey Hanzah, how are you?" Jeannie asked.

"Well, I have to say, I am pretty glad to have you all here and to know my sister will be returning soon," Hanzah answered with his head held high.

"Ah, so the Masters have come to a decision?" Harrison asked.

"Yes. I know it is difficult for you, friends, but they have chosen to take the peace deal for the sake of our captured people."

"Jeannie and I are happy for you, buddy. After all you've been through—all you've both been through—it'll be so great if this can bring you and your sister back together."

"If? No. *When*," Hanzah corrected. In his mind, it was a certainty—at least, it was until Harrison's wording caused doubt to sneak in.

"That's what Harrison meant, I'm sure," Dominic chimed. "It's just a matter of when now."

"Of course," Harrison nodded. "My apologies. You *will* see her again, I know it."

"Thank you. And I hope you all know even once the deal is made you have the protection of our people. We would never let the Keagans hurt or mistreat you. The Morrell-V'ahani alliance remains strong."

"It's good to hear you're on our side, Hanzah," Harrison said.

"We'll always value you and your friendship, no matter what

happens." Something was beginning to feel off as Jeannie did not look him in the eye as she spoke.

He paused for a moment and furrowed his brows. "What is it?"

Jeannie's eyes widened and the others hesitated. "Nothing . . ."

"I know you may not agree with this deal, but you will do nothing to jeopardize it, will you?" Hanzah asked, scared of what their disagreement might cause them to do.

"No, no. It's not like that—" Dominic started.

"Well what is it?" He said, whipping his focus to Dominic. "Please, tell me. I know it must be hard with what they have done to you all. But if you tell me, I swear I will communicate your concerns to my people. Perhaps we can find a better way, but do not take this into your own hands."

"No," Harrison shook his head. "Hanzah, this *is* the best way, and we understand that completely. I mean, look, our parents and brother were burned to the ground, and for a while, Jeannie and I thought we were alone in this world. I'm sure I speak for us both when I tell you how hollow the feeling was. But then we discovered it wasn't the case, and we became whole again. We no longer had to travel our paths alone, and we had someone we could grieve with. The difference it makes…well, it makes all the difference. Now this is your chance to be reunited with your sister and have that peace of mind, too. There's no way we could ever take the opportunity away from you, not after all you've given for us. But—"

"We need to leave, Hanzah," Jeannie cried, only now facing him straight on.

"No, you cannot leave me," he said, welling up at the idea. "You are my family."

"We'll always be your family," Dominic promised as Jeannie nodded fervently. "But right now, here in the Mountainlands, you're trying to find your place. There's no better way for you to do that than with your people. But we need answers, too, and we won't find them here. What we're looking for lies in the Riverlands—in Harran. It's our home, Hanzah."

Though he knew they were right, his sadness did not lift so easily.

"When the time is right, we'll see you again, Hanzah," Harrison said. "It'll be our responsibility to reunite the Morrells with the re-established V'ahani of the Riverlands. But if we don't all make our own way, we won't be able to do that. You know we need something to offer your people that we just don't have right now. When the time comes, we hope you'll be ready to stand with us again, much like our fathers did. We hope you'll remember our bond, because I know we will."

Hanzah sighed long and hard, fighting to hold back his tears. He hated that even as he gained his sister back, he would lose his friends. But deep down, he understood, so he gave a soft nod to Harrison, to Jeannie, and to Dominic.

They all approached him in an embrace, as if they'd been holding themselves back, too. He wrapped his arms around them, and felt Jeannie's hot tears on his shoulder, knowing she felt his same sorrow. After a minute of taking in their embrace, Hanzah stepped back.

Wiping away a tear from Jeannie's cheek, and looking at her with what smile he could afford to give, he pledged, "I will stand with you, my friends. And we will restore the mountains they raised."

After waiting some time in her usual chair, Latera heard several footsteps. At this point, she was no longer intimidated by her physically helpless position, but despite this, her body continued to shiver when restrained. It irritated her to no end, which perhaps fueled the degree of confidence she felt in speaking her mind.

"Why have you done this?" Latera's voice was shaky, but only because of her tremors. "Do you realize the position you have put me in? Now they will never trust me! I will get nothing more."

Slow footsteps circled her once again, and the silence in between each one was thick. By now though, Latera only thought it obnoxious. "Enough of this game," she sighed. "Tell me who you are. I need to know it if you want anything more from me."

"Hmm, is that what you think this is?" the voice asked. "Do you think this is a game?"

"Who are you?" Latera asked again.

"Hey, hey, hey, I never said you were wrong. You wouldn't be too far off at all if you do think this way. Clovis does treat it like a game. To him all of life is a game—like chess. To him, you're all pieces on a board. And he doesn't even play by the rules. He moves you wherever he might choose. Because he is the master here, and this is his board."

"Enough of this, tell me why you slaughtered those hogs," Latera ordered, though she assumed it'd be to no avail.

"To him a pawn is no different than a king or a knight or a rook." The man continued to ignore her. "Let me ask you, what do you think of yourself as? If I had to guess I would say a queen. No cliché in it just because you're a woman and all—a queen is the best piece on the board. By far the most versatile."

"You know what?" Latera started, having heard enough. "I am the damn queen. I am the queen because that is what I am in the eyes of my people."

"There, you see? This is how you play the game! But why is it they see you this way?"

"Because I have fought for them," Latera answered. "Because I have evolved for them."

"No, no, my dear. They're only safe because the Keagans allow them to be," the man said, this time in a franker, less cheery tone. "Not only safe, but alive and present on the board. You see, the Keagans have control of it—always have. Tell me, how does it feel to be at the mercy of your captors?"

"The time will come where neither the Mother nor my people will have mercy on you, and I will ask you the same," Latera spat defiantly.

"It seems you haven't been *listening* again. In this place, Clovis is the only god. Your Mother holds no sway. You are at his mercy, his will. And you will be kept in this position as long as we like."

"He is no god," Latera objected, insulted by the very suggestion. "Only the Mother controls this world."

"Latera, Latera, Latera," the man said as he came to her side and grazed his hand from one shoulder, up over her neck, and to the other shoulder. She wanted to bite that hand for the insolence of the gesture. He was goading her. Reminding her of her bonds. "He is, though. He has the power. He has the control. And he sets the terms. It's something you will come to see more and more as the days go by. I mean hell, he even decides who lives and who dies. No one can even kill without his command—not under any circumstances. If they do, they're punished. Power and punishment, they are the two tools of any god, are they not?"

"He is not—"

"Ah, ah, ah. That's the way it is. You have no power; you have no sway, little queen. You're a piece on our board and currently a captive at my mercy. The same way a queen can't jump off the board to take out the player who decides where she goes, you can do nothing you are not told to do. So, for future reference, sweetheart, when you see those hogs out there, bloodied and massacred, fight the urge to question it. Fight the urge, and don't you fucking dare come in here looking to make demands. You're in no position to do anything of the sort."

His hand moved from her shoulder, down her arm, and to her hand. Instinctively she pulled away, causing the ropes to burn her wrists even more.

"Get your hands off me!" she screeched,

"What are you going to do, Latera? What *can* you do? Do you see now just how powerless you are?"

Lifting his hand away from hers, he ripped the sack off her head.

Latera stared into the eyes of Walter Keagan and could form no words.

He stood up straight, straightened his ridiculous clothes, and cleared his throat.

"Do you understand now, little queen?"

His voice had changed in an instant. Gone was the raspy, deep tone. Now his own nasally squeal was as clear and crisp as day.

191

So that was how he'd done it. That was how he'd tricked her.

He cleared his throat again. "I am relieved to drop the act, my dear. It did a number on my throat, you know. In any case, we have no more use for you and therefore no more use for the secrecy," Walter said.

"I do not think so, Walter Keagan," Latera said, recovering from the shock, her anger growing.

"Oh? Are you making the mistake of thinking again? The Tokali's secret has been exposed, and they'll pay for keeping it. What more use could you be? Our deal is done."

"You are right. It has been done," Latera said. "But there is more information I can bring you. The things the Tokali were saying both before and after the hogs in the field…I can tell they are up to something more, and I believe it involves Clovis."

Walter stared down at her hard. "I don't think so. I think you're lying. Desperate for something…but for what?"

He was clever, this one. But she was prepared for this.

"I am not lying, but if you do not want to believe me, do so at your own risk. It means little to me if they succeed where I did not. I will not weep at the death of Clovis Keagan."

Walter considered her another moment with narrowed eyes. She realized he no longer leaned on a cane. He was recovered then. What a shame.

"Okay, I'll bite. What do you know?"

"I want to speak to Clovis," Latera said. "I will speak to him directly or not speak at all. As you like to remind me, *he* is the one with the power to grant me a new deal."

Walter stiffened at her insult. Ah, so he did not like the reminder.

"What do you want?"

"I will tell Clovis," she said. "Though we can begin with my being untied. I have no weapons and am no threat to you. Enough of these senseless restraints. You see what they do to me."

"Well now you know how it feels, *princess*."

So Walter still held his grudge about being her people's prisoner. She said nothing, merely staring at him.

Walter pursed his lips. "Very well," he said, pulling out a blade. He hesitated for a second before cutting her wrists free. She rubbed at the burn caused by the tightly bound rope and waited as the shuddering subsided. She exhaled, stretching her arms and legs to loosen her tense muscles.

"But you will not be speaking with Clovis," Walter announced.

"I—"

"I do wonder, though, what more can you be after besides safety for the V'ahani?" Walter pondered.

She smiled at him. *Let us see what you offer me, Walter Keagan.*

"We can start with the obvious—freedom. Everyone wants that, but we both know you can't have it in its entirety, so that's out of the question. Next would possibly be power…another thing everyone craves and of which you currently have little."

Walter considered her, his head at an angle. Latera maintained her silence.

"Hmm…I suppose we could give you a bit of that among the natives, as long as you submitted to us, of course. If you'd like to play that game, just say the word." He paused, tapping his chin. "The last option though—and what I think would be the most likely—is vengeance. Now that, I can understand. Maybe you still want the Tokali to suffer for what they did to your people? If that's the case, maybe you fit in here more than I initially realized. Is that it, your highness?"

"Do not call me your highness," Latera demanded. She was tired of his little comments demeaning her place amongst her people. "I would not mind freedom, but I know you cannot give it to me. As for the other two…no. Bring Clovis here, and I will make you all another deal. Or do not, but know his death will be on your head. I wonder what your cousin William will think of that."

Latera folded her arms again and lifted her eyebrows at Walter in expectation.

And this time, Walter shrugged.

"Well, well, little queen, you've surprised me. I'll give you that." The smile faded from his face, and his eyes showed his intent as he said, "I hope you know what you're doing, because I doubt you understand who you are dealing with."

A tingle of fear trailed down Latera's spine, but she sat up straighter to hide it.

After a few seconds, Walter turned to the men standing at the door. "Well?" he asked impatiently. "What are y'all dilly-dallying for? Go!"

One of the guards took off, and they waited in silence. Walter paced around the room the entire time, while Latera sat back into her chair, fidgeting uncomfortably as the time passed. After what seemed close to an hour but was likely much less, Clovis slithered in. He brought a lackey in tow with him. Latera recognized the man from somewhere before—the Square? Yes, she recalled now. It was one of the men from Clovis's inner circle, the silent, slimy one. She thought his name might be Devin.

Her attention flicked back to Clovis, the urge to be ill overwhelming her. Clovis looked the same as always and wore an ever-present twisted grin on his face. How she despised this grotesque animal. But she fisted her hands beneath her crossed arms and strived to appear unaffected.

"Well, well, well, if it isn't the queen bitch herself," Clovis said. Latera was getting tired of being called that and wondered if they all referred to people as game pieces in private. "How'd that bacon out there look to you? Personally, I like my meat bloody, but did it look too raw for your tastes?"

"I believe you are in danger." Latera had no desire to be reminded of the grisly hog massacre. "I can find out what kind for you, but as with all helpful things, there is a cost."

"You're damn right I'm in danger," Clovis snorted. "I'm in it, around it, and I'm goddamn one with it."

"Even so, the Tokali have something planned I can help you get ahead of—if I am given the time and resources to work it out of them," Latera said, trying to persevere through Clovis's bolstering.

Clovis coughed and raised a hand in a dismissive "out with it" gesture.

"What I need is two things, but only one is for my own benefit," she began, worried making requests of him directly might be far more difficult than it was with Walter. "First, for my people, I want equal housing. Use whatever standard you please to determine who gets which homes and who must stay in the shelters we are currently crammed into, but if we cannot have freedom, we must at least have equality."

There was a pause as Clovis turned back to Devin and Walter.

"The Tokali won't like that," Walter said.

Latera felt sweat break out on her forehead, which she was quick to wipe away. *This had to work.*

A repetitive nod from Clovis amplified Latera's stress.

"Deal."

"What?" Latera asked him in shock.

Walter seemed unsurprised Clovis had ignored his concern, though he let loose an extensive sigh.

"Tell me what your second demand is, so I can be on my way," Clovis practically groaned. "Don't bother givin' me none of this pleased, grateful shit neither. This ain't no kind of mercy I'm affording you, and y'all are only alive to appease my brothers. So, get on with it, I've got places to be where my talents can be utilized."

Latera blinked once, pushing away the queasy thought of whatever "talents" meant. "Okay, well there is only one other thing I need: the release of the prisoner, Gannon."

"Impossible," Clovis dismissed. "That dumb bastard disobeyed my direct orders for the world to see. This place is run on fear, and I ain't compromising that for a law breaker."

"Well then, I am afraid I cannot help you. After what was done to the hogs right after their confession to me, the Tokali will never trust me again without some kind of gift."

"Forgive me for interrupting, Clovis, but if she were to deliver the boy directly to the Tokali, wouldn't they know she was spying for us?" Devin asked, speaking for the first time since their arrival.

"Devin, you know, you're a weird cat sometimes, but this is why I have you around," Clovis chuckled. "What you got to say, girly?"

"They can know I am talking to you, and it does not have to

be an issue," Latera answered confidently. "I can tell them he was negotiated as part of the surrender of my people in the North."

"But they haven't surrendered yet," Walter started.

Clovis looked at her sideways. "No, this is good." He wagged a finger at her. "I'm not gonna lie, I don't like you at all. You're too impressive, and if I were in charge, I'd end you for it. But, I can respect the way you think in that twisted little head of yours. You're like a poisonous lizard—when you're at your most vulnerable, you're at your most dangerous. I can be like that, too."

Internally revolting at the idea she shared any characteristic with Clovis, Latera nonetheless nodded. "So, will you grant my request?" she asked.

"Yeah, he's already taken a good beating or two, so he'll be released," Clovis conceded. "But if you don't bring my boys here the information within the week, I'm giving them my permission right now to lock both you and him right back up. You understand?"

"Yes, I do."

One week.

"Also, his release ain't gonna be a public thing where you're some kind of hero. You can make sure Malik and Adila know we approved of this out of good will, but you tell them word on it ain't to get out. If it does…same consequences I mentioned and worse."

"Understood," Latera affirmed. "And you can trust me to get this information in time. I will find out before they are able to act, I swear it."

"You should hope you do," Walter said. "Or restraints will be the least of your worries."

"True. Though whatever information you get won't matter." Clovis straightened his clothes out and motioned for Walter to follow him as he headed towards the door.

"What do you mean?" Latera asked, her mind racing to the possibilities.

"The surrender you fabricated about your V'ahani in the North—it ain't as much a fantasy as you might think. I'll be heading up there to the Riverlands myself to handle some things as early as tomorrow." Clovis stopped with a grin and turned towards Devin, who remained in the middle of the room for some reason. "Devin—before I forget, you'll be coming with me."

Devin's face lit up like he'd been given a gift. It was disgusting to witness such adoration.

Without eye contact, Clovis turned back to Latera. "But yeah, I'll be heading north. Once I finish a few initial things, it'll be time to talk to your leaders, who'll have no choice but to surrender. You'll tell of my absence to no one, though. Not your people, not theirs. Walter will lord over this citadel with an iron fist while I'm gone, and you won't even get the chance to beg for a cell if there's any suggestion of my absence spread around here."

Latera blinked hard to cover her shock at the bombshell revelation. "If you will not even be here, why have me carry this out?" she followed.

"Because, I'd love nothing more than to be given a reason to gut them when I return," Clovis laughed as he and Walter walked out the door.

Thank the Mother he's gone. A sense of relief swept over Latera as Clovis left the room.

The idea he would be away from the Hold for any period of time was too wonderful to comprehend. So wonderful she stood up and moved towards the door in a daze.

Devin darted in front of her and put his hand on it, blocking her exit. She recoiled at his nearness but placed a bland mask on her face. What did this one want with her now? More intimidation to please his master?

"We'll deliver Gannon to his brother when the sun goes down and there won't be anyone around to make a commotion," Devin said with a grunt. "Provided they're still at Malik and Adila's home, he'll be returned before the morning."

"Very well," Latera nodded, but Devin only continued to stare at her. Her sense of unease grew. His gaze felt slimy in some way. It gave her the desire to bathe.

"You know, someone once told me the most valuable resource in all the world—even more than material wealth or power—was a young woman's beauty." Devin ran the back of his hand over her cheek. Latera winced at his touch. This wasn't intimidation—this was something else. "And how true it must be, for the daughter of a fallen foe to be alive and standing tall in the lands we claim. Despite your negotiating skills, I see such innocence in you, my queen. Soon you won't have to disguise it any longer."

Latera felt rage overtake her. How dare this creature think she was his anything? How dare he touch her this way? It disturbed her to her core. She needed to get away from him. But she did not step back from the door. She'd not allow him to goad her into losing the ground she'd won.

"Can I go now?" she said sharply.

Devin backed off from the door, and Latera swiftly maneuvered herself out. She sprinted home to change into her hooded V'ahani-white coat. Since wearing the clan colors was illegal in the Hold, she wore it underneath her brown outer coat. This is how she'd send her true message.

Latera remained in her shelter until the sun began to set. When the last rays of light were fighting for their place in the sky, she set off for the Tokali homes.

The crowds had subsided almost entirely when she reached a corner just down the road—and visible—from Elan's door. Pulling up her brown hood, she waited there for some time until the darkness thickened. A torch's crisp flame on the corner flickered and lit her figure on the street. She waited and waited without as much as a movement. She felt no need to fidget here in the comfort of the dark.

From seemingly out of nowhere, two Keagan men marched up to Elan's door, a hunched figure too weak to walk on his own between them. A small sense of victory filled Latera, which was bolstered when the door opened and Shelton charged into his brother's embrace. Almost as soon as Shelton had Gannon, the Keagan men stormed off, but the Tokali filtered out the door and remained outside for a moment.

That was when Latera's eyes locked with Warrick's—though she assumed he couldn't see her own from under the hood. Latera scanned the streets around her—the coast was clear. When she removed her brown hood and swapped it for her white one, Warrick jolted in recognition. In that moment, the Tokali began to file back inside, but Warrick remained. Latera moved closer to the flame on the corner and raised a hand in the air to wave, again causing the outer brown garment sleeve on her arm to fall to her elbow, revealing her whites. Warrick followed suit with a wave, much to her excitement. With a nod he ran back inside.

It had begun.

*

A week had almost passed since William had arrived in New Berkeley, and there was a tempered excitement inside him. While the heartbreak of Leroy's death continued to eat at him, the previous evening his father had finally set a time for them to discuss his business plan for the Murrieta and the East the next day. Their meeting would take place on their last full day in New Berkley before they'd set off on their journey back to the Murrieta. His father had invited him to talk in his office prior to a family trip to the horse track. In the past week, he'd introduced William to new, prominent figures in town and taken him out to the finest of restaurants. After the first night, Judith and Henry had always been invited to join them, and while Judith had enjoyed the entertainment, she was growing antsy to get back to the Murrieta—a place she now even referred to as "home." This pleased William to no end. So, though none of this was the purpose of his trip, William was happy with it nonetheless. But now, his time here would truly pay off.

William paced the room anxiously as Judith dressed in preparation for the event at the track.

"My moment is here, and for the first time in my life, I'm gonna make damn sure he hears me out," William said to his wife as he buttoned up the cuffs of his sleeves.

"As you should, baby," Judith chimed, sitting in her corset and pulling up her stockings. It was a process she was likely used to and didn't think much of, but William felt light on his feet as she eased the stockings around her long, slender legs. He stared at her for a moment, biting his lip with a grin until she caught the look and smiled back.

"What?" she giggled, as she slid on her dress and started on the buttons.

"You just don't even—" he started with a laugh that turned into a more serious sigh. "It's just after what went down with Leroy… I've been thinking a lot, and you know, you're the best thing that's ever happened to me. When I see you, I get this feeling inside me I can't even explain. It's not simply bliss anymore, either, it's like a necessity. Like all the things you've given me have taken the place of my heart, pumping the blood through my veins, and it's made me twice what I was before. I love you, Judith."

Judith walked over to him and wrapped him in her arms. He felt as if there was a great battle raging inside him but in her arms, he was shielded. With his face buried in Judith's shoulder, he began to choke up.

"There are things eating at you, and those are the things you need to say to him," Judith encouraged him. "I know you, and I can see it in you, baby. As much as I appreciate your love—and I do more than you could know—if you don't release what you've been holding onto since you were a boy, you'll be consumed by it all."

"But that's the problem. I could shout it at the top of my lungs, and it won't make a difference, because he doesn't hear me."

"He set the meeting, didn't he? Maybe he's changed in his age."

"Not about this. The meeting is all business."

"Well if that's the case, this deal just ain't meant to be."

"No, it has to be. I didn't spend all these years getting to this point for nothing. The hell I've had to go through, the things I've had to see, the things I've had to *do*."

"You can't have a deal with your father with this pain—pain he caused—festering inside of you, William. Deal or no deal, you need to tell him how you feel," Judith ordered. "If you don't, I will. And if he's still heartless enough not to see you for what you've become, so be it. Then *he* can rot inside for the rest of his days until he dies sad and alone, but you, you will continue on your path toward the man you want to become. I believe in that man. It's why I married you. And you've come such a long way. Together, we'll do better for the people whose livelihood rests in our hands than your father ever could. We'll do that with or without him. But as for this deal, if there is any hope of it going through, it has to start with honesty."

"The deal *will* be made," William said again, to which Judith rolled her eyes. "I've come too far for it not to come together the way I planned, Judith. But I'll clear out what's been bothering me too, okay? I will."

Judith nodded, and William kissed her, holding her silky cheeks in his hands and pulling her face gently into his. What started as innocent lip-locking was quick to evolve as their mouths opened, accepting each other in. Once their tongues began to embrace, the fire was sparked, and Judith eased William gently back onto the bed. She climbed steadily and intimately on top of him, her stocking-covered legs emerging from her silky, only partially buttoned dress. William couldn't help but move his hands up her legs, feeling the smoothness all the way up her thighs and beyond. *This is exactly what I needed.*

Judith was always what he needed, and he was so ready to have her. As they were beginning to get aggressive, a knock at the door interrupted them.

William turned and let out a growl. "Who the hell is it?" He became enraged when he saw it started to crack open. "Good lord don't come in here now!"

The door slammed shut and from outside Cassius informed, "It's me, William. Henry and I are ready."

William looked painfully at Judith. "Our business here isn't finished, but thank you, my love."

"Our business will never be finished," she said sensually and eased her way down his body. Her hands dragged down every inch of his chest until her face was right below his belt. He fidgeted pleasurably as she held a kiss there before they raised up to finish preparing themselves.

"I'll escort Judith down in a moment, Cassius," William called through the door. He heard Cassius's footsteps fade down the hall after he did.

William collected himself, waiting a few painful moments, before he went to the corner to relieve himself. He didn't want anything interrupting the meeting with his father. Once he finished, he slicked back his long, greasy hair, straightened himself out and took a deep breath. But when he felt down his sides, he realized he'd forgotten his gun and holster in his distraction. After what happened at the casino, he'd be sure not to take any risks when it came to Leonard's apparent enemies, especially not in public places like the horse track. William spotted his holster on top of the dresser, but his stomach turned when he saw it was empty.

"You haven't moved my gun since last night, have you?" William asked.

"No, I haven't." Judith finished sliding her earrings in before turning to him. "You don't think…?"

"That's exactly what I think. This had to be Forrest's idea, that sick, conniving sociopath! As if I can't be trusted? Leonard's own blood! And who is he? Nobody! A leach. Not in the least bit worth any intimidation. With or without my gun, nothing's stopping this deal from happening."

"That's right, baby. Don't let it change anything, okay? Just do what you came here to do. And remember, I love you."

"I love you too, Judith, and I will. Soon we'll be going back with a big chunk of their stack," William said with a grin. They locked arms and left the room together.

"William. Judith. You both look ready to watch some ponies," Leonard called once he spotted them coming off the stairs. He stood together with Forrest, Myrna, Cassius, and Henry.

"We are, indeed," Judith said.

Leonard rubbed his hands together. "So, we all ready to go?"

William couldn't believe his ears. He'd not have this meeting put off again. "Sure, we're ready as soon as you and I have the talk we planned."

"Of course, we'll have our meeting first." William could tell he was less than thrilled.

Forrest simply stared at William with unshaking eye contact. "I'm gonna be off to the track," he said, as if to protest. *Predictable from the asshole.* "Cassius, come along and take me there. We need to see to it our bookies remember they're our bookies when the first gun pops."

"Mr. Abigale, are you sure you won't be needing me to take you over today?" Cassius asked Henry as Forrest turned to leave.

"It's all right, Cassius. We still have several hours until the races begin, so I had planned to take Judith along the scenic route through the countryside on the way there. We're gonna stop by where we used to live and hopefully run into some old friends."

"Very well." Cassius followed Forrest out of the office.

"I have business at the casino," Myrna said to Leonard. "I'll meet you at the track, as well."

Leonard nodded, and Myrna left. Once she was gone, his father gestured him toward his office. "Shall we?"

William stepped forward into the office.

"I need to go back upstairs and use the ladies room if our trip might be long, Daddy," William heard Judith behind him.

"Good idea, I think I might—" The slamming of the office door cut off the rest of Henry's sentence.

At long last, he was alone with his father.

He looked around, contemplating where to begin. His father's office was dimly lit, even this late in the morning, with the curtains only slightly drawn. It looked much the same as it had the first day of his arrival into town—papers and notebooks scattered all around on the desk and shelves. This reminded him of Daniel's desire to always keep notes on his thoughts and activities. Maybe he got it from their father.

When Leonard pulled him back a seat, William spotted a revolver sitting atop his desk. It looked very similar to his, but without a closer look he couldn't tell. He wasn't going to start their conversation with an accusation. But when he settled into his seat, the barrel just so happened to be pointed right at him. *Another intimidation tactic.*

For some reason, though, the barrel altogether hypnotized him, and for a moment he forgot where he was.

"I know that stare," Leonard said with a grin, as William snapped his attention away from the weapon. "That's my stare. It's a void, is it not? We try to focus so hard, and every day the epiphany becomes a little bit clearer."

"What epiphany?" William asked.

"The epiphany that whatever we're searching so fiercely for in that void is something we'll never find." Leonard looked straight at William with excitement as if this was a subject they both thought extensively about.

Admittedly for William, it was. Though he struggled to put any reply into words as he pondered it.

"As I was saying though, I know this meeting took long to come together. Forrest likes to take extra precaution and wanted to get to know y'all first. After this week though, he determined y'all aren't likely to do anything against our interests."

William was bothered by the last suggestion but pushed it aside. "I'm glad to hear it. This week has been eye-opening, I can tell you that. I've been waiting a long time for this opportunity, and I'm grateful to be in this room with you."

"Good to know. Gratitude is a good thing to have earned from those who fall in line. So, shall we get down to it? What exactly are we doing here, William?"

William struggled with Leonard's words. What had he meant by "those who fall in line"? Was he talking about heirs? "Well, I'd like to get to that. But there's something I need to say. I need to get this bit out before we talk business."

Leonard snorted as he sat back and crossed his arms. "Then spit it out."

"First, I need to know what happened in the casino. You ain't told me a single thing about it, and if you're in danger here, I need to know."

"My being in danger is none of your concern."

"Why in the hell not?" William asked.

"Because yours ain't been none of mine since before it counted!"

Well, that answered more than one question for William. The truth stung, but it was the closure Judith had been talking about. It was better to know his father would never care for him than to hold out false hope for them ever being anything besides business partners. Part of him wanted to scream in his father's face, but the strategist in him didn't allow for it.

"I see. Well, that's a shame to hear, especially after I came back here to present the opportunity for you to have what you've always wanted," William said, carefully holding onto his emotions.

"As if you could ever give me anything I couldn't give myself, boy."

Boy? That's it.

William felt his control snap in two, and he couldn't even bother to be regretful about it.

"I'll have you understand, Leonard, I made myself into something I thought—hell I knew—you'd have to be proud of. It's clear to me now that's gone to shit, but either way I ain't no boy anymore. I'm a man with power in my own right. And so, I'll speak my damn mind on this: For you to still not give two shits about the wellbeing of your own damn son—and after all I've done to prove myself worthy—it's downright evil is what it is!"

"You couldn't begin to understand, William."

"Then make me!"

"You need to make a decision right now if that's what you want, *boy*." Leonard stood up from his seat. "You gotta look me square in my fucking eyes and tell me you're ready for this step. And let me tell you something, you ain't. You never could be."

"I wouldn't have come all this way if I wasn't ready for you." William stood up as well as he spoke, at this point in a blistering rage.

"All right then, let's start with the latest!" Leonard ripped a book off the table and threw it into a wall. "I knew that boy Leroy was your right-hand man's son all along!"

William stood and stared at him, speechless for a moment.

What did Leroy have to do with—wait how did he know about Gregory?

"Yeah, that's right! I know more than you can even begin to comprehend, William, and you know why that is? Because I'm obsessed with it all—every last part of this disgusting, extravagant lifestyle. It took time and growth to get there and boo-hoo that I didn't see it till after y'all were born. I cared more about y'all at first than you could know and honestly thought that clean life was what I wanted when I was a younger man, but it just ain't. It isn't enough. So, I began to acquire a desperate thirst for it all: the violence, the thievery, the whores, the power, the power, the power, the power, the cruel, intoxicating, beautiful, fucking power! And I couldn't have it both ways, so I made a choice, long ago, the same choice you just said you're ready for but you ain't. You ain't ready to make the sacrifices you'd need to in order to get to where I am. Especially if you can't understand how the distance between us actually benefitted y'all. Y'all should be thanking me!"

With every word, Leonard had grown increasingly frenzied. He was throwing objects around the room and thrashing his arms around. William had tried to fight him back defensively, not aiming to hurt him, but Leonard kept coming. "Listen, I—"

"You nothing! You and your brothers are nothing because you don't get it. As insane as Clovis is, he seems to be the only one of you three who understands what he is. But you and Daniel? Nah, the two of you are lost!"

"Don't you dare speak of us as if you know anything at all," William snarled, his chest puffing up at the insults hurled at his brothers.

With those words, his father stopped thrashing around the room.

"I know all about you and your little operation in your jungle over there," Leonard scoffed. "If you'd have let me finish, I'd have told you I didn't only know of Leroy or Gregory, but I also had my men question his slut of a mother to see what she could tell me about your partner. I needed all the information I could get on you prior to your arrival. As it turns out though, she had nothing of use even after the beating began. All she could tell us was the juicy little nugget that Gregory Calloway was a working stiff loser. And as for her, she was so bored of him she faked her own son's death to get rid of him and carry on whoring around. While I didn't know I was gonna have issues with some rivals that night, my thought is a boy so unfortunate is better off dead than in this world anyway."

"You beat an innocent woman for information on me?" William sighed, feeling equal parts anger and guilt. He'd done a lot of things, but beating women wasn't one of them.

"Yes. Yes, I did," Leonard grinned. "So, if you're wondering whether or not the death of your best friend's son is on your head, well…I mean, I'm not saying it's not."

William felt awful about Leroy, but he wasn't responsible for his death. Just where was his father going with this? "Now wait just a minute—"

"He was in the casino because of what I did to prepare for—who?" Leonard asked.

"That's not releva—"

"Look, you wanna pretend it's not on you, fine. You've only proven to me you can't cut it. Like I said, you ain't ready for the next step."

Leonard stared him down a moment. William stared right back.

Did his father honestly think his refusal to carry another death on his head which wasn't even his responsibility meant he failed some kind of test? What was the man getting at?

"Just what—"

"Let's cut to the chase. I'm just gonna tell you how this'll go," Leonard said.

"Goddamn it! No!"

"Your operation in the Murrieta…I understand it, and it is as brilliant as you think it is. And I know your aim in coming here was to be partners. You thought maybe having Henry over there with you would sway me somehow. But it won't, and so that isn't what's going to happen. There'll be no deal made. So, this little Keagan 'gang' of yours will be no more. You and your brothers will be my employees. I'll define y'all's cuts, which'll still be healthy, don't you worry. But y'all will not be my partners, because people work for me, not with me. The only exception to that rule is Forrest, who'll be overseeing the operation and will be taking up residence in your mansion there to ensure things all go according to plan."

His father couldn't be serious. He couldn't possibly take away all William and Daniel had built.

"What's going to happen now," Leonard said in a relaxed tone, as William's mind raced. "Is we're gonna go enjoy these races today. Then tomorrow, Forrest is gonna head back with y'all across the Chorisma, and you're gonna give him whatever he comes to need. Do you understand me?"

No.

"I said, do you understand what I'm saying?" Leonard asked again.

NO.

"All my life you've talked about this choice I'd have to make," William started. "Even brought it up again right here, as if this were my one and only time to make it. I think if you've taught me one thing though, it's the exact opposite of what you've said. The life you live, it ain't decided based on a single choice, but on a collection of them. And you know what? It took coming here to realize I don't need your approval, after all. I don't even know who you are, but I know I ain't got no love for you."

Leonard's expression twisted sour, but William was already reaching for the gun, lifting it directly into his father's face and pulling the trigger.

But the gun was empty.

Leonard smiled again and let out a whistle. William heard heels clacking toward the door before it swung open—Myrna. Two pistols in each hand, she smiled at him, as she took aim. William heard a single *pop* as blood splattered out of the side of her head. Judith appeared in the doorway with William's pistol in her hand. Leonard didn't hesitate. He unsheathed the knife from his boot and lunged at William. William fought back Leonard's attempts to dig the blade into him, blocking it at times with the barrel of the gun he still held, dodging his stabs entirely at others, until he was able to lock his arms to keep his father far enough off.

"William, should I shoot?" Judith asked, visibly shaking with the gun pointed.

Leonard looked up at him with bloodshot eyes and was foaming at the mouth. "Yes! Do it, you fucking coward! Tell her to shoot! This is it, William! This is your moment! You want your piece of the pie? You're gonna have to take it! Make your choice!"

Rage poured out of William. The rage of a neglected son, who, after so many years of trying, still came up short. The rage of a brother, who witnessed Daniel's lack of nurturing, who witnessed what Clovis had become because of a lack of much needed attention and care. The rage of a best friend, who'd have to tell Gregory his son was dead *again*. And the rage of a man, who could have lost his entire world to an old man's greed.

"Maybe it is my moment, maybe it isn't," William grunted as he turned the tables on Leonard, who howled as William twisted his knife-wielding wrist. "But yours has come and gone." William released his ferocity, and it found its expression in the hand that smashed his father's face in with the handle of his own gun again and again until not even the rattle of the old man's breath could be heard.

When it was over—when it was all finally over—his hands were covered in blood. He looked down at them and wondered how long they had been this way, and if they'd ever be clean again. Looking up at Judith and Henry, who had joined her at the doorway, he whispered, "We need to leave right now."

CHAPTER 10

JNHALE, EXHALE

Even after rushing to the harbor, making their way on the first ship departing for the Murrieta, and landing back across the Chorisma in Doreshire, William remained on the knife's edge. Judith, Henry, and he were forced to leave Cassius behind when they fled, and they'd likely have to steal horses to make it back through the Passage. While they successfully snuck out of New Berkeley, the need to look over his shoulder remained. He also struggled to accept his grand vision for a deal between the East and West was all but ruined. As much as his father had been cruel to his last breath, William felt like a piece of him had died there with Leonard—then again, a new piece had likely formed, too.

It was late in the night when William, Henry, and Judith reached Doreshire. William tried to ensure they remained hidden as they snuck through the streets.

"I'm exhausted and feeling sick," Judith said with a groan. "Can't we stop this running now and get some rest at the inn?"

William couldn't deny he, too, was running low on energy, as he had hardly even blinked his eyes shut since the escape. He directed them into a shadowed edge of a building and paused to contemplate his options. "Doreshire isn't as safe as it may seem for us. Even if my father's operation hadn't expanded deep into the Murrieta, this town is corrupted with his men. Word travels fast. We won't be safe here for long."

"Unfortunately, my love, he's right," Henry said to Judith. "Leonard has spies and couriers in this town, so we must not be long. Perhaps though, we could just get a short rest at the inn, William? If Judith is feeling sick, we'd be taking a chance by not addressing it."

"Are you sure it ain't just you're a little nervous, baby?"

"William Keagan!" Judith blurted in a hushed roar.

William realized his mistake as he saw her brows furrow at the insult. "All right, all right, I'm sorry. We'll go to the inn, but we can't stay there all night. If they were true to their word, Bronson, Nova, and Kai should be nearby sometime tomorrow to see us back through the Passage. Hopefully they'll be around earlier rather than later. We'll have to steal some horses, which should be easier to do before dawn, so we'll get a couple hours rest and be off, okay?"

The others nodded, and they all crept through town in the shadows toward the inn. When they reached it, William was sure to be very short, polite, and calm with the innkeeper, avoiding drawing any undue attention to his party. As drained as he was from a long day on the run, William didn't sleep that night. He cared for Judith, rubbing her back and running his hands through her hair while she slept, but he remained sitting up in bed and looking out the window of their room. As soon as he could see the darkness beginning to lift in even the slightest way, he woke Judith and Henry.

While they readied themselves, he walked out of the inn and toward the road leading out of town. When he reached the outskirts, he squinted into the distance, but he saw nothing except birds circling overhead. William prayed again Bronson's word would be kept. Without Bronson and Nova as a guide, he knew the way back would be even more difficult.

In the distance, three riders came into sight. It was still very dark, but he could just make out dust clouds kicking up behind their horses as they moved with the utmost haste. His heartbeat picked up. He was exposed in the middle of the road. If they weren't friendly, he'd need to run—now. But when he saw how small the third rider was, child-like small, he realized it must be Kai. He relaxed until he processed the fact that they'd neglected to slow down, still riding like hellhounds were behind them. It could mean nothing good. As they approached, Bronson, Nova, and Kai, Bronson reached out a hand to William, and he grabbed it, scaling up the side of the horse at Bronson's back. The horses were headed straight for the inn.

"We saw you come into town," Nova said over the gust in their wake.

"How did you see—"

"There is no time to waste!"

"What do you—?" William started until two loud *bangs* rang out—this time from inside the town—followed by ricochets. He panicked and realized there was no time for questions. The gunshots could only mean one thing—Leonard's men had found them. "My wife and father-in-law are at the inn!"

"We know," Bronson exclaimed. "Take out your gun, we gotta

hold these guys off while Nova and Kai fetch them."

William presumed in the night word had passed into Doreshire of Leonard's murder, and the men he no doubt had here had organized to hunt them down. How many would be after them? As he loaded his gun, he noticed Nova and Kai rode with their hand on their horse's skull and their eyes closed. Their horses rode much faster than Bronson's, and soon enough, they were charging at the inn before hastily darting to the back of it. Another round of gunshots rang out, allowing William to spot the attackers taking cover behind a building across from the inn. He unloaded his pistol in a fury. When fire was returned, he assumed he'd missed and Bronson ran their horse behind the cover of a saloon next to the inn.

They could hear their attackers shouting orders at one another as the guns were reloaded.

"Aim your weapons at the inn!"

Bullets rained down upon the inn. William tried to keep track of how many distinct guns it sounded like were being fired, but he was too panicked about Judith and Henry being inside.

"Judith get out of there!" he screamed. "Goddamn it, get out of there!"

"Hold your fire!" a voice called. William peaked out from their cover, leaning over Bronson's shoulder, to see a bloody man stumbling out the front door of the inn. With the sky a bit lighter than before, he squinted and saw it was the innkeeper, who fell to his knees before landing face first into the dirt road. Panting heavily and fearing for his loved ones inside, William's gaze was fixed on the pool of blood emerging from underneath the fallen innkeeper. The back door of the inn opening in his peripheral was all that could pull him away.

They were alive!

Nova and Kai helped Judith and Henry up onto their horses, and they darted from the back of the inn and took off on the road out of town. As soon as they emerged, the shooting continued, but Nova and Kai's horses moved like lightening, straight out of danger.

Bronson spurred his horse on. Once they were a safe distance away, William looked back. Birds were now launching themselves down into the attackers. Like a swarm, they attacked and contained the men, so none followed. In no time at all, the town drifted out of sight and below the horizon.

For a while, the horses remained on the main trail through the Passage. But as the sun was just starting to paint the morning sky in long strokes of blues and reds, Nova veered off it and led them up the hills atop the canyon walls. William worried about all the beasts he'd heard inhabited these parts, and when he began to spot them, his initial fears did not lessen.

On the days-long trip back, they spotted groups of hogs in the tree lines, grazing elk with tremendous antlers, birds of all colors and sizes, mountain lions, the occasional wolf, and even a spotted leopard—William's favorite. Their power was a wonder for a city-born fellow like William. Yet, while the magnificence of the wildlife was beautiful, its deadliness was never in question. After what William had just seen with the birds back in Doreshire, birds were as much of a threat as the mountain lions. But luckily, none of the animals they saw now gave them any trouble.

About a day's ride later, Judith was feeling particularly sick, so they stopped to make camp for a bit and rest. Once again, William sat with her to try and tend to her. She lay in his lap, waiting for water, which Nova had ordered Kai to go fetch. William worried about her seemingly worsening condition, but he didn't want it to show for her sake, so he aimed to distract her.

"I've just been thinking about that spotted leopard, again, love."

"Oh?" Judith said, a little too weak for William's liking.

"Yeah, when Nova slowed the horses down to get closer to it, the way it roared back…it was so intimidating it made me feel humbled, you know? It made me realize how fortunate we are to be in this kingdom. I mean, our presence in it is a gift, baby. We gotta be sure to try our best to improve it, if we can, and this trip put how to do so into perspective, I think."

"Can I still fix up Doreshire?" William dried the sweat off her pale face with his shirt.

"Of course, you can, my love. You're gonna make that little town as grand as you'd hoped and make a lot of folks real happy."

Judith smiled and closed her eyes, making herself comfortable against him.

He knew how excited she was at the prospect, but, in truth, it'd take some time to secure the Passage and also to clear Doreshire of the grip of his father's gang. They'd be safe in Fayette though, where they controlled the town and could reinforce their defenses. Leonard's influence had never extended in a significant way to the Murrieta, which is how he and his brothers had built their gang. But in time, he'd make sure Judith got her wish—he'd promised after all.

"I need to rethink some things though, too," William said.

"What's that?" she asked.

"Well I don't know how I'm gonna talk to Daniel about this, but I don't know if we're handling Clovis the right way. I mean, I love my brothers more than anything in this world—next to you, of course. And Clovis is my blood, so I have and will continue to try anything I have to. But on the docks, the father we saw there—he was a broken man if I'd ever seen one. And he didn't even blame Clovis for it. He blamed me, Judith."

"That's nonsense."

"Is it, though?" William wondered. "I just don't know anymore, but I gotta talk to Daniel about it. The plan to rule over this place with an iron fist—these people deserve better. I mean look how they're helping us now, you know?"

Judith said nothing in response.

"Baby, you all right?" William asked, but still she said nothing. Kai ran back to the camp with a canteen in his hand. "Come quick, Kai!"

Kai nodded and darted over. William sat Judith up and poured water carefully into Judith's mouth. "Judith?" he asked. "Judith?!"

Henry, Bronson, and Nova, who'd been a little ways away, ran over on hearing William's panic.

"Is she okay?" Henry asked with a crack in his voice.

Judith choked on the water, coming to, and Nova came around behind her and patted her back. "Here, let me," she said, extending a hand to William for the canteen. Nova proceeded to hold Judith up and give her the water. "What are you feeling, Judith?"

"A little light-headed," Judith mumbled. "Kind of nauseous."

"When was the last time she had something to drink?" Nova asked the others. "Could she be dehydrated?"

William shook his head. "Not long enough for it to be a serious concern. So, I don't believe that's it."

"What else are you feeling?" Nova asked Judith again. "Tell me everything, please."

"Pressure, like I have to pee, but I went not too long ago." Nova looked to William once Judith finished.

"She uh...she did as soon as we stopped," William said.

Nova felt at different parts of Judith's body until she abruptly froze in her tracks. "Judith, when was the last time you bled?"

William's heart skipped a beat as he waited in anticipation for an answer. Judith's eyes widened as she realized what Nova's question meant.

"You are pregnant," Nova said as she smiled.

Tears began to fill William's eyes. If Nova's guess was true, which he begged any gods that might exist it was, he was going to be a father. Henry and he exchanged a laugh and a hug William needed as much for the excitement as he did to keep himself from falling over. He felt joy; he felt terror; he felt anticipation; and he felt alive. This would be his chance to do right by a child he created with all the love he had inside him. He released Henry and kissed Judith's lips, which were salty from sweat, but he didn't care.

"We should ease up on our ride back now that we know this," Nova acknowledged to Bronson and Kai.

William didn't want to jeopardize his unborn child, but he also knew what they were running from. "How far in are we?"

Bronson seemed the first to understand. "We're deep into the uncharted trail and over half way to Fayette. We're as safe as we can be, William."

William nodded. "Let's slow down."

The rest of the journey took longer due to their shortened pace, but William felt like he was on a cloud. Time was hardly even a thing to him anymore as his mind raced about the possibilities of fatherhood. After some more days of travel and rest and tending to Judith, the scenery was beginning to become more familiar. Soon enough, Fayette came into view, and William's underlying tension eased. This was his power seat. Here, they were safe. At the edge of the town's borders, Nova, Kai, and Bronson stopped their horses to let the others off.

"This is the end of the road for us," Bronson said as William stepped down and helped Judith off.

"I could never repay y'all for all you've done. But I tell you what, I'm gonna do all I can to rid y'all of them Highlanders soon enough. When that day comes, I hope I can see y'all again."

"Whether it is the Highlanders or someone else who tries to harm our lands," Nova began, intently looking down at William, "in the end I know the majesty of this place shall live on. It was designed as such. Do not ever forget that, William Keagan. You have chosen to be a part of it, so you will either contribute to its greatness or you will fail. This land does not suffer leaches. So, I hope you choose the former option going forward."

"I will." A hint of the guilt he hadn't done so thus far took William for a moment. But he put it in the back of his mind. "I promise you, I will."

With the journey to New Berkeley and back now behind them, they walked toward home.

Daniel thought the negotiation had gone very well, but he was glad for the window of time he'd been given. The V'ahani wanted him back in four days, and he would be. In the meantime, though, he needed to rectify his broken promise to hear out the people of Harran. Deciding a quick check-in on the town was the best course of action, he ordered his men to hold their post while two escorted him back.

On the return trip to Harran, he was asked several questions by his escorts about where the negotiations with the V'ahani were headed. He told the men he felt surrender was imminent, but to hold off on sending any word until it was finalized. Their original scheme to take the hostages seemed to have worked. He doubted the clan would be foolish enough to risk their peoples' lives.

This, too, would make William's eventual presence all the more beneficial when the time came. Daniel felt confident they were headed toward a peaceful resolution and the beginnings of a trade partnership, like William and he had always planned. What he still had questions about is what would come *after*—and what it would mean in regard to Clovis. But he didn't tell his escorts any of that. Instead, he told them he'd need one of them to continue on from Harran to Fayette, to inform Gregory Clovis's services wouldn't be necessary in the North after all. After doubting his own abilities, Daniel now felt he had things under control and he'd developed too much of a liking for this town to conscionably unleash Clovis on it—or maybe on any other town ever again for that matter. He said he'd also need word sent to Gregory that when William returned, Daniel needed a one-on-one meeting with his brother up here as soon as possible. Daniel knew they needed to investigate these rumblings together.

After the speedy, day-or-so journey down the River White, Daniel reached Harran. He was greeted by the angry glares of the townsfolk and was soon swarmed by the Keagan men he'd left in the town. They were all shouting about making requests and saying they had news. To this nervous lot, their news probably seemed earth-shattering, but the scene was more amusing to Daniel than stressful.

"One at a time, one at a time," Daniel ordered, raising his hands into the air for quiet. "I only have so long here, so I'll handle each of y'all's requests one-by-one—and I won't hear another until the last is finished. You there, you first, please."

"Sir," the man Daniel pointed to, and the same he'd appointed sheriff not long before, followed. "A man by the name of Cassius is here to see you. Told him you'd be back shortly, and he's been waiting outside the jail door pretty much since."

"That's good news, Sheriff. Means Billy must be back. You," Daniel said, turning to the first escort, "stay with us for now. If Cassius is just stopping in, y'all should be able to ride down to Fayette together to deliver my message. Man's as capable a guide as I ever seen. For now, though, lead the way, Sheriff."

The whole crowd of Daniel's men followed him along to the jail. He could feel the anxiousness in their every step and vowed he'd get to the rest of their requests shortly. When they reached it, there Cassius sat—as the Sheriff suggested. There were rings around his eyes and his foot tapped rapidly, but he otherwise sat up perfectly straight.

"Cassius!" Daniel greeted, going over to shake his hand. "How was y'all's journey to the East?"

Cassius stood in response and took a moment before shaking Daniel's hand. He said nothing at first, but his eyes were on the men. Daniel caught on.

"If y'all could give us some room, please," Daniel called to them. They followed suit and once they'd backed off enough, Cassius's eyes turned back to Daniel.

"Daniel, things got kind of complicated back East. I only just caught up with William and headed directly here for two things. First, you should head toward Fayette once you've wrapped up these negotiations with the V'ahani I've been hearing about, and second—" Cassius said.

"Wait. Complicated? And you were separated?" Despair overcame Daniel for his brother. He knew if a deal didn't go through as William had hoped, it'd break him down. "Did something go wrong?"

"I think that'd be best left for him to tell you," Cassius said. "It's some family business I should probably stay out of, but yes, we were separated on the journey back until I caught up with him in Fayette."

"Why?"

"It really is family business, Daniel."

"I suppose that's fair." As they spoke, Daniel continued to worry what could have happened. "But, I was hoping William could come up north. I've got quite a few things to chat with him about this place, and they'd be better done here."

"I see. Well, I can pass that message along to him, but I do think it's better you head down south, Daniel, if I'm honest."

The deal must have gone awful for Cassius to be pushing this hard for him to head toward William. But he'd wait for direct word from William; surely, he'd send a letter explaining things shortly. "I'll think it over. But what's the second thing, Cassius?"

"This is minor business I opted to handle on the side of coming here to deliver that message. But I'm here to bring your prisoner back down to Fayette for his judgment, as you requested a while back."

This was not what Daniel expected to hear. "You mean the dimwit 'mayor'?" he asked, pointing at the jail with a raised brow. "Y'all went all that way to New Berkeley and back, and you want to take this man to Fayette now?"

"Well, might as well while I'm here, I figure." The hoarseness in Cassius' voice caught Daniel's attention.

"All right. But hey, I got another prisoner now—tried to kill me in the night as a matter of fact. How's about I send you down with my escort here and the two of y'all take these—"

"You know, I'm thinking it might be best if I just take this one to him for now," Cassius interrupted. "I can handle it alone."

"All the same . . ." Daniel said, slightly bothered by the rudeness. "I need this man to deliver a message for Billy now that he's back. So, whether you take one prisoner now or both is of no concern to me, but I need him to tag along with you. There'll be a murderer up on your horse with you, too, so better to have someone watching your back wouldn't you say?"

"Very well," Cassius said with a deep breath and a sigh.

Without another word from Cassius, Daniel had the sheriff

remove a cuffed Charles Langston from his cell and out of the jail.

"Time to hang the Mayor, is it?" Charles cried as he was dragged out and toward the horse. Daniel locked eyes with him. "You'll never be the Mayor of my town, you hear me? I know that's been your intention all along—to strip a good man of his title and dignity."

"I can't say I much consider myself a good man, but I'm sure-as-shit-certain you ain't one either," Daniel snorted back as Charles was lifted atop the horse behind Cassius. His hands, cuffed behind his back, held onto nothing but the saddle. Daniel's messenger, too, was fetched a horse. "Say hi to the gallows for me."

"You just keep on pretending your position is real now, Daniel Keagan," Charles called, the irony not lost on Daniel who chuckled. "Somewhere inside all frauds is the desire to be exposed." Charles was sterner this time, to which Daniel stopped laughing.

"Yeah, I've come to find that," Daniel said as Cassius and Daniel's messenger kicked their horses into a trot. "Who's next?" Daniel rolled his eyes and slicked back his hair as he turned to the others.

The other three men who remained spoke up at the same time, with Daniel only able to make out pieces of what was being said. From what he could gather, it was all about the townsfolk.

"Good lord, you first," Daniel said, pointing to one of them.

"I think I can speak for the three of us when I say we've heard rumblings, sir," the man relayed. "The people of Harran, they ain't happy you didn't hear out their concerns. There's plans to rebel. And we know it to be true on account of we've seen it again."

"Seen what again?" Daniel asked with a bitter taste in his mouth.

"The sign, sir," another man said.

"Hey, I was gonna—" the first started.

"The 'Welcome to Harran' sign," the third added.

"It's just been out and about," the second said. "What I mean is, we ain't seen it in one place, but each of us seen it pop up real mysterious-like in different locations around town. Each time we tried to tear it down, too, but for each we do another pops up."

Daniel looked to the Sheriff and his escort. "Both of you, with me," he ordered. "Thanks for the information, gentlemen. Keep alert for anything else suspicious, you hear?"

"Yes, sir," they said in unison before walking off, the first man grumbling about how they interrupted his part of the story.

Daniel stormed into the rundown jail to see Johanna casually leaning against the wall of her cell, like she didn't have a care in the world.

"Oh hey, hun, fancy seeing you—"

"Stop with the act, Johanna! Who else is part of your little revolt? Just come on and say it—now! I know the love you got for the people of this here town, and I respect that. I mean hell, if you didn't try something as hateful as to smother me and stab my pretty-ass, smiling face I'd let you right on out of this cell without another question. But even so, I've gone and called off my brother, who would've done even more damage to each one of y'all than you tried doing me in my own bed. So, go ahead, out with it. I ain't afraid to call him back, but I want peace."

A dark grin crept over Johanna's face. "I don't know what you're talking about, hun."

"Quit calling me that, you demonic slut."

"Oh, and here he comes, ladies and gentlemen. The real man behind the charm and the fancy clothes and the greasy hair."

Daniel felt his face grow red and instinctively slicked his hair back. "Look, I didn't mean…no one needs to get hurt, is all. I don't want none of that, so please tell me. I swear there won't be any consequences against them. Please."

"No one needs to get hurt?"

Daniel grabbed desperately for the bars of the cell. "No, not at all."

"You, I believe, wouldn't hurt us personally. I at least feel fairly confident you wouldn't."

"Of course not. I want peace here in Harran, I do."

Johanna edged closer to Daniel, placing her hands gently onto his where they rested on the bars. Her grin vanished, and he was drawn into her gaze, which appeared to be filled with a sadness that was both sincere and vulnerable. Leaning closer to him she moved her mouth between the bars toward his ear. "Then don't allow us to be hurt, Daniel."

Daniel couldn't move. He was in a trance in her eyes, frozen in place. Who was this person? This wasn't the woman he shared his bed with. The soft look in her eyes now—the touch of her hand to his—this was the real Johanna Fontaine. And perhaps this was—

SHUG! Click-click. Daniel and his men dove to the floor.

SHUG! Click-click. Again came the blare and reload of a shotgun.

"Get your heads d—!"

SHUG! Click-click.

"Daniel Keagan, come on out with your hands up, you hear?" a man said from outside, as Daniel realized the shots hadn't been fired into the jailhouse.

"And get myself blown away? What kind of crazy you think I am?"

"Perhaps not crazy enough, per se, but a bit misguided."

It couldn't be. "Donald? Donald, is that you?"

"It is boyo. Now how's about you go and let miss Jojo outta there. Come on out with yer hands right up there in the air and yer gun tossed out to the side. We can settle this nice and easy now."

"I'm on your side, Donald. I swear I am. If you do this now though, I won't be able to protect you. No one will."

"That there is a risk we the people of Harran find ourselves willin'a take," Donald contested. "We had somethin' good here. We had family, like you have yours, only ours didn't thrive at others' expense."

"Daniel, what do we do?" the sheriff asked.

"Man, I just—," Daniel groaned, his mind racing. His attention snapped back to Johanna. Hers was also still fixed on him, and her demeanor remained the same as when they were against the cell. "Uh, y—you know, Don, it's not just family y'all got here. It's something more. Family stays with you no matter where you go, but not everywhere you go is this place." Daniel's eyes locked with Johanna's as he spoke. "What y'all got here, it's a place you feel like you fit in. It's one where you can just be you, because who you are can make this place even better. That's Harran for y'all, and it's what I want it to be for me. And I swear, if you give me the chance to make it to your seventy-fifth birthday with you, I'll do that. I'll make this place the one I've been looking for my whole life and have never truly found. I'll make it my home, and together we'll make it better."

"He means what he's saying, Donald." Johanna's surprising support meant a lot to Daniel.

"Quite the endorsement there, fella, seein' as it's comin' from the dame who was fixin'a slice a couple new holes in yer face." Daniel's spirits lifted. "But what Momma Schneider always use-ta say was actions, well those speak louder than words. So, I ask ya now, what is it yer gonna do ta prove what ya said here ta be true?"

Daniel thought hard. His intention to help was genuine, but he honestly was drawing a blank. "I don't—"

"I think I have an idea," Daniel heard the voice of Debra Kennedale from outside the jail.

"Debra?" Daniel called back in shock. "Goddamn, y'all got the whole town out there?"

"As a matter of fact . . ." Debra started but stopped. "You're in meetings with the V'ahani though, yeah?"

"That's right."

"And we take it by the lack of your men returning with you, those talks aren't done?" Cassie Kennedale asked.

"You would be correct," Daniel answered, in confusion.

"Then how about you take us up there with you when next you talk to them?" Debra asked. "That way we can be there to witness and ensure the people of Harran remain informed of the plans of the Keagans."

"You kittens sure you're okay with the danger and all in bein' around such negotiatins?" Daniel could make out Donald asking in a quieter tone.

"Of course, we know what's at stake," Cassie said to the hotel owner.

A thought jumped into Daniel's head. "Kennedales, I can do you even better. I can take you to the negotiations, sure. But in doing so, I can take you to see the Morrell children, too. If all goes well, I'll ensure they see you again."

"Jeannie and Harrison are alright?" Debra shrieked, and Daniel heard a happy commotion outside.

"Alive and well. And very much having a hand in our talks, as a matter of fact. Perhaps your involvement and presence could even get us to earn a degree of their trust."

The enthusiasm outside continued to build until Donald began shushing the crowd. "As much as we'd all love ta run 'round in our little nickers about this proposition, what's ta say ya won't have off with our lovely future-seein' ladies once ya head back up? We'll be needin' some collateral if we're to trust ya and let ya outta there in one piece I'm afraid, Daniel."

Daniel turned reluctantly to the sheriff, whose mouth dropped. "No, you can't be serious."

"We'll be back in no time at all, and I ain't yanking these peoples' tails. I mean every word I say. Even if I gotta get into it with William over this, so be it. I've seen the damn light here, and you'll be taken care of, I swear to it. I'll do what it takes and won't let no harm come of you."

The sheriff rolled his eyes and gave a dismissive nod.

"A couple of my men remain here, as you know, Donald. So does the sheriff. Providing you take care of them, they'll remain under your supervision in *your* hotel, till we return. That's my deal. And they're valuable as hell to me up here, you better believe that. I ain't got much help beyond them. Those men I got up there at the camp wouldn't last me with the V'ahani to the north and y'all to the south. But it's a non-issue because I mean to keep my word."

There was a pause for a few minutes' time. Daniel sweated profusely through every second of anticipation. The nervous looks on his men's faces remained, as did the look of intensity from Johanna. He sent it back to her and, in some twisted way, there was something between them again. He was still terrified of it, but the risk was intoxicating.

"Alrighty then, Daniel," Donald called. "Come out slowly, with yer hands to the bright blue. There won't be a barrel lookin' in yer direction either. And don't be forgettin' ta let Jojo free."

Daniel followed the order, first unlocking Johanna from the cell and then gesturing for his men to lift their guns in the air. He felt there were two possible outcomes as he tiptoed toward the door—they'd either exit and be lit into oblivion, or Donald would keep his word, and they'd carry on about their arrangement.

As much as his mind played over and over the possible hail of bullets that could ultimately be about to tear through him, in that moment Daniel recalled the words Johanna had said earlier: *Then don't allow us to be hurt, Daniel.* Her words now made clear to him the depth of his responsibility—the impact he had and would have on all those around him. He decided that no matter which scenario played out, he'd be the first one out the door.

For a moment, Daniel paused and looked back at Johanna

with a grin. She returned one right back to him before he spun around and marched straight for the door. Turning the handle, and with the smile slapped across his face, he opened the door and became engulfed in light.

CHAPTER 11

WATERSHED

The four days following the first negotiation had passed, and Dominic was ready for the next step of his journey. His purpose was restored now that he'd united with the Morrells. He didn't think his debt to their father could ever be repaid, but acting as their defender helped him to satisfy it. It gave him direction, too—especially knowing Harran had fallen. How he couldn't wait to go back now and find a way to restore it to the place it was. And while he'd miss Hanzah, he would not be all that upset to be apart from the V'ahani for a while.

So, when Varek gave the order for his people to mobilize across the bridge again, Dominic alerted the Morrells.

"Jeannie, Harrison. It's time."

"How will we do it?" Jeannie asked as she prepared her things.

"We'll see how it goes here first and figure out the rest after."

"Whatever comes of this meeting, we'll handle it," Harrison said to his sister.

"I know we will."

"Thank you again for forgiving me—both of you," Dominic said with his hands pressed together. "I swear I will not let you down again."

Jeannie pushed her hair back behind her ear. "You made the decision you did to protect us, Dominic. You didn't let us down."

"I already told you too there's nothing to forgive, except for you to forgive me for doubting you in the first place."

Dominic nodded, as warmth spread through him. He'd come to love the Morrell children as he imagined he would love his own. "Well I'm glad to hear it. Now let's go get this over with so we can go back home."

With that, he followed them over the bridge and into the field. The V'ahani around them filed in, again led by Varek, Orrin, and Hanzah, with the rest of the Masters and councilmen behind them. The air was heavy with anticipation as Dominic took his place to the right of Jeannie and Harrison, some V'ahani guards lining up on his left. When Varek turned around and spotted him, the Grand Chieftain sent a grumpy look his way. Dominic didn't even flinch; he'd promised himself he wouldn't fear the Keagans or the V'ahani ever again.

It took some time for the Keagan camp to respond, but soon Daniel made his way out into the field.

Dominic watched as Varek took a deep breath and began, "We have—"

"Hold on one moment please, Chieftain," Daniel called with a hand in the air. "As a sign of goodwill, I want to make a gesture first for your friends the Morrells." Doubt filled Dominic, but he remained still as Daniel turned and waved back at his camp. A moment later, none other than the Kennedale sisters emerged from the trees. A shock traveled through Dominic. Were they friends or captives? Was it further proof of Daniel's turn or was it a trick?

Jeannie waved both arms at them. "Debra! Cassie!"

Raising a hand before her to hold her back, Dominic remained suspicious. "It could be a trap."

"He's right," Harrison said. "Hold back."

The sisters were presented by Daniel as if they were on display. "These two are dear friends of the Morrell children, and I just wanted to reunite them in the spirit of unity, since that's what I intend to bring to you." Dominic spat forcefully at the ground. "In the truest sense, that's my intention, despite all that's happened."

A frown extended across his face, Varek folded his arms. "A kind gesture for those who have lost their kin, and they may be reunited once we are finished here. But this is not the purpose of our assembly. As Grand Chieftain of the V'ahani, my concerns are for the V'ahani alone. As such, we will accept your terms for our surrender—given the V'ahani of the Riverlands will be returned to us safely. We do not make this decision lightly and only do so for the well-being of our people. Do not fail us, Daniel Keagan."

Dominic's heart sank to hear the official confirmation of surrender, and it sunk further at the sight of Daniel's satisfied grin. "That sure is good to know," Daniel exhaled.

A loud *pop* echoed through the field. Before Dominic could react, blood sprayed all over his upper body and onto his face. He clutched the sides of his head as his ears rang blisteringly in his shock. He fell to a knee from the disorientation. Collapsed on his left was a V'ahani warrior who had been shot between his heart and neck. As Dominic tried to comprehend what was happening, he could see chaos had erupted in the field.

"Stand down!" he heard Daniel Keagan yell back at his men.

"Stand down, you stupid bastards!"

Varek ran back to his guard, pushing Dominic aside, but it would be too late for the bleeding-out fighter. Looking back to the Keagan camp again, Dominic could now see a scuffle among their men. A storm of grizzlies seemingly appeared out of nowhere, surrounding and roaring ferociously at the enemies.

Dominic ran over to Harrison and Jeannie, desperate to make sure they were okay. Other than the look of shock on their faces, they were unharmed. He heard Daniel yelling again, this time at the V'ahani.

"No, please! This was a mistake! Don't do this, it was a terrible mistake!"

The grizzlies did not cease in their monstrous intimidation, but one Keagan came forward with another in his clutches, a gun pointed at the captive's head.

"Daniel—Daniel I have him," the gunman exclaimed.

"Daniel Keagan, our deal is finished," Varek called out, still hovering over his man. "You tell your brothers it will be war between us."

"Bring that psychopath before me." Daniel appeared hysterical, craning his head in anger at his camp and back at the V'ahani. "Grand Chieftain, please. It doesn't have to be this way. I will kill this man myself, please. I'll show you this was a mistake. Goddamn it, bring him to—You!"

There, on his knees before Daniel was Collin McCormack. It was clear to Dominic the bullet that broke the peace was meant for him. Collin still hadn't let go of Dominic embarrassing him, it seemed. The man couldn't stomach being bested by a magician—

or perhaps it was holding the title of the guard under which the Morrell children escaped Harran. Either way, Collin had tried to kill him twice now. Blind rage filled Dominic, and he let it loose without a qualm.

"I swear to the heavens I will kill you if it's the last—!" Standing up and beginning to charge toward the other side, he was caught and held back by the V'ahani leaders. He could only struggle in resistance as he was restrained.

Daniel took out his pistol, cocked it back, and aimed it at Collin's head. "Do you realize what you've done?" he asked.

"You send him over here, or you and your men will be overcome by our grizzlies," Varek demanded.

"You need me alive, Daniel," Collin said with a gasp.

"Bullshit he does! Pull the damn trigger, you yellow-bellied hick," Dominic fumed, still fighting the V'ahani clutches.

"I was there at the fire. I was one of Clovis' leftover men in Harran, and I'm the only one who'd be willing to tell you what really went down at the Morrell home when it was burned to the ground. The others, they'd be too scared and threatened. He's indoctrinated them. But I know the truth, which you need—I know you do."

"No!" Dominic was beside himself. How dare that snake use his crimes to stay alive? "No! No! No!"

Harrison ran to his side and said, "Dominic, please. If he can tell him the truth, we need him alive too."

It made him furious and numb to admit it, but Harrison was right. He needed to calm down for the Morrells.

"Get him back," Varek ordered, motioning to the men that restrained him. "My order was clear, Daniel."

"I—I need more time. This is information I need to know if y'all want peace. I'm sorry, but I can't turn him over yet. It's about stopping my brother Clovis. And I will stop him. If you just give us more time . . ."

A gasp and a death rattle made Dominic's stomach turn. The fallen V'ahani warrior had perished.

"There can be no more time," Varek howled to a dejected-looking Daniel Keagan. "You have already allowed one of my men to be murdered at the hand of one of your own!"

"No, please—" Daniel begged.

"Leave the Riverlands! That is the new order. Our people will be returned unharmed, or you and yours will bleed. If your brother Clovis is the boulder blocking that stream, then you will deliver him to us for judgment, or you and your people will bleed. If you do neither of these things, there will be a war in these lands—and it will be one you cannot and will not win. Hear me, Daniel Keagan, for your efforts, we will give you time. But your time is limited—do not forget that. And unlike your gang, we have eyes throughout the skies. We will monitor you constantly until you deliver upon our wishes."

Dominic's feelings were mixed when Varek turned and ordered his men back across the bridge with the deceased in tow. On the one hand, there would be no truce with the Keagans and V'ahani, which meant they might finally rid the Murrieta of Keagan influence. But it also meant there may be war. While they were now one step closer to revealing the truth to an unsure Daniel, Collin McCormack, his greatest, most unrelenting adversary, remained alive.

With the V'ahani turning back toward the bridge and the Keagans retreating toward Harran, Dominic, Jeannie, and Harrison stood together in the field, facing the Riverlands. As Dominic wiped the blood from his face with one hand, a small hand grabbed his other from behind. He looked to his side and saw Jeannie staring longingly in the direction of Harran. Harrison walked up to his other side, waving to the Kennedales, who waved back as they retreated into the woods.

"I'm not sure what we'll find when we do make our way back into Harran," Jeannie said to Dominic. "But no matter what we go through, Hanzah was right, we are family. And my father would be so grateful for you, Dominic, because we wouldn't have made it this far without you."

Dominic gripped her hand more tightly and told her, "Nor I without you."

*

Standing by the doors of his mansion with Gregory, William waited for Henry to come downstairs. Looking out from the porch, William acknowledged how good it felt to be back in his kingdom again—back to normal life. Well, relatively so. He still needed to wrap his mind around the events that took place in New Berkley, which is why William had decided to see Henry and Gregory off into town rather than joining them in meeting up with the rest of the family. Maria and Judith had decided to take the girls off to the circus to see the progress Blanton had apparently made in a few short sessions with the strongman and encouraged everyone to get out of the house with them. While he would've liked to head to the circus, too, he needed a few hours alone in the mansion to craft a letter to Daniel. A week had passed since their return, and he hadn't gotten a chance to clear his head and figure out what was next now or how to put it into words.

Gregory released a deep sigh beside him, which William echoed in response.

"You're sure you're okay to do this?" William asked Gregory. "I know the circus can't be the first place you'd want to be right now."

When he had told Gregory of all that happened in New Berkeley, his best friend was very emotional. But since that moment, Gregory's face hardly showed any sign of animation. He would sigh frequently, and it troubled William deeply, but he also realized a positive change would occur any time Gregory was around Blanton. Some kind of bond had formed between them, and William couldn't be more appreciative of Gregory for helping to encourage his young cousin—and vice versa for that matter.

Again, Gregory sighed, but it was not as much of a pout this time as before. "What you did for me when I came into the Murrieta…with no real obligation to do so, you gave me a home and a purpose I thought I'd lost completely. I'll always do whatever you need, Billy—including chaperoning a circus trip."

"Gregory—"

"No, no, I didn't mean it was a chore. I just meant I'm happy to be needed by you and the others. After you took me in, for a while I blamed all my short-comings on that evil woman who I called my wife back—"

"They sure as shit are all her fault, you know that," William tried to assure him. "You ain't done no wrong by her or your son."

"No, I know, but it's not the point." Gregory wiped his hulking hand over his face. "The point is I'm sad, Billy. I am so far beyond sad. And somehow, I've always been this way. Honestly, I—I think everyone always has some kind of sadness inside of them. But even though it'd be easy to feel like someone's always trying to make my life miserable, I still find solace in two things. First, I know those who do wrong will always be the saddest and deadest on the inside. Second, I have something to hold on to—I'm needed here. Which is why I have to go to this circus. Because I know Blanton's nervous about it, and he needs me there to support him. And for me, there's joy in supporting him."

William nodded and put a hand on his friend's shoulder before pulling him in for a hug. Gregory was a physical giant, and his heart was just as big.

"You are needed here, Gregory. I couldn't do all this without you in my corner."

And it was true. Even during his grieving, Gregory did not waste any time in suggesting they station men along the road leading to Prayer's Passage, just in case any of Leonard's men survived the Highlanders and attacked Bronson and Nova. The extra precaution and the personal guard they'd installed on the family helped William feel better.

Footsteps behind them signaled Henry's arrival.

"Afternoon, Henry. So, you saw the ladies off this morning?" William asked him.

"Saw them off, no. But Maria told me she was gathering the kids and meeting Judith there—poor bug's still not feeling the best in the mornings, I hear?"

"Yes, she's taken to sleeping in late to try to avoid the illness in the mornings, so I left her with a guard by her door. She wasn't up there last I looked though, so I'm sure my man took her into town to meet up with the others once she was feeling better. I sent two guards with Maria and the kids, as well, so please feed all three of them as part of my thanks when you meet up with everyone."

"Great, will do. See you in a bit."

"And Gregory," William stopped them before they went. "Tell Blanton I said good luck."

Gregory nodded with a soft grin, and they departed. William reentered the mansion, determined to have a satisfying meal before he headed to his study and started strategizing his next steps. In the halls, he found a butler and requested he ask the chef to prepare his favorite meal—roast pig. He did his best thinking on a full stomach. The butler confirmed and darted off, while William made his way to the dining room.

In the time it took him to arrive, his spot at the head of the table was already made. He plopped down into his cushioned, wooden seat as if he were settling into a cloud. With his eyes closed, he took a deep breath, in and out, and suddenly he was in his zone. He eased his eyes open, staring down into his empty plate, only this time he wasn't sucked into the void. This time, he realized, in this, his father had been right—there was nothing there. And the realization lifted an incredible weight off his shoulders. There was nothing left to search for. There was nothing in the void—and Leonard was gone. The world he lived in was now his own.

The door connecting the dining room to the kitchen swung

open, and Cassius came in, carrying a silver cloche he placed in the center of the table.

"Cassius! Where have you been?" There was also another man with Cassius as well, whom William did not recognize.

"Cassius? Who's this?" William said, unsure of what to think.

The other man pulled rope out from behind him.

"Uh, what are you—? What the hell?" William protested with a shriek as he moved to stand, but Cassius threw him down into the chair as the unknown man restrained him. He tied William's wrists to the chair so tightly it almost felt they could break in two. Cassius walked to the other end of the table. "Goddamn it, stop this! Cassius, what the—mmm!"

From behind, the man had gagged William, and though he kept trying to scream in fury, it was useless. Cassius stood perfectly still at the opposite end of the table, staring at him without flinching as William tried to resist, kicking away from his seat. But the man behind him was strong and held him firmly in place until William gave in and went quiet. Now at their mercy, William groaned in anger once more and fixed his attention on Cassius.

"This is Charles Langston," Cassius began, gesturing dismissively at his partner. "Charles, this is William Keagan."

"Nice to meet you," Charles said in a cheerful way that infuriated William. It had to be sarcasm, even though the man didn't give as much as a chuckle.

"That'll be the extent of you talking," Cassius said calmly to Charles.

"But hold on there," Charles started. "I can contribute as much as—"

Cassius held his hand up and shook his head. "Enough now." The handle of his pistol twinkled in the light. "Charles is a simple man, William. And by simple I don't mean he is a basic fellow. What I mean is he's just kind of slow."

"Hey I—!" Charles protested.

"Your father had people everywhere, and Charles, like me, was one of those people," Cassius interrupted.

William couldn't care less about the idiot's backstory but was horrified to hear of his father's control in his own domain. How had it snuck in? How deep did it go? How had he not sensed it? And now, was that control transferred to Forrest?

"Charles though, was sent off to a quiet town to send back information which was more or less irrelevant, because he'd proven himself to be only somewhat loyal and a much greater nuisance. Isn't that right?"

"Now wai—"

"So, Leonard, the astute politician he was gave this fellow a silly title, knowing he'd inflate it, and now look where we are… somehow he proved useful after all. I did need another man, and he was the closest."

William only squinted his eyes at Cassius in betrayal. *This traitorous rat.*

"Now I'm not sure if you know why we're here, William, but you should. You did this, not us."

William let out a muffled denial but realized how futile it was. Even so, he was unable to keep from reacting. Leonard did this— not him. Leonard wanted to dismantle all they'd built. Leonard was obsessed with power. Leonard was an old rotten soul-sucking bastard. And Leonard put him in a situation where it was obey or revolt, live or die.

"I've never wanted to live this kind of life—being a Swiss army knife for a madman isn't pleasant." William rolled his eyes. The man seriously wanted pity even as he was about to murder him in cold blood? "But my place in this world is what it is. It's what I'm good at, and I've tried to escape it in the past, but it was always for nothing. Leonard and Forrest just wouldn't let me go. I did one thing for your father at a time when I didn't even necessarily like him but needed a favor, and from that moment on, he kept asking, and later demanding, and now, here I am, doomed to walk this road. But you...you damned yourself to find me on it."

William felt a tug at his pant leg. He looked down at a snail's pace to see Blanton was hiding under the table beneath the curtain. Horrified, William opened his eyes wide and tried to covertly nod his head at his cousin to ensure he stayed out of sight. He couldn't stand for the boy to be in danger. Blanton followed the silent order, much to his fleeting relief.

"Now, I'm not gonna pretend like I don't know why you'd want to kill your father," Cassius sighed as he pulled his revolver out and loaded the bullets one-by-one. "The man could be difficult—impossible even—and I myself know the pain of a neglected childhood. But you had to know there'd be consequences you wouldn't be able to handle. Not even from his men—but from Forrest alone."

William began to groan again, trying to tell Cassius through the gag to shoot him and save the speech. He'd done what he'd done. For better or for worse, he was willing to pay the consequences for ridding the world, and his family, of his father. Daniel and Gregory would pick up the pieces. William's only regret was he'd never see his child. But he pushed the thought away, determined to die like a man. Cassius cocked back his gun and stood with it by his side.

"Do you realize how close Forrest and your father were?" Cassius asked, eyes squinting in frustration. "Those two grew up together, and they were the only friends they each had. They were brothers, William. Same as you and yours."

No one had the bond William and his brothers did, especially not with Leonard.

"Well, know this," Cassius exhaled. "Know your father wouldn't have wanted this, even after you did what you did. While it may be Forrest's order that led me here, you need to realize you chose this the moment you touched Leonard, the moment you chose to play the game. It's a shame, too. I was starting to kind of like you. But like I said, I got a job to do."

William heard the front doors of the mansion open.

"Blanton! Blanton!" It was Gregory.

Before William could make a sound, Cassius lifted his finger to his mouth and his gun to the door leading into the dining room. Charles Langston fidgeted, moving slowly away from William and toward the kitchen door, holding there when Cassius ordered him to.

"I'm going to search all the rooms," Gregory said. He was close. He must've been in the hallway.

"I'll be outside until you find him," Henry followed.

William grew hysterical. He couldn't let Gregory walk into his death, so he began to howl at the top of his lungs from beneath his gag. The steps slowed outside the dining room by the door for a brief moment. When the door crept open, Cassius opened fire, getting only two shots off before he started shrieking in pain, grabbing at his knee and firing a third shot into the table before him. Gregory charged in, and William continued to howl, now trying to call Blanton's name. Cassius's expression was panicked when he saw Gregory, and he tried to lift his gun again, but Gregory sent two bullets through his throat and chest before he had the chance. William noticed Charles Langston dash away through the kitchen, but he didn't give a damn about anything except making sure Blanton was alive. Gregory was about to run toward the kitchen, having noted Charles exited, but William continued yelling in protest until he came back and removed the gag.

"Blanton!" William cried, as a pool of blood spread on the other side of the table where his cousin had been. "Goddamn it, Blanton!"

"Don't tell me he was under there!" Gregory gasped, running over to lift up the curtain.

William couldn't move with his hands tied, so he used his feet to try and lift himself up.

"Are you all right?" Gregory asked.

"I'm sorry," Blanton began to cry. "I shouldn't have been here. I'm so sorry."

Gregory hugged him, and William sat back down in the chair to take a deep breath in relief. "No, you saved my life, Blanton. You're a hero."

After a few minutes of the boy sobbing and coming to his senses, Gregory came over to untie William.

"Is everything all right?" Henry had entered the dining room next. With his wrists unbound, William turned toward him. "I heard gunshots. Came around the back in case the element of surprise was needed. What the hell ha—"

Henry stopped mid-sentence, staring right at the other end of the table. The gun he was holding fell out of his hand. William turned to see what he was staring at and saw Blanton had lifted the hood of the cloche Cassius had delivered. Judith's head sat atop the silver platter, facing his end of the table.

Time stopped. There was no sound. There was no taste on his tongue. There was no color in the room. He saw his name, "Billy," mouthed repeatedly on Gregory's lips, but he heard nothing. His wife's dead eyes stared at him from the silver platter. William stood up slowly as Gregory tried to restrain and embrace him. Henry remained in place cursing every possible god and Blanton sprinted out of the room screaming. When William reached the cloche, he climbed up onto the table, fell to his knees atop it—knocking dishware to the floor, and pressed his head against Judith's. It was cold—it was so cold—but so was he. With Gregory trying his best but failing to get him down and console him, William remained there, looking straight into his wife's opened eyes as his began to water. Within an instant he became filled with ire—not at Leonard or even Forrest, but at himself—as he only now understood the choice his father had made all those years ago.

*

Latera needed a fake plot and a real one, and she needed both fast. Clovis was now gone, and she thanked the Mother daily for that, because this would be her chance to make some kind of escape.

Despite Clovis's threats, Latera sent word to her people in the North right after that he was coming. There was no way she could let them be surprised by his presence. She also pleaded for them not to accept the Keagan rule. In her message, she explained that things were all right for them at the Hold for now. She argued that they could survive until the V'ahani found another way.

Although she worried about leaving her people here, she could do nothing more for them from within the Hold. The webs she'd woven were already too intricate, and, if she stayed, the consequences would be harsher on her people. The Keagans would torture her by torturing them. She needed to break from them for their own protection. She needed to appear the sole rebel, the outlier, and not their representative. In that way, she could keep them safe, even as she fought to free them. Plus, she had one big advantage now—Clovis' men couldn't kill without his sick orders.

With Gannon's release and the relocation of the clans within the Hold already beginning, the wheels were beginning to turn. As she walked the streets, she saw difficult families being selectively removed and orders being given for others to house V'ahani. The Tokali took exception, and their protests filled the air. Escalation of this conflict was what she was banking on. While Latera knew there would be risks, she also predicted the Keagans would shut down any physical disturbances. Until that happened though, she needed the spark to ignite and cause enough distraction for her to make an escape.

Her first stop would be for Winona and Mika—she'd need some of her own people on the journey with her and wanted to directly ensure the safety of her best friends, at least. She first checked their shelter, guessing the Keagans wouldn't be willing to help those who were closest to her—and she was right. The two sat on their cot, looking around dejectedly as many of the others around them were ushered out of the tight shelter. Latera waved them over to a place away from the commotion.

"Is this you again?" Winona asked, to which Latera nodded and looked around to ensure no one would hear. "The gifts you have given us never end. But Latera, how did you—"

"We need to leave here now."

"But we have not been ordered to leave this shelter," Mika said, confusion in his voice.

"No, not the shelter. The Hold. You must come with me if we are to escape the Hold. It is now or never."

Mika's eyes widened. "What are you saying? What about our people?"

"Latera, what is going on?" Winona asked.

"Our people are in as good of a position now as I could have possibly achieved for them here. Would you disagree?" The two shook their heads. "Good, but they are still not free, are they? And neither are the Tokali. That is the next step in my mission to save us all. And I cannot complete it from inside these walls, where we are constantly watched and unable to utilize the gifts of the Mother. So, I must escape, whether you come with me or not. But I know I will need your help and strength, so please trust me as you already have. I know I can lead our people to freedom."

"*We* know you can," Winona corrected with a smile, as Mika nodded his agreement. Latera beamed and gave her friend a hug before Winona whispered for Mika to gather a few essentials. Latera already had hers hidden under her outer garments. Once the couple had what they needed, Latera led them over to the Tokali homes.

Underneath her outer garments, she still wore her whites, and she returned to the same corner she stood before, across from Elan's home. The tension on the streets was building, and debates were spreading everywhere. Though the colors of the clan members were not being worn, the distinction between the sides was more obvious than ever.

After a period of waiting at the corner, Latera had enough. "Come with me," she waved her friends on as she marched straight for Elan's home, fighting through the growing crowds. Latera knocked on the door several times—but there was no answer. She decided to try one more time and knocked again. This time, the door opened, but she was met by a woman of the Keagan gang.

"Is this your new relocation?" she asked, waving her in. "Come inside."

Malik, Adila, and Elan came to the door, carrying their belongings. Latera was stunned and felt her face flush when they sent her angry glares. She never thought they'd be forced to give up their home—not with their status.

"So, this is how it is going to be, girl?" Adila spat in disgust.

"Perhaps you would have seen this coming when you uprooted my people from our home. After all, do you not deserve the same treatment you give to others?" Adila drove Latera crazy.

"This is what they want, Latera," Elan pleaded.

"I am counting on it." Latera stared him down as they left their home.

When Malik and Adila walked out the door with their things,

almost all Tokali in the streets stopped in their tracks. Cries of unfairness and disbelief could be heard. They all seemed to wonder how two of the most beloved of their own could be put in this position. The Keagan woman ran out attempting to calm the shouting, but it was to no avail. Latera realized this was the spark she'd needed. The disagreements were slowly turning into spats, and soon enough, sides were being drawn.

"We have to go now," Latera said to Winona and Mika as they pushed out the door of the home.

"Latera!" she heard Warrick call out. Looking around, she spotted him at the same corner she had been earlier, accompanied by Hammond, Shelton, and Gannon. Elan must have also heard the call, because he whipped around and looked at them with confusion. Ignoring him, Latera ran over, Winona and Mika in tow.

"Warrick told us what you did for Gannon, and we cannot thank you enough," Shelton said. Gannon, who still had some bruises and the beginnings of some scarring, waved gently with a grin.

"Let us repay you by getting you out of here," Hammond said. "We know where we can hide to escape this scuffle."

"I am glad I could help you, and I appreciate your gratitude, but my friends and I are leaving the Hold. I came here only to see if any of you wished to join us," Latera said as quietly as she could but still needing to talk somewhat loud over the riotous commotion.

"Just the three of you?" Warrick asked. "Without weapons? Even with this madness, you will be shot down as soon as you enter the field by the tower guards. At best, one of you could live."

"It is a risk we are willing to take," Winona said in Latera's support.

Gannon covertly revealed the handle of a rifle on his back. "You will not take it alone." Somehow, he'd hidden it under his thick coat. "We will help you escape. We will come with you."

"What?" Warrick asked nervously.

"He is right," Shelton said. "We cannot stay here any longer. These worsening conditions are not her fault. They are ours. And they will not get any better unless we stop the Keagans."

"It is as I have been saying since we gave in to them." Hammond's chest puffed out as he acknowledged he was right. Latera almost chuckled at his brazenness in such a dire situation. "I am in."

"But what will we do, even if we are successful, Latera?" Warrick asked.

"There is no time to discuss it now, but I promise it will be clear in time."

"What will be clear?" Elan asked from behind them. She wondered how to handle his presence and weighed the potential of his betrayal. He'd not hand over *his* friends, she decided. So, honesty it was.

"We are leaving, Elan," she said. "We are leaving so we can fight for the freedom of our people from beyond these walls."

"Is this true?" he asked, turning to his friends.

"It is," Hammond said, seemingly the only one confident enough to reply. "All of us. You can tell them and get us killed, or you can accept this and move along."

"Have you told Pharaoh?" Elan asked.

"You know what his response would be," Shelton said. "How could we have told him?"

"Good," Elan said, much to Latera's surprise. "Let us go. I am coming with you."

Though she felt uncertain Elan's presence was a good idea, there was no more time to waste contemplating. "So be it, but we need to leave now."

Hammond nodded and hurriedly led the group through the riots and toward the gates of the Hold. There were both physical and non-physical altercations throughout the streets, and the Keagans were struggling to keep it all in check. When they reached the path to the gates, she spotted the two guards up in the watchtowers, their attention turned to the inside of the Hold, rather than the outside. She saw the first was a Keagan, but recognized the other to be Pharaoh, and worried about what it might mean for them.

"Stop them!" Latera heard Walter Keagan shout from behind. A gunshot which increased the frenzy, followed his exclamation.

Pharaoh and the other guard swung their attention toward them. As their group ran through the gates, Latera knew she needed to act to ensure their safety. She paused outside the gate and called to the wind, reaching a hawk from the woods beyond the Hold. When they connected, Latera ordered it to attack the Keagan guard in the tower. The distraction worked momentarily, and her friends ran around the hog carcasses as the hawk ripped the rifle out of the hands of the guard.

"Latera!" she heard Winona shout from across the way.

Latera froze at the base of the wall, unsure if it was even worth the risk of Pharaoh shooting her down. Flooded by thoughts of freedom and of her brother and of her people, she began darting across the field anyway. The hawk was shot down the moment she began running, and a second shot landed by her feet, making her yelp in fear. Before her, Gannon whipped around with his rifle, killing the Keagan guard with one shot. She was relieved to see that Pharaoh stood there in shock with his rifle by his side—he was not so far lost as to shoot his own friends. Walter Keagan joined him at his post and began wrestling furiously with him over the gun. Latera whipped back around, and in her terror, her legs picked up to a speed she didn't know they could. Elan ran towards her. When he reached her, he shielded her with his body as best he could.

A *bang* blared from atop the walls.

"Pharaoh, no!" Gannon cried as Latera and Elan froze and turned. Latera's heart broke as she saw Walter lift the rifle and shove Pharaoh's lifeless body over the edge of the wall.

"Pharaoh!" Elan echoed, even as they both turned and ran toward their friends.

Walter's bullets whizzed by them and into the dead pigs. As they passed him, Gannon waved them on, "There's another! Run faster!" and turned with them to run toward the woods.

Another? There must be another marksman joining Walter on the wall. They'd never make it. At the panicked thought, Latera stumbled to the ground into the rot, sliding on the vile sludge. Elan darted to her side, dragging her behind the cover of two hogs, as Gannon continued on ahead of them.

"I am so sorry, Elan," she cried aloud. "I did not think...I am so sorry."

"It is not your fault, Latera. But we don't have much time. Are you ready?" he asked. "We will make it, okay? I promise you, we will make it."

Latera nodded as a bullet snapped into their cover, startling her. She took a few breaths and nodded again at Elan. As she crouched in preparation to sprint again, two quick shots blared out from the trees before them. *Gannon.* When she looked up above their cover, she could no longer see anyone on the wall, only a spray of blood in their place.

Latera and Elan sprinted hand-in-hand toward the trees. When she crossed the threshold into the forest, she released his hand, fell to her knees, and kissed the ground of the forest floor. Looking around at the others, she rose to her feet. They consoled one another over Pharaoh's death, which she felt for. For once, she was united with them, even if it was in grief.

Winona approached her, placing a gentle hand on her shoulder, before dropping to a knee. When Winona knelt on the ground, all eyes fell upon Latera, but she could only look at her best friend before her and wait for whatever was next.

Winona smiled. "Where can we follow you now, my Chieftess?"

$\sim$

CURIOUS ABOUT WHAT HAPPENS NEXT?

Continue to Amazon to buy the next book in the series now:

https://www.amazon.com/author/nbaustin

Need more than that?
Check out Nicholas Austin's website!

linktr.ee/nbaustinbooks

ABOUT THE AUTHOR

N.B. Austin is the author, screenwriter, and blogger behind the Civilands Series. His first novel, *Crimson River*, was a finalist for the *2016-2017 BooksGoSocialDaily Book of the Year Award*.

Based in Austin, Texas, but hailing originally from Long Island, New York. University of Texas at Austin educated. His experience as writer and editor for several scholastic newsletter publications combined with a passion for song writing, soon inspired him to divert his attention to storytelling.

Find more about N.B. Austin, including his blog and details on free book giveaways, at:

linktr.ee/nbaustinbooks